KOSTAS KROMMYDAS

CAVE

OF SILENCE

C000000019

Sponsored by
REALIZE
Via Donizetti 3, 22060 Figino Serenza (Como), Italy
Phone: +39 0315481104

To Marina and Vaia,
for the horizons we explore together.
To my father, for the worlds he has created through the
stories he told me these past forty-five years.

≈≈≈≈≈≈≈≈≈≈≈

"It takes a minute to have a crush on someone, an hour
to like someone, and a day to love someone. But it takes a
lifetime to forget someone."
Oscar Wilde

≈≈≈≈≈≈≈≈≈≈≈

Many thanks to Simone Arnaboldi,
Errikos Tzavaras, Iris Gioti, Andreas Manolikakis,
Lilia Dimaraki and Chrisovalanti Leftaki

Contents

Introduction

As much as I tried to free my hands, the thick ropes tying them to my back refused to budge. Through a slit in the torn fabric wrapped around my head, I could see the gathered people, their eyes filled with fear and hatred. Someone roughly tightened the cloth over my eyes. Everything drowned in darkness. Screams surrounded me. I felt the threatening crowd inch toward me. My heart pounded in my chest. My breath came out in shallow rasps. Thick beads of sweat trickled down my neck and back as I swayed my head in a desperate attempt to peer through the cloth. I struggled to move away from the approaching throng of people, but deep roots had grown from my feet, digging into the earth, pinning me to the ground. Gathering every remaining bit of my strength, I jerked my head upward. At last, the fabric slipped and I opened my eyes in horror, waking up.

A gentle sea breeze brushed against my skin. I was dripping with sweat. The faint red light that tints the horizon to announce the coming day filtered into the room through narrow slits in the wooden shutters.

I lay still for a few moments, waiting for my throbbing heart to slow down. The early colors of dawn played across the brightening sky. Once I could breathe normally again, I got up as softly as I could and stood at the balcony doors. The beauty unfolding before me soothed me. The mild breeze dried the moisture off my naked body.

A sliver of a moon was still discernible, as if making a last stand against the arriving sun before slowly bowing out.

Further out, a small boat was indolently entering the port, carving a white trail on the still surface of the water. To my right, the imposing masses that loomed unmoving, as if suspended from the sky with invisible thread, cast imposing dark shadows on the blue waters. One of the shadows looked almost human, a body that had lain down on the rocks a long time ago and become one with the boulder with the passage of time, its frozen space forever staring into the vastness of the universe.

I always felt awed by these bizarre land sculptures, awed and irrationally afraid that they would suddenly come loose and crush everything beneath them.

Fears do not fade with age after all. You always stumble upon them, inexplicably, as if someone has carved them inside you, deeply and irrevocably, to follow you and rise up even at the most wonderful moments of your life.

Absorbed by my thoughts and the images of the waking day, I did not sense Anita rise and come toward me until she wrapped her arms around me and rested her head on my shoulder. I felt the heat of her naked body seep into mine and stepped back ever so softly to bridge any gap between our bodies. She hugged me tightly in response.

We stood there silently, afraid that sound, any sound, would mar the perfection of that moment. Our heavy breaths were all that could be heard, her body perfectly fitted against mine.

Turning to face her, I saw in her eyes that she had wanted to share with me the rising dawn. Spontaneously, our lips met and our hands reached out to explore every inch of flesh.

Through half-opened eyes, I saw our figures against the early morning colors reflected in the mirror across the room. It was like a shifting painting, the shapes altering as our bodies moved, until the outline blurred into an indeterminate shape.

≈≈≈≈≈≈≈≈≈≈≈

I was holding her so tightly her feet no longer touched the ground. Locked in my arms as she was, she wrapped her legs around my waist as if executing a dexterous dance move, seeking our absolute union.

Untamed passion set the rhythm of our movements, while the first rays of sunlight peeked through the thin curtains fluttering in the gentle breeze.

We stayed there kissing, breathless, waiting for the intensity of our feelings to subside, letting ourselves wallow in them.

"Good morning," I said, brushing away the long brown locks that fell softly in her eyes.

Her smile lit up the room. "Good morning," she replied softly.

We gazed deeply into each other's eyes and then burst out laughing, not knowing why, and not caring to find out. We just let ourselves sink into the unforced intimacy of the moment; kissing and teasing each other until a knock on the door sharply brought us back to reality.

The crumpled sheets on the bed and our clothes flung across the whole room betrayed the magical night we had spent together. I caught a glimpse of the hotel telephone on the floor, the receiver off the hook.

"What time is it?" she wondered and moved to pick up her phone from the bedside table. "Ten missed calls...Oh no, it's already nine thirty," she gasped and hurriedly wrapped herself in one of the loose sheets. "Who is it?" she asked looking at the door, although she already knew it could only be one person.

"It's me, Miss Hertz. Electra."

Anita cracked the door open ever so slightly to prevent the girl at the door from seeing me standing naked across the room and sheepishly greeted Electra.

Electra was a production assistant, looking after the actors and in charge of their schedules. Short, sweet and slightly overweight, she pulled back the hair hanging down the unshaved half of her head. "Good morning, sorry to bother you, but I've been calling your room and your cell phone, and I realized you must have overslept, we are due on location at ten, and the monastery of Aghios Mámas is a bit far away," she said in one breath.

"I know Electra, I'm very sorry. I must have forgotten to set my alarm and the phone...I guess I did not hang up properly. I'll be down in five minutes, okay?"

"Yes, Miss Hertz. The others will have set off, but I'll wait for you."

"Thanks, I'll be as fast as I can. Again, I'm so sorry and please call me Anita, okay?"

"Yes, of course, Miss Hertz...errr, Anita. Sorry," Electra said and, before Anita had a chance to close the door, added in a louder voice, "Good morning, Mr. Voudouris. Have a nice day; I'll let you know soon what time you're due on set on Monday."

She walked off, leaving both of us with the same stunned expression on our faces. We were aware everyone knew about us, but not to the extent of knowing when and where we met. We were in the middle of shooting and had to be more careful. It did not matter that our lives seemed to be following the script we were filming, we had to be professional about it.

Electra had just shattered the illusion of secrecy we were under up until that moment, although we both knew that whatever was happening between us would not affect our work. We were fully conscious that we were mixing work with pleasure and we were handling that in the best possible manner, as we had done from the first moment we'd met, at the screen test.

On my side, I had been feeling lucky to have been cast in such a sought-after part. Now, simple as it sounds, happiness had been added to that heady mix despite the short amount of time that had elapsed; despite the fact that we were only just getting to know each other.

She was already famous, mostly in Europe. Not even thirty yet, she had a career that anyone would envy, with parts in international films, awards, and acclaimed theater performances. I would have never imagined she would be so unaffected and approachable in person. Not a spectacular beauty, she had a unique, strange allure that won others over. Her eyes, the way she moved, her expression; everything about her was captivating.

I watched her dash around the room getting ready and realized how much I wanted this relationship to last. Did she feel the same way about it?

Putting an end to my musings, Anita came near me, a small smile on her face. "Just think what they must be saying about me. I'm late on set, I sleep with my co-star..." she said and kissed me goodbye.

I took her hand, trying to keep her near me for another moment. "I don't know how much sleep *you*'re getting...I've hardly gotten any," I said teasingly, and then, in a more serious tone, "People may be talking but they stop when the camera starts rolling Anita. That says a lot about you. You are an amazing professional and perfect for this part. I'm so happy to be in this film with you, to be acting alongside you."

We gazed at each other, letting our eyes do all the talking and jumped at the sound of the ferry boat's horn as it entered the port.

"Isn't that your ferry?" she asked.

"Yes, I guess," I hesitated, still caught up in the moment.

"Then you'd better hurry or you'll miss it." She looked at me sweetly as she moved toward the door.

"You're right; I'd better get back to my room and pack. You know I would have loved to stay and spend these three days with you, right?" I asked as I walked her to the door.

"I know, but I understand how important getting to that island is to you. First ever visit."

"Not exactly *first* visit…"

"That time doesn't count, nobody saw us," she said, giving me another kiss and not seeming in any hurry to leave the room. "Anyway, it's only three days, they'll fly by, and we'll be together again before you know it."

"I wish you could come with me. Maybe I should put this trip off and we could go together when filming is over," I suggested, stroking her hair.

"Don't tempt me to say yes, when I know how much it means to you to get there now. I'll be here, waiting for you. Go, find your answers and then we'll go together and stay awhile. Promise, Dimitri? And we'll go to Krifó and visit the Cave of Silence again."

"I promise," I said, and kissed her, trying to hold on to the flavor of her lips for the coming separation.

She took another look at the mess in the room and hesitated.

"Don't worry. I'll tidy up before I go... Maybe I'll leave something for the cleaning lady to do, too," I said and winked.

She looked at me, eyes twinkling with laughter, picked up her bag and made her way to the stairs. I watched her walk away and felt our being apart, even for these few days, start to weigh upon me.

As she arrived at the top of the landing, she turned toward me and, a shadow of worry fleeting across her face, said solemnly, "Dimitri, be careful!"

That was the first time I had ever seen her worry. That same look had crossed my mother's face when I had announced my intention to visit the island. She was adamant I should not go. When she failed to dissuade me, she made me swear not to tell anyone my grandfather's name or the reason for my visit.

I had taken it upon myself to carry out her brother's last wish before he passed away. To have his body cremated in Bulgaria, as cremations in Greece were not possible, and scatter his ashes at his birthplace. He'd left the island as a young child and never been back; at least, that's what he claimed. He wanted, even in this manner, to stay there forever. So, someone had to carry his ashes there. But neither my mother nor my two distant aunts had any wish to be involved in this. That had to mean something, but what? The reasons behind that reluctance remained unclear.

Uncle Nikos lived in northern Greece, in Thessaloniki, and never had a family or any other close relations. He was a lonely and reclusive man with a wonderful voice; a gifted singer. When I used to ask him as a child how I could learn to sing like him, he used to laugh and say with a forlorn sigh, "When you drink from the spring at Mantani, at the top of the mountain on our island, you'll sing beautifully too, Dimitri." But when I would declare that as soon as I was old enough I would go to the island and drink the water, he would become solemn once again. He'd look me in the eyes and say, "No one from your mother's family will ever return there." Then his face would cloud over, belying that Uncle Nikos regretted the words he had just spoken.

No one ever explained what those words really meant; not my father, who passed away fifteen years ago, nor my mother, who avoided the subject like the plague. All I knew was that she had left the island as a very young child with my uncle Nikos, just before the end of the Second World War. The Germans had just executed both my grandparents and others from their village. I was, as they never tired of telling me, the only male left on my mother's side.

So, when I got cast in this film, I took it as an omen, the shooting taking place in a location so close to the island. My three-day break, when I wouldn't be needed on location, was a window of opportunity to carry out my mission. No one knew that the small metal box in my suitcase contained my uncle's ashes. Not even Anita.

My mind preoccupied with all these thoughts, I was staring blankly toward the landing where Anita had been standing minutes ago when I suddenly realized the cleaning lady had stepped into the corridor and now stood staring at me standing naked by the door, stunned.

"I'm sorry," I stuttered with a deep blush and closed the door.

Berlin, three months earlier

Anita hurriedly zipped up the suitcase that was lying on the bed in her sparsely and tastefully decorated bedroom.

One wall was mostly glass, a stunning view of the center of Berlin, which looked clean and orderly, as if it had just been built.

On the wall facing the window stood a closet covered in mirrors that reflected the view, and the staircase that led to the floor below, a loft-like space that contained the living and kitchen area.

Facing the bed, a collection of paintings and photos hung on the wall. A large black and white photo stood out among the other frames. It showed two women, smiling and holding a one-year-old baby, in what looked like an antique shop. The baby was Anita, and the two women her mother and grandmother.

Script pages were scattered all across the room. She was hurriedly trying to gather the loose sheets in one pile when the phone rang. "Anita Hertz speaking," and then, as if the line was bad, "Who is this? *Mamá!* I was just about to call you. Yes, almost ready...I have a taxi waiting downstairs. I'll be over in twenty minutes... I have to hurry up. I hope *Yiayia* is up and I get to see her....Great!"

Hanging up, her glance lingered over the photo for a moment and she smiled fondly. She hurriedly finished gathering the papers in a neat pile and, once order was restored, pressed the remote control button. The blinds in the bedroom and downstairs started to noiselessly come down, plunging the apartment in a dark twilight.

She picked up her suitcase and made her way to the living room, with its two comfortable, red, designer sofas and marble fireplace, the hearth now filled with candles as the weather was warmer at the end of spring.

On the coffee table lay a dark metal tray filled with a collection of pebbles, which at first glance seemed to have been randomly put together. Upon closer inspection, the colors blended together to form an impressive abstract mosaic. A smaller suitcase and a laptop bag stood by the front door.

Anita cast one last look over the room to make sure everything was okay and struggled to shuffle both suitcases out to the corridor. She set the burglar alarm, turned off the lights, and locked the front door.

Downstairs, in the building's lobby, the waiting driver quickly picked up her suitcases and carried them to the waiting car.

"*Vielen Dank,*" she thanked the driver and then got in the back seat, registering the surprised and admiring glances the middle-aged driver was casting through the rear-view mirror before starting the engine.

As soon as the taxi joined the evening traffic toward her mother's house, Anita sank in the leather seats and looked out at the urban scenery flashing past her window. She had always been an observer; enjoyed taking in the landscape and people around her, no matter where she was. In all these years as an actress, the words of her teacher, the great Kurt Rainus, never left her. *You become a better actor and a better person if you never stop observing in life and searching for the truth.*

The Memorial to the Murdered Jews in Europe came into view, its 2,711 concrete slabs, unmarked tombs arranged on a sloping field, casting a shadow of isolation, oppression, and menace on the visitors wandering through its maze of corridors.

Anita, too, had felt awed and distressed whenever she had been there, especially at nighttime, chilled by the darkness cast by the slabs. She thought of them as human bodies lying still, frozen in times, silently screaming for justice beyond death.

The driver's honk, a rare sound in Berlin, brought her back to the bright present. As if suddenly remembering something urgent, she took her phone out and dialed a number. "Good evening, this is Anita Hertz...How are you?" she said in Greek.

The driver, somewhat startled, stared at her through the rear-view mirror, but Anita ignored him, absorbed in her call as she was. "I'm flying to Athens in three hours...No, I haven't received it yet...That's fine, I'll see you at my hotel tomorrow morning then. Thank you. See you soon."

She hung up and looked out the window to get her bearings. The driver's voice brought her attention back to the car's interior once more. "You're Greek?" he asked in the same language, eyes firmly on the road.

Overcoming her initial surprise, Anita smiled and answered politely. "My grandmother is Greek but has lived here most of her life. How about you, are you Greek?"

"My father is. He immigrated to Germany forty-five years ago. He married my mother, who is German, and they had me and my sister. It's a nice place, Germany, but not like Greece. Many Greeks came to work here."

"Yes, that's true, many..." she agreed.

Cave of Silence

"It's a strange world. During the war, the Germans executed my grandfather, but my father came here and loved the country and a German girl... funny, isn't it?"

"Love is stronger than war. Nothing can stop it," she answered with a knowing smile.

"Your Greek is very good though."

"Thank you! I spoke Greek at home, both with my grandmother and my mother. My mother used to teach at a Greek school in Berlin. I went there too, and then studied Greek literature."

"And acting!" the driver added meaningfully, to show her he had recognized her.

"Yes, acting too," Anita replied with an awkward smile.

The ringtone of her cell phone interrupted this rather uncomfortable conversation.

"Hi, *Mamá*, I'll be there in five minutes...Yes, in the taxi now. See you shortly."

She hung up, staring absentmindedly at the screen for a moment before turning back to the driver, who had been patiently waiting for her to finish the call.

"Things are not easy in Greece at the moment, are they?" he asked with a sad nod.

"Greece has been through a lot worse and everything will be fine," she replied curtly, as if reluctant to discuss the matter any further.

"Let's hope so..." he replied, picking up on her mood and falling silent.

A few minutes later the car pulled up in front of her mother's house.

"I'll be back in ten minutes and then we'll head to the airport," she said, slinging her laptop bag over her shoulder.

"I'll wait, *kein problem*," he reassured her, still smiling.

≈≈≈≈≈≈≈≈≈≈≈

Despite her seventy years, Michaela had a face as fresh and warm as the sun on a spring day. The resemblance between the two women was striking and anyone could easily guess they were mother and daughter.

Thirty-five years had passed since she had met and married Anita's father, a US soldier stationed in Berlin. By the time her husband announced he had been recalled back to his country the marriage was on the rocks, so she chose to remain in Germany and filed for divorce. Anita met her father rarely, whenever he visited Germany to see this distant daughter, and relations between the two of them were rather formal. Every time they met he would try to persuade her to leave Europe and try her luck in Hollywood, but Anita had no wish to do so. She was happy with her life as it was and wanted to stay close to her mother and grandmother.

≈≈≈≈≈≈≈≈≈≈≈

Walking up the garden to the house, Anita saw the beaming face of her mother waiting impatiently at the door and felt a warm glow.

Michaela greeted her daughter with a kiss and ushered her into the ground floor flat. In sharp contrast to Anita's apartment, the room was heavily decorated and bursting with artifacts, the remnants of her grandmother Eleni's antique shop. The business had passed on to Eleni when her husband's family perished in the Battle of Berlin, just before the end of World War II.

Anita knew very little about that time in her grandmother's life. All she knew was that the antique shop was one of the few buildings left standing after the Soviet bombardment and that her grandmother had had a lucky escape. "God owed me that," Eleni used to say, never giving away the full meaning of those words.

Whenever Anita and Michaela pressed her with questions, hungry for more information, Eleni would change the subject, insisting that one should let sleeping dogs lie lest they wake up and bite. She would then purse her lips together as if determined to honor a vow of silence.

≈≈≈≈≈≈≈≈≈

"Did you take everything you need? Are you sure you haven't forgotten anything?" Michaela asked with a frown of concern as the two women entered the apartment.

"Don't fret, *Mamá*, it doesn't matter. It's not like I'm heading into the wilderness," Anita said soothingly. "*Yiayia?*" she asked looking around the living room.

"Your grandmother's expecting you, Anita. She is better today, although overall she is getting worse every day. When she found out about you going to Greece, she wasn't very happy. She's not spoken a single word since."

Michaela put her arms around Anita's shoulders and gently guided her toward Eleni's room.

They found the ninety-year-old woman propped up against a cluster of comfortable pillows on the large bed. Her neatly coiffed hair and pretty nightgown showed how eagerly she had anticipated her granddaughter's visit.

Rina, Eleni's Georgian carer, was sitting in an armchair beside the bed knitting and keeping up a happy, aimless chatter. As soon as she saw them enter the room she got up, greeted Anita, and, wishing her a safe flight, discreetly exited the room to give the three women some privacy.

Anita paused before the bed for a moment and glanced around the familiar room, which always transported her back to her childhood; back to those moments when she would lie by her grandmother on the big bed and listen to that tender voice tell Greek fairy tales, soothed by the melodic sound of words whose meaning she was still learning.

Long white organza curtains hung from the ceiling, diffusing the daylight into a soft warm glow that filled the room. An old dressing table with a three-panel mirror stood by the wall on the left of the room, cluttered with knick-knacks. On the wall across the bed, a large frame was prominent: a faded sepia photograph of a crowd gathered at a harbor, cloth bundles and trunks littering the quay, waiting for the coming steamship that loomed large on the horizon, clouds of black smoke escaping its funnel, announcing its arrival.

It was the only photo from Eleni's youth. It was fuzzy and the faces were somewhat blurred, as this was a blow up of the original, small photograph and its sharpness had been sacrificed in the process. The original photo had been lost on the day Eleni had picked up the enlarged framed copy from the photographer's. She had been terribly upset, crying for days. Clearly, that photo had meant much to her.

She had told them the picture had been taken during her student days in Italy. The man holding her in his arms was a fellow student, who had been very much in love with her. Eleni claimed she had not felt the same way, but the photo told otherwise—she was leaning against his chest, eyes shut, enjoying the moment with all her senses.

Anita bent down to kiss her grandmother's wrinkled cheeks, the familiar, beloved scent of lemon and lavender a warm, welcoming cocoon. She was going to miss that scent when... She shook her head to chase the gloomy thought away. No morbid thoughts now that she was saying goodbye.

Eleni opened her arms invitingly, with a tender smile and the lively sparkle of a much younger woman in her eyes. Anita sank into her grandmother's affectionate embrace for a moment, and then sat beside her on the bed. "My beautiful grandmother, how are you?"

"How do you find me, Anita?" Eleni asked in a playful tone.

"You look wonderful, *Yiayia*. It's nice to see you smile, it makes you even lovelier..."

"You, my love, are beautiful. I think you take that from me," the elderly woman joked.

Michaela, who had been watching this tender exchange glowing with happiness, came and sat down on the other side of the bed; three generations laughing together, the eldest squeezing their hands tightly as if wishing to infuse them with all her warmth.

Before their laughter had subsided, Eleni turned to Anita and sighed. "You are going to be away for quite a while, my love. Be careful."

"I'll be careful, *Yiayia*, don't worry! It's only work, but I'll be careful."

"Your mother said you're going to Greece. Is that so?"

"Yes, *Yiayia*, I'm flying to Athens today." Anita took a deep breath: "I'll stay there tomorrow and the day after I'm going to an island near Turkey. We'll shoot most of the film there. I'll be back in three months, and finish filming here..."

The moment the words "island near Turkey" left Anita's mouth, Eleni fixed her gaze on the framed photo on the wall and stared at it mesmerized, as if trying to see through the painting into the distant past, oblivious to anything else her granddaughter said.

Unaware of the change that had come over her grandmother, Anita chattered on. "I'll call and we'll Skype, so we'll be able to see each other..."

Michaela, more used to the elderly woman's lapses, stroked her hand and turned toward her daughter. "I think we'd better let grandmother get some rest. You don't want to miss your flight..."

Anita nodded and hugged her grandmother. "*Yiayia*, I'm going now. I love you, don't you ever forget that."

Eleni's eyes were moist, but it was hard to tell if she was saddened by the thoughts crossing her mind or because she had been staring at that photo unblinkingly for so long, still frozen after the mention of Anita's journey.

Feeling the weight of the young woman shift as Anita started to get up, she suddenly grabbed her arms and pulled her closer, until their faces were only inches apart.

"When they come, you hide in the mountains so they don't find you, you hear?" she whispered fiercely in a shaky voice.

Anita, taken aback, was dumbfounded for a moment. Then, realizing her grandmother was in a state of confusion, she promised in a sad voice, "Yes. I'll be careful. Don't worry, I'll be very careful."

Digging her fingers into Anita's arms, Eleni spoke once more, in German this time. "I should have gone with him..."

Her grasp weakened as if all her strength had been exhausted by that last sentence and she could not hang on to Anita any longer.

It was the first time her grandmother had ever spoken to her in German and Anita was taken aback. She stood staring at her grandmother for a moment, trying to make sense of what had just happened. She kissed her forehead and stood up. "I love you *Yiayia*."

"I love you too, Anita," Eleni replied, returning to the present for a moment.

As she turned to leave, Anita's coat belt caught on one of the drawer handles. Bending down to untangle it, she noticed a case on the dresser, an old hunter case pocket watch inside it. She had never seen the watch before and was puzzled to find it there. Already running late, she gave it no more thought and started moving toward the living room, followed by her mother.

One more time, she turned toward her grandmother and waved goodbye, but the old woman remained unresponsive.

Rina, who had been patiently waiting outside, rushed back to her place by Eleni the moment the two of them came out of the room.

Noticing Anita's sad expression, Michaela gently cupped her daughter's face. "Don't be sad Anita, my love; your grandmother is very, very old now. If only we are as lucky and live as long as she has."

"I know, but it's hard seeing her like this," Anita replied swallowing hard. Michaela stroked her daughter's cheek.

"Even so, my sweetheart, she is still with us and we should be thankful for it."

Anita nodded and pulled her hair back as if trying to shake off the sadness. "I have to go now, I'm late and the taxi is waiting... The driver's Greek you know."

"Really?" Michaela smiled, trying to lighten up the mood.

Still unable to brush off what had just happened, Anita turned the conversation back to what had just happened in the bedroom. "Why do you think she spoke to me in German? Who was she talking about when she said she should have gone off with him?"

Michaela shook her head. "Your grandmother has been saying a lot of things I don't understand lately. It's as if she's remembering something, but it's all very confusing. I can't make sense of any of it."

Anita raised her eyebrows quizzically. "What about the watch on the dresser, *Mamá*? I've never seen it before."

"I only saw it for the first time the day before yesterday. When I asked her about it she said "memories" and nothing else. Yesterday, I asked her again and she didn't answer. You know how *Yiayia* is with all this old stuff. Her trunks are filled with it. Some remind her of something, others she just likes to have. Maybe it's your grandfather's. It doesn't matter, go now or you'll be very late."

Anita hugged her mother and gave her a kiss goodbye. "I'll call you when I get there. I love you…"

"I love you too, Anita. Take care."

Michaela reluctantly let go of her daughter and stood outside the front door, watching Anita get back into the taxi and drive off.

≈≈≈≈≈≈≈≈≈≈≈

Very few people got on the ferry boat with me. It was only a local shuttle, connecting five or six islands in the area, and the locals had nicknamed it the "Titanic."

I laughed when I heard the name—even more so when I saw it. It was so old and so small it could barely hold twenty cars in its garage.

"The Unsinkable" was its other nickname because in all these years it had never had any trouble at sea despite ferrying goods, mail, newspapers, the sick and the pregnant, winter after stormy winter. I gave a small prayer that its age would not catch up with it on my first crossing.

Climbing the salt-encrusted stairs, I wondered how many people it must have ferried in all these years and what stories it could tell.

No one asked to see my ticket, so I kept walking. Once inside the indoor seating area, I decided to ignore the locals' advice and have a coffee on board. I had had so many pleasantly sleepless nights I desperately needed the caffeine. The much-maligned ferry boat coffee would have to do. It was a two-hour crossing and I had to keep my wits about me, so I headed straight to the bar. "Double espresso, please."

The bartender, a slightly funny-looking young man who appeared to be in his early twenties, looked at me with a puzzled and surprised expression. "Greek coffee and *frappé* only, buddy," he said.

"Double Greek coffee then," I said, fumbling for my cash.

"Sugar?" he asked, waving the small copper coffee pot in my direction.

"None, *skéto,*" I smiled and he looked impressed, presumably at my ability to down such a bitter drink.

While he prepared my coffee, I looked around at the seating area, taking in my fellow passengers. There had been barely fifty people at the port, mostly foreign tourists loaded with camping gear, who had headed straight up to the sea breeze of the upper deck. The rest, a few Greeks, were locals from the islands on the ferry's route who were either visiting a doctor or friends and relatives. At one end of the room, a TV set was blasting the morning news at a volume that was hard to ignore. I turned back to the bar when I heard the bartender's cheerful voice. "Here you go, my friend. Double Greek coffee, on the house."

I stood there with a banknote in my outstretched hand, trying to understand. A cheeky grin lit up the barman's face. "You're an actor, right?"

I was taken aback and mumbled something that sounded like yes.

"Thought I recognized you, I saw you in a play last year. You look taller on stage ..."

The fact that he recognized me, had seen me in a play and was buying me coffee so generously, made me feel so embarrassed I did not know what to say. I was not used to it as I had never appeared on television. Getting recognized was a rare occurrence and never ceased to amaze me. I thanked him warmly and politely said that really, there was no need.

He dismissed my objections with a brisk wave of the hand. "What are you talking about, it's not often we get a celebrity on board."

He said this loudly enough to turn a few heads, which stared in curiosity, trying to spot the 'celebrity'. No one seemed the least bit impressed, and looked away soon enough. I thanked him again and took the coffee cup. I lingered at the bar.

"Are you from Athens?" I asked him.

"Yes."

"Do you go to the theater often?"

"Not really. My girlfriend likes plays so we go once in a while. Are you going to be in anything this year so we can come see you?"

"No, not as things stand at the moment. But it's early days."

My hand was getting scalded by the hot coffee cup, so I made toward the armchairs to leave it on a table. He carried on in a louder voice, as if we were the only two people at the bar, "And you're here for a film now, right? That movie."

That's when I caught on to the fact that this guy was truly well informed, and I laughed. "Yes, that's what I'm here for. You really are up to date, aren't you?"

He placed a newspaper on the bar with a smile. "I spend a lot of time on this boat, buddy, and read everything. You'd be surprised at the things people leave behind when they get off."

Unable to contain my curiosity, I moved back toward the bar. "Can I borrow this for a moment?" I asked.

"Sure. It's even got an interview with that German star, the one who is half-Greek. And a photo of you with her," he winked, handing over the paper. "When I go to the bridge, I'll bring you today's paper. Even more photos in that one, but the Captain's reading it now."

He stressed "captain" in a way that clearly showed the man was not exactly his favorite person.

I thanked him again and sat down to enjoy my coffee, leaving the newspaper on the table before me. The drink was not as bad as I had expected, although that was probably an unexpected perk of my celebrity status in the eyes of the bartender.

I leaned back in the faded armchair and opened the newspaper. There was a photo of Anita on the front page, and the headline read: "On the set of *Lost in Time* with Anita Hertz. Exclusive interview and photos." The truth is I had never really paid any attention to the press before. But when I joined this huge production, I discovered what a big part newspapers, magazines, interviews and, unfortunately, gossip played in promoting a film.

Anita's photo brought her before me in flesh and blood. I could still taste her skin; I could still feel her body brush against mine. Although we had only parted a few hours ago, I wanted to see her again, right there and then. Maybe I was afraid that leaving her so soon would dull our budding affair. It was intense and beautiful, and a new experience for me. I did not know how she felt about us being together in the future, but I still felt optimistic. Neither one of us held back in demonstrating our feelings; we understood each other and worked together as if we had been doing it for years, yet without that numbing sensation that routine brings to the lives of people who spend so much time together on an everyday basis. Often, we'd just sit together without speaking, happy to just be in each other's presence.

I could not understand how we had become so close in such a brief amount of time, nor did I care to. What I felt deep inside sufficed. Whenever I saw her, my blood coursed faster through my veins. Every time our bodies met, I slipped into another dimension. I feared dwelling on the whys and hows would diminish the intensity of the experience.

I looked at the photos and smiled when I saw the one of us together. It was a promotional photo, and I remembered that day as if it were yesterday. I had felt the current that passed between us as we'd stood side by side for the first time; it was impossible to ignore. She, too, could feel the chemistry. I'd wished like a small child that the photo shoot would never end, so that I could stay near her.

I'll never forget the first time we were together on our own.

On one of our rare days off, Mihalis, who worked as a general helper on location, took us to a beach on my mother's island in his speedboat. The beach was locally known as Kryfó, hidden-away. It lay just across the water from where we were filming.

He initially kept our exact destination a secret, just telling us that he was taking us to a secluded beach of incomparable beauty.

I felt an inkling about where we were going when I saw the direction we were headed toward and asked for the name of the island. As soon as my suspicions were confirmed, my first impulse was to ask him to turn back. Seeing how happy and relaxed Anita was, though, made me hold my tongue. Anyway, given how secluded Mihalis claimed the spot was, there was very little chance of us running into anyone.

It took forty minutes to get there. I have traveled much in my life, but never had I seen a beach like that one. Literally a hideaway, it could only be reached by boat or after an arduous trek through the mountains.

The beauty of the place was breathtaking, as if God had summoned all His artistry and inspiration to create it and then tuck it away from human eyes.

A river came down from high up the mountain, arriving on a large stretch of virgin sand, crowned by two enormous rocks. Beneath the rocks and hidden from view was a cave, a shelter to fugitives and secret lovers, as Mihalis pointed out in a voice laden with meaning.

The locals called it the Cave of Silence—the still silence that engulfed you once you were inside; the silence of all the secrets the Cave had kept over the years.

During our crossing, Mihalis had shared many colorful stories about this blissful spot: stories of pirates who'd come here to bury hidden treasure; of the couple who had met here to enjoy a few stolen moments of love during the Nazi occupation; and his own story of how he would meet his wife here in the early stages of their romance, to escape prying eyes and local gossip.

It felt strange to set foot on my mother's island for the very first time in such unusual circumstances and in this manner. I knew that I'd be back again in a few days. I tried not to dwell on it and turned my attention to Anita, who seemed enthralled.

Mihalis left us on the beach with some food and drinks and said he'd be back in the evening. It was a warm, sunny day, we were all alone surrounded by the most beautiful scenery and, although nothing had happened between us until then, it was not long before we succumbed to what we had been feeling from the first moment we'd had met.

When our lips touched for the first time, I felt as if time stood still. And as soon as we walked into the Cave of Silence, we realized how much we wanted one another.

I am still not aware of how I overcame my fear of closed spaces that day. I rarely entered caves, always seized by an irrational fear that I may never be able to get out. That day, however, I could sense nothing other than Anita's presence and the turmoil it stirred inside me.

She spread the sheet we'd brought with us in the center of the cave and beckoned me to lie down next to her. We made love as if it were our first time, as if we had never made love to anyone before; as if we were only just discovering a hidden pleasure and we shared a look of intensity and incredulity, wondering whether what was happening was truly real. Adam and Eve, on earth.

A small lake had formed inside the cave, a pool of water dripping from the cave walls. It reflected what little light could enter the cave onto the ceiling, casting a kaleidoscope of fluid shapes and the shadows of our bodies onto the wild rocks. Our moans of pleasure echoed before being swallowed up by the silence.

The rocks were scarred with carved initials and names, an odd testament to those who had been there before, a brotherhood of visitors who had known this place and left a relic of their story behind. We did the same before we left. We found a place high up on one of the walls and I carved our names on the rough rock with a penknife—right beside two other names that had faded with the passage of time. You could barely make out *ELENI* and an *M*. Time and brine had taken away the rest. How long ago had these names been carved? Were Eleni and M. still alive today? Years from now, would someone else be trying to carve their name next to ours, see our faded names?

We stayed on the beach until dusk when Mihalis returned to ferry us back. If we weren't working early the early following day I would have asked him to let us spend the night there, in the Cave of Silence.

Ever since that day, I felt that I had reached the destination I'd always been searching for; like I'd become a different person, the person I had always wanted to be...

≈≈≈≈≈≈≈≈≈≈

My reverie was interrupted by a man sitting at a nearby table, who spoke loudly at the television set. "Unbelievable, people can be barbarians."

I turned to the TV set and suddenly, as if someone had just turned the volume up, I heard the newscaster announce that the upcoming video was distressing and unsuitable for younger viewers. I had not heard the introduction to this news item, so I stared at the screen trying to make out what the story was about.

The scenes unfolding on the screen shocked me so much I was unable to turn away, despite the revolt I felt. Shot somewhere in the Middle East, the video showed a woman, her hands bound behind her back, blindfolded with a scarf and kneeling on the ground. A braying crowd of men, women, and, shockingly children, had gathered, stones in their hands, and as far as I could make out from the shaky footage, were getting ready to hurl them at their victim. Thankfully, the video ended there and resumed only at the end of the stoning, the camera zooming in on the woman's lifeless body covered in blood-splattered stones. The caption at the bottom of the screen read *WOMAN SENTENCED TO DEATH BY STONING FOR ADULTERY.*

The newscaster, also shocked by what had just been screened, stayed silent for a couple of seconds and then resumed the broadcast.

The sudden contrast between the sweet image of Anita on the beach and the brutal execution of that poor woman had shaken me so much that, for a moment, I felt my extremities go numb. I wondered how it was possible for one human being to do this to another and, in this instance, how so many people took on the part of executioner in this monstrous killing so willingly. Surely that was a woman they'd known, who'd lived among them, yet no one seemed to feel any pity for her.

I wished I hadn't watched any of it, that I could have stayed wrapped up in my reveries. I glared at the man whose loud voice had brought me back to reality and the TV set and turned to face the window behind me, trying to escape what I had just seen.

An elderly man was staring at me with a look of sympathy, as if telling me to calm down and forget what I had just watched. Our eyes met and, for a moment, he seemed familiar, making me wonder whether this was someone I knew. I gave him a tight little smile to convey my thanks and he returned my gesture with a slight nod.

I picked up my coffee cup and took a large sip. I don't know why, but at that moment my mother begging me with all her might not to set foot on the island where she'd been born came to my mind. I leaned back and closed my eyes, transported to the scene that had unfolded at her house three months before.

My mother's house, three months ago

The truth is, my visits back home had become increasingly rare these past few years. My relationship with my mother was not to blame; the man who had been sharing her life during that time was. I never expected my mother to remain single and not have a partner as she grew older. After all, she had spent ten lonely years following my father's death from cancer. I knew how difficult that had been, how much she missed him, so I never felt bothered by the presence of a new man in her life. It's just that my relations with Kostas were almost non-existent. He ignored my presence and I reciprocated.

My mother had had a difficult childhood, as had her brother, Uncle Nikos, especially during the War. When the Germans executed my grandparents, the orphaned siblings had been forced to flee their island on a small boat. After a day at sea with no food or water, they washed up on a nearby island and were rescued by some monks. When the Nazis learned that the two children were being sheltered at the monastery, they burned it to the ground. Once again, Mother and Uncle Nikos escaped by the skin of their teeth and went into hiding. At the end of the war, they were taken to Athens, into the care of some distant relatives. Growing up, they managed to stand on their own two feet; my mother finished school and married my father and Uncle Nikos moved to Thessaloniki.

My mother always claimed not to remember much, but I sensed that most of what she recounted had been indelibly etched in her memory despite being so young at the time;

practically an infant. The only heirloom that had survived that time was the cross her godmother had given her at her christening, in accordance with religious custom. According to Uncle Nikos, she'd had a secret christening at sea.

Uncle Nikos certainly remembered a lot more than my mother, but his lips were tightly sealed. He'd buried those painful experiences somewhere deep inside him and did not want to share them with anyone else.

Before leaving Athens to start work on the film, I decided to go visit my mother. Not only would I be absent for quite a while, I had to pick up my uncle's ashes, kept in the steel box that would accompany me on this trip.

She let me in with a smile on her face. "You can still let yourself in the house with your own key, you know."

She'd just had a haircut and her short white hair made her look more vibrant, giving more character to her wrinkles and the story they told.

I smiled back and blurted out the first excuse that popped into my head. "I've lost my keys."

She didn't fall for it. "Don't lie. We are alone. Kostas is out and won't be back for a while."

"I like your hair, *Mamá*," I changed the subject playfully patting her head. "I've never seen you with short hair before."

"I thought it was time for a change, even in my old age, Dimitri. Sit down. Have you had anything to eat? Would you like me to get you something?"

"I'm okay, I've had lunch," I replied looking around the room.

Not much had changed since I'd moved out, and, for some strange reason, I liked that. I felt like a pilgrim, revisiting the temple that held my memories, everything we had shared while my father was alive. Waiting for him to come home from work, hanging onto the door, waiting for the sound of his keys in the lock...even at that moment, I looked at the door thinking that he'd walk in and take me in his arms.

I was glad to see the photo of the three of us was still hanging on the wall, my parents grinning and beaming with pride at their eight-month-old son. They looked so happy! When Kostas had moved in I had feared that my mother would have felt obliged to take the photo down, but it hadn't happened. She still honored her past.

I sat on the couch and let my eyes wander over the magnificent sea view framed by the balcony doors before me. My mother had filled her balcony with pots bursting with all kinds of flowers. This time of year, it was a cornucopia of color, and the heady flower scents combined with the sea view made you forget you were in an apartment, tricking you into thinking you were sitting in the most wonderful garden. I missed this relaxing blend of green and blue, a constant absence in the urban downtown apartment where I lived.

While I sat on the couch thinking about my father and lost in the view, my mother had been busy in the kitchen. She returned carrying a large glass of freshly squeezed orange juice, which she placed before me with a smile. "Drink it," she said as if I were a ten-year-old again, and sat down beside me.

I took a big sip. Once again I felt like my childhood self, my mother holding the juice in her hand and waiting for me to gulp it down as I hopped on one foot, late for school as always, my father waiting at the door to drop me off and I dashing off, straw still dangling from my lips, leaving the juice half-drunk,.

"So, you're leaving tomorrow..." she said in an altered voice, the bright smile on her face replaced by a worried frown.

"Yes, tomorrow morning and I shoot my first scene the day after." I tried to speak in a light-hearted manner, to make her feel some of my joy at the prospect of the brilliant break that had fallen into my lap. She tried to look happy for me, but it was clear her mind was elsewhere. "Congratulations, I'm so pleased for you. I hope all goes well and it's a hit..."

She took a long pause. I kept quiet, feeling there was something else she wanted to say. But her pause just grew longer and she seemed to struggle to express what was on her mind. I knew it had something to do with the island, and I tried to help her out by speaking first. "Everything is going to be fine, *Mamá*, don't worry. But perhaps now is a good time to tell me why you don't want me to go there. I think I'm old enough now to know the reasons behind this. Whatever it is, please tell me and I'll be careful. But I need to know, in case I need to protect myself in some way."

My mother sighed and seemed to summon all her strength. She took my hands in hers and looked at me, determined, intense, her eyes welling up. "If you do exactly as I tell you, Dimitri, you won't need anyone's protection. If you insist on going there, you'll go there, scatter your uncle's ashes, and not mention a word of it to anyone. You must *never* mention your grandfather's name. Don't tell anyone that you are connected to that place, in any way. And leave as soon as your work there is done. Can you promise me that? Can you?"

She fell silent once again as a teardrop made its way down her wrinkled cheek. I tried to contain the anger rising in me. Her secrecy, her refusal to explain made me unhappy and ill at ease. What *would* happen if I were to reveal that my grandfather was Yiannis Reniotis, that I was the son of Maria Reniotis?

My mother could read me well. Regaining her composure, she pressed on. "When you come back, we'll talk about this. I'll tell everything I know. I haven't been lying when I said I don't remember that much. Your uncle kept secrets, even from me. He didn't like to bring up the past. Maybe it's better if we don't either. Only pain and bad memories..."

I could see she was upset and I did not want to make her feel worse, so I decided to let the matter rest. "Okay. I'll do exactly as you say."

"Promise?" she asked once again, as if wanting to make sure.

"Yes, come on now, you're making me feel like a little boy..."

She looked me in the eyes once again and walked out of the living room toward my own bedroom.

I felt bad for pressing her but, at the same time, my curiosity was getting the better of me, increasing over the years. Having gotten tired of asking and receiving no answers, I'd done a little digging of my own in an attempt to shed some light on this family mystery. All I'd found out was simply a rehash of what little my mother had shared. The Germans had burned down most of the village and executed many of its inhabitants. For many years the village remained abandoned, until about fifty years ago when some of the locals returned. No one from grandfather Reniotis' family had ever gone back.

I was well aware of the temptation to break the promise I'd just given, find out as much as I could when I was there. But I also felt scared. Should these "bad memories" be left alone, as my mother advised? At that point, I really wasn't sure how I would handle this once I got there. All I could tell myself was that I would focus on my work and take things one day at a time.

Another box filled with secrets was now on the coffee table before me. The box containing Uncle Nikos' ashes, wrapped in linen, looking almost like a macabre gift. My mother had just placed it there and now stood gazing at it, transfixed. "Uncle Nikos left for Thessaloniki straight after his military service. I rarely saw him after that. If he hadn't felt it was his duty to look after me, he'd have left sooner. Even at my wedding he only came to the church and left straight after the service. I don't hold it against him. I just wish we'd spent more time together."

Her voice cracked when she uttered these last words. I got up and held her in my arms.

She seemed to come out of her trance, wiped her eyes, and said in a steadier voice, "We'll have to sort out all the inheritance paperwork when you come back. Not that he left much..."

"All I want is for you to be happy, *Mamá*. You've had more than your share of unhappiness, more than enough. Now, I just want you to be happy."

I kissed her forehead and she gave a little smile. "Yes, let's forget all this for now. Tell me about the film. I saw your co-star on TV and she mentioned you, said you get on very well. I'm not sure I've seen her in anything, but she

seems familiar somehow. Her face rer
What's her name again, Anita…?"

"Hertz."

She picked up on how my vɔ
mentioned her last name and gave me
"She's a pretty girl, seems very sweet. She speaᴋ
Greek; you can't tell she's German. Were her parents ᴄ
I couldn't understand. She looks more Greek than Germaᵢ.
anyway."

The truth was, I knew very little about Anita. I hadn't asked her anything personal at the screen test; I only knew what I'd picked up from various sources here and there. "I know her grandmother is Greek and her mother taught in a Greek school in Germany. We haven't had a chance to talk."

I felt her give me a piercing look and shifted awkwardly on the couch.

"Now you'll have all the time in the world to talk, you'll be spending so much time together," she said.

I purposely ignored the little hint and decided to put an end to the conversation there and then. "We'll be very busy with work, but if I find out anything else, I'll be sure to let you know."

She picked up on my wish to change the subject and played along. "I'm very happy for you, Dimitri, I'm sure you'll do a great job. Just be careful. Be humble, and keep your head down. You know how people can get when they see someone succeed."

I wasn't one to brag and play the actor card in any case, but my mother was right. Many people had already started acting differently around me once they'd found out I'd gotten this part, making snide comments behind my back which reached my ears through others who thought that

e way into my good books. In any event, I thought I'd
be cautious.

Our time was running out. Kostas was sure to return
shortly and I wanted to avoid running into him. "*Mamá*, I
have to go now, I still have some errands to run before I
leave."

Her eyes moistened once again, and she gave me another
hug. "Go. Have a safe journey. Don't forget to call me when
you have a moment, I don't want to be bothering you. When
you get to the island, find out where the spring is, and
scatter Uncle Nikos' ashes, as he wished. But don't forget
what you promised—not a word to anyone."

She said all this in a light-hearted manner but I could feel
how anxious she was. I tried to reassure her as best as I
could. "I promise. Don't worry if I don't call often. We'll be
very busy and I won't have a lot of free time."

"I understand, but please call me before you set off for
the island."

I picked up the box containing the ashes and headed for
the door. She accompanied me to the elevator, kissed my
cheek, and waited with me while it arrived. "Have a safe
trip. Be careful..."

"Yes, yes, I'll be careful," I said in a little-boy voice. "I'll
eat all my greens, I won't swim far from the shore, and I'll
get a good night's sleep every night."

We both laughed. I stepped into the elevator. "I love
you," I said just as the doors began to close.

"I love you too."

Just before the elevator doors met, I caught the
frightened look which had returned to her eyes. She
realized I saw her and gave me a quick wave. I saw my
reflection in the steel doors, a tall man holding a box of

ashes, and felt a chill run down my spine. Trying to shake off the irrational fear that gripped me, I told myself everything was going to be okay, that all these secrets were probably exaggerated family stories. I pressed the ground floor button and thought of Anita and how much I was looking forward to seeing her again.

≈≈≈≈≈≈≈≈≈≈≈

Anita, dressed in a long white dress, was trying to shelter from the searing sun under a giant umbrella that seemed ready to take off at any moment, the strong gusts of wind shaking it perilously. She was the only actor present that day. People were milling about, carrying things and getting ready to shoot the scene, while Rita was vainly battling to keep Anita's hair intact despite the strong wind.

Clutching a handful of papers in her hand, Electra hurriedly made her way toward her, full of apologies. "I'm so sorry for the delay, Miss Hertz. We won't be ready for you for another twenty minutes. Is there anything I can get you? Water? Anything else?"

"I'm fine, I have enough water, thank you very much, Ma'am," she teased.

Electra smiled and shrugged at the same time. "It's not easy to call you Anita. I'll get used to it eventually."

"Thank you, Electra, I'm only teasing. Call me whatever you like. Well, it seems I have time for a little sightseeing. I'll walk to the monastery. Thank you, Rita, I think you've done all you can."

Anita picked up a shawl from a nearby chair to cover her naked shoulders as well as her head and headed off in the direction of the monastery. "If you need me sooner come and get me, please."

"Don't worry, we will," Electra replied and turned to Rita, thinking Anita was out of earshot. "She is really great, isn't she? Friendly and professional at the same time."

Rita nodded in silent agreement.

Built on the edge of a large rock, part of the monastery hung suspended over the sea below. Constructed entirely of stone, it looked more like a small Venetian castle than a place of worship, with its tall tower and turrets. Were it not for the crosses decorating the rooftops of the two churches, a visitor would be easily fooled as to the building's true nature.

This was the only day they would spend at this spot, shooting a scene where the female lead visits an abandoned monastery and stares wistfully into the distance when she finds out that the man she loves has left forever. It was a small scene but would take the larger part of the day to shoot. Fastidious as he was, the film director wanted it to be as perfect as could be.

Her long white dress flapping in the strong wind, the edges of her shawl rising behind her like a pair of wings, Anita looked more like a fairy queen than a visiting pilgrim. She walked through the main gate and headed toward the highest spot to get as broad a view as possible. All day they hadn't come across any of the monks, just the man who had been entrusted with opening the gate for them when they arrived. Everything was still, calm, silent.

As she climbed up the stairs leading to the tiny church perched on the highest point of the rock, a sweet, unusual scent filled the air. It wasn't perfume or some plant. It was unlike anything she had smelled before. She stepped into the small, paved courtyard circling the tiny church, whose door stood open. The smell was now more intense than ever and Anita realized it was coming from inside.

She hesitated before the door, wondering whether she should go in. Unable to resist the temptation, she stepped into the church's dark interior. Waiting for a moment for her eyes to adjust to the change of light, she took another couple of steps and, eyes growing accustomed to the trembling flames of the votive candles, stood before the altar. She could just about make out the wall to her right, faded images of various saints slowly coming into focus. She could tell the smell was coming from there, but not what it was.

With a start, she suddenly noticed that someone else was in the church with her. A monk was sitting on a chair against the wall, his black robes and the obscure candlelight making him nearly invisible, so much so that Anita could have sworn the man wasn't there when she first walked in. Realizing that he had startled her, the monk spoke to her in a soft, tranquil voice. "Good morning, my child."

Anita tried to regain her composure. "Good morning. I'm sorry to disturb you. I didn't see you when I walked in."

"You didn't disturb me, my child." He smiled but remained seated. "I knew you hadn't seen me, but I thought you came in to pray, so I kept quiet."

Anita could see him clearly now. He had the voice of a young man, but he was at least eighty. His face was narrow and thin, covered with a heavy white beard. The way he sat, immobile, made him seem like he was part of the church fresco behind him. Feeling awkward, she made a small move toward the door, but the monk was quick to reassure her. "Stay if you wish to pray, my child."

Anita had no intention of praying, she just wanted to admire the church, but could not resist his calm, soft voice. So she smiled her thanks at the old man and admired the altar and the church while silence engulfed them both once again. Feeling braver, she turned to the monk and asked, "What is the smell? I've never smelled anything like it before."

He stood up and moved past her, stopping before an icon encased in a stand made of wood and glass. As he walked by her, Anita felt the sweet smell grow stronger, almost as if it were coming from him. She moved toward the monk who was pointing at the icon. "This is where the smell comes from, my child, from the Saint's icon."

Anita took a closer look at the icon. She wasn't sure that she believed in miracles, but at that moment she felt as if she believed what the old man's calm, assured voice was telling her. A bead of sweat ran down her forehead, the climb and the heat inside the church catching up with her.

"Come, let's step outside and get some fresh air," he said and moved to the door, his long robe rustling at every step.

Anita gladly followed the old man out to the courtyard. When she saw this otherworldly man turn into more ordinary flesh and blood in the bright daylight, she could not help but notice that his eyes were the color of the stormy sea. She'd never seen eyes that shade of blue before. He stood there gazing at her, deeply serene. His strange eyes seemed to smile at her.

She had heard one of the crew describe the man while they were at the beach, and realized he must be the Abbot. Tall, ascetic, he resembled the saints and martyrs on the church walls. She put out her hand and introduced herself, unsure of what was customary when greeting an orthodox monk. "My name is Anita. I'm here with the film crew."

"I know, my child," he replied with disarming forthrightness. "I am the Abbot of this monastery. We are pleased to welcome you here."

"I know... that you're the Abbot, I mean. You have done a wonderful job here. The monastery is perfectly preserved. It must take a lot of work to keep it like this."

"With God's love and help anything can be achieved, my child," he replied humbly.

Anita shifted uneasily under his intense gaze, and asked another question to suppress the awkwardness she was feeling. "I don't know much about its history. When was it built?"

He did not immediately reply but stood still, facing the sea, looking out at something invisible in the distance. For a few moments, neither spoke and all that could be heard was the whistle of the sharp breeze and the waves crashing at the feet of the rock.

The old man raised his voice so he could be heard, his gaze still locked on the horizon. "At the beginning of last century, there was a small building on this spot. The monks would stay there when they came to look after their fields and animals that were kept in a nearby barn. They eventually built some rooms and a church. The island was conquered by the Italians in 1912, but the locals lived peacefully with them. Bad things started to happen when the Germans arrived. During the occupation, many locals whose homes were burnt down by the Germans sought refuge here. Just before the end of the war, the Germans burnt down many houses on the island. My child, many bad things happened...and not just by the Nazis."

He turned to look at Anita, who felt guilty for a moment for being German. Unaware, the old man continued. "One of the locals informed the Germans that two children were hiding here, a three-year-old girl and her brother, who was older. They had escaped from a nearby island and had washed up on this beach, hungry and exhausted. The Nazis sent some soldiers to arrest them, but the children ran away. That's when they set fire to the monastery in reprisal. Nothing was left standing, everything was turned to ash."

He took a big breath and tried to steady his wavering voice. Anita was looking at him, spellbound.

"The children then disappeared and no one knows what became of them. The monks started to search the ruins to see if anything could be salvaged. Under the smoking ashes, the young novitiate who had found the children on the beach discovered the icon of St. Mámas, intact. This miracle inspired the monks to rebuild the monastery on this site, named after the Saint. With the help of God and the love of our fellow men, we managed to complete construction a few years ago. That's when the second miracle happened and continues to this day. You saw it yourself: the icon's odor of sanctity."

Anita listened to the story with great interest, nevertheless believing that there was a rational explanation for both miracles. As if reading her mind, the monk asked, "Do you believe in God, my child?"

She didn't know whether to answer truthfully; to tell him that, to her, God was man himself and what he did or did not do. Wishing to avoid a long discussion, she chose to say something she truly believed. "I believe in love and what happens from a place of love. That is truly a miracle when it happens..."

The old man was silent for a moment. He was about to speak when Electra's voice interrupted them, coming up behind them. "I'm sorry to interrupt. Miss Hertz, you are wanted now," she said, nodding to the monk who was trying not to stare at her half shaved head.

"I'll be with you in a moment Electra, thank you." She turned back toward the monk. "I'm sorry, I have to go now."

"God bless you." He raised his hand in a gesture of benediction.

Anita turned to follow Electra who was already walking ahead, hesitated, and turned back toward the monk who was still looking at her.

"The boy who saved the children on the boat and found the icon..."

"You are looking at him," he readily replied as if he had been expecting that question, then turned and began climbing the stairs that led to the monks' quarters.

She turned away reluctantly and started making her way back to the set, ruminating on the story she had just heard.

Rita walked up to her on the beach and starting fixing her hair while Electra handed her the script and urged her to have one last look. Holding the papers in her hand, Anita turned back toward the monastery and saw that the old monk was now standing at the front gates, watching them. She raised her hand and waved, and he returned the greeting. Her mind once again focused on her work, and all thoughts of children and war were soon forgotten.

≈≈≈≈≈≈≈≈≈≈≈

I woke up with a start. Lost in my thoughts about my mother and what had happened at her house, I'd drifted off to sleep. I looked at the clock over the ferry bar and realized I'd been sleeping for at least a half hour. If the armchair had not been so uncomfortable, I think I could have slept through the rest of the crossing. The place was quiet now, most passengers having moved to the upper deck and the remaining few fast asleep. I thought about going outside but the newspaper that had fallen on my lap caught my attention.

I picked it up, took a gulp of cold coffee, and turned the pages until I found the interview. A double page spread, filled with photos, the headline reading, *ANITA HERTZ, LOST IN TIME... AND THE GREEK ISLES.* I read on.

Famous actress Anita Hertz arrived in the Aegean a few days ago to begin filming 'Lost in Time', director Dimitri Liberopoulos' new project. An expensive Greek-German production, it will be shot mostly on the Greek islands and in Athens. Greek actor Dimitris Voudouris also stars in the film, making his debut on the big screen.

At this point, an announcement cackled over the ferry speakers, but the sound was so bad I could not make out a word of what was being said. I ignored it and went back to reading.

A man and a woman meet on a Greek island ten years after their first meeting and a relationship that ended abruptly. They resume their old love affair during the few days of their stay. But a secret that comes to light will change their lives forever. We traveled to the Aegean and spoke with the movie's star, Anita Hertz.

Miss Hertz, few people in Greece know that you have Greek grandparents and love our country very much, although you haven't spent a lot of time here. Tell us about your ties to Greece.

I don't think you need to be Greek or have Greek ties to love this country, it's a place anyone could easily fall in love with. My grandmother is Greek. My mother is a teacher and she taught at a Greek school. We spoke mostly Greek at home.

Do you believe in the twists of fate, which is really the main theme of this movie?

I believe people shape their own destiny with their actions; the choices they make. We set events in motion and their repercussions, not some higher power.

This is your first time in Greece, isn't that a bit strange given your love for the country and your family's ties?

Well, fate is certainly not at play here. (Laughter). I just did not manage to come earlier, even though I really wanted to. Every time I'd plan a visit something would come up; work or other obligations. I'm very happy to be here, and even happier that the reason behind my trip is a wonderful film. It's clearly a case of perfect timing.

The film is a love story. It looks at how love becomes an all-consuming force in the characters' lives. How important is love in your life?

Look, I think people actually choose who they fall in love with, in a way. It may seem random but it isn't. Their life, choices they've made along the way, they all bring them to someone who's also arrived there through the choices they've made. This is also what happens in the film. These two people meet at some point and then they lose touch only to meet again when their lives and choices make their paths cross again. Of course, this doesn't mean that this time round it will work...

So everything is a matter of choice?

Almost everything.

Have you ever been hopelessly in love?

I looked up and tried to remember when she'd given that interview. Was it before or after our visit to Kryfó? I couldn't be sure so I went back to reading, anxious to read her reply.

What's important is to see, to examine the lives of the main characters of the film. Their stories are the reason we are here on this island, not mine.

I smiled. A master class on how to handle press gracefully and protect your privacy, a lesson I would strive to learn. And another indication of how seriously Anita took her work, how she remained professional at all times; except with me, of course. Maybe this was an interview she had given before anything happened between us after all. I decided to go with that option; it suited me better.

I must have had a very curious expression on my face, for it certainly aroused the curiosity of the old man who was sitting nearby, staring once again. Still smiling to myself, I read on.

A Greek actor, Dimitri Voudouris, is the male lead in this film, even though he's inexperienced. This is his first film part and you are a very experienced actress, but reports say it's working out very well. What is that like?

Dimitri is a very good actor and a pleasure to work with. He is very professional; I don't see him as 'inexperienced' as you say. On the contrary, I feel like I am working with a talented and seasoned actor.

Could you ever fall in love with someone you work with?

Well, never say never, but probably not. At least, that has never happened so far.

So she must have given this interview a while ago.

Could you ever pretend to be in love with a co-star, to generate more publicity for a film, to help promote it?

I don't think I can pretend in anything that has to do with real life. I have strived very hard to keep my personal and professional lives separate. Although sometimes it is hard, I think I have managed it.

What do you think of Greece now that you're here?

I must confess that I've been impressed, not just by how beautiful it is but by the Greeks themselves. Now that I am getting to know the people, working with them, I find that I feel comfortable with the lifestyle, with people's attitudes.

I guess you'll be visiting more often from now on?

That's certain. Unfortunately, it doesn't just depend on me. But I love the place more and more with each passing day and I would like to come back again soon.

≈≈≈≈≈≈≈≈≈≈≈

I looked at the photos accompanying the interview, especially the one of the two of us. I felt that they were also pieces of the puzzle of my relationship to Anita, that they added to what I already knew about her and made me admire and want her even more.

The sitting area was getting hot and stuffy. I needed to get some air, to feel the sea breeze. I left my rucksack on the armchair, folded the newspaper neatly, and placed it on the table. Walking past the bar, I saw the young bartender sitting on a low chair and playing a game on his cell phone.

"Could you keep an eye on my things, please? I'm stepping outside for a bit."

"Yes, of course, don't worry about it. Keeping an eye on everything in here," he said without looking up from the screen. I laughed and stepped outside nonetheless.

The engine made the small deck shake as the ferry groaned and heaved, leaving behind a white trail of foam. Passengers were lying down on the white benches, surrounded by bags and suitcases. Others had pulled up plastic chairs close to the railings and sat gazing out to sea. The sky was clear and you could see far into the distance. To my left, I could just make out a blurry mountainous outline that I guessed must be my mother's homeland. It did not seem that far, but the 'Titanic' was a slow boat.

I rubbed my hands together to scrape off the salt from the banister and pulled up a plastic chair. I sat down, stretched my legs on the railings, and looked out toward the island.

The slight tinge of fear I had felt whenever my mother spoke of her homeland returned and once again I wondered what would happen if I revealed who I was once I got there. The only rational explanation I could come up with was that my mother's family must have become embroiled in some local feud, a vendetta with another family that was not ready to be forgotten. Despite this being the 21st century, there were places in remote parts of Greece where the culture of vendetta persisted and even young people had lost their lives to it. How someone could hurt an innocent soul to extract vengeance for something in the past, an injury someone else had inflicted, was beyond me.

The more I thought about it, the more I was inclined to follow my mother's advice. After all, what ties did I really have to this place beyond an obligation to carry out my uncle's dying wish? Moreover, the desire to be with Anita, to spend as much time as possible with her, was becoming all-consuming and pushing my curiosity about my family's history and its secrets to the background. Were it not for my uncle's ashes, I probably wouldn't be sacrificing precious moments with her to visit the island at all. A love affair of a few days and my life was already changing.

I felt a hand tap my shoulder and a newspaper was thrust in my face. "Freshest news on the boat. Coffee-stained by the captain himself, but still readable," the young bartender said, sneering as he mentioned the captain's name.

That boy would have made a great comedian, I thought as I picked up the paper and thanked him.

"I'm Thanasis," he said and I shook his hand.

Not only was the newspaper well and truly stained, it was one of those gossipy papers that carried a lot of allegations and very little news. Buried in one of the pages was a small, gossipy article that made me catch my breath. *LOVED IN TIME. ANITA HERTZ- DIMITRIS VOUDOURIS.* Beneath the headline, a blurry picture of the both of us, kissing. Blurry, yet clear enough to make out who it was. I read on.

Exclusive pictures from the island. According to our sources, the two leads are not only LOST IN TIME on their island location, but also LOST IN LOVE with each other. This photo confirms all the local gossip. The film is due to open in Athens at Christmas, and we wish all the best to the new couple.

It was clear someone had taken this picture on their cell phone and sent it to the paper. I also wondered for a moment whether that someone worked for production, keen to gain any publicity to promote the film. We had been very careful when we were out and about, and I could not remember any locals being around on the night the photo was taken. We'd been alone and had had the small winding streets of the island's town to ourselves. Or so we thought.

My phone vibrated and I shifted in my chair trying to extract it from my back pocket. A text from Anita: "I miss you..."

I stared at the screen. Had she read my thoughts? At that moment I wanted to turn back, jump off the ship and swim back to her, just to see her even for a moment. I quickly typed, "I miss you too. I wish you were here with me," and pressed send. I could have said so much more, wanted to say so much more. But I knew she was working, and I didn't want to distract her.

My eyes flickered between the screen and the sea, but then I saw the old man who had been staring at me in the living room struggling to untangle a plastic chair from a stack of chairs beside me. Without thinking, I shoved the phone back in my pocket and went over to help him.

"Need a hand?" I asked, already pulling one chair up while holding the others down. The top chair finally came free and I straightened it and beckoned him to sit down.

"Thank you, young man."

"You're welcome," I said as I returned to my place. He kept on staring at me in the same way. I wondered once again whether I had seen him before, whether this was someone I had already met. I smiled awkwardly and he returned the smile, the puzzled frown of a man trying to figure something out still on his face.

"Is this your first time on the island?" I heard him ask. I felt my guard go up straight away. Was this someone who knew who I was? Or was I being paranoid, a result of my mother's ceaseless warnings? I felt defensive and decided to reply with a small white lie. "I've been here once before with my parents when I was young. I don't remember much, though."

He didn't seem surprised by my answer. Maybe I was worrying without reason.

"It hasn't changed much, my boy, in all these years. Are you here on business or holiday? I heard Thanasis downstairs say you are an actor."

Maybe that's why he'd been staring at me. Maybe he was trying to figure out if he'd seen me on TV or something like that. "I'm filming on another island and I thought I'd visit yours for a couple of days. I heard it's a beautiful place."

"Beautiful and secluded, but we like it that way."

I couldn't figure out whether he was saying that they liked the peace and quiet or disliked visitors. I decided to go with the first option. "That's what I'm looking for. A couple of days of rest so I can get back to work," I said, leaning back in my chair.

"That, we can provide," he laughed.

His smile was open and sincere and I felt a bit ashamed of my suspicions. The poor man was just being friendly, trying to thank me for getting his chair or bored and wanting a bit of company. "I'm Thomas," he introduced himself.

"Dimitri," I said and got up to shake his hand. His palm was warm and rough, calloused.

My phone vibrated. I apologized and looked at the screen; another message from Anita. "Are you there yet?" I figured she must be on a break and decided to call her. I dialed Anita and apologized to Thomas at the same time, saying I had to make this call. I picked up the newspaper while I waited for the phone to ring and moved back into the seating area where I would have more quiet and privacy. The phone still wasn't ringing by the time I went in. I took a closer look at the screen and realized there was no signal. I tried again, but nothing was happening.

"No signal here, my friend," Thanasis informed me.

I tried to hide my disappointment. "When do we get to the island, Thanasis?"

"In about an hour, at most," he replied, taking up his post behind the bar once again. "Buy you a coffee?"

"No thanks, I think I'll take a nap until we get there. Here is your paper, and thank you."

"You can keep it if you like."

I opened the paper, found the story about Anita and myself, and pulled that page out. "Only bit worth keeping," I winked at him and made my way to a couch.

I tried calling Anita once more, but to no avail. Putting the phone back into my rucksack, I felt the cold metal of the box containing Uncle Nikos' ashes. The last thing I saw before I drifted off to sleep was the face of Thomas, back at his table, looking at me.

≈≈≈≈≈≈≈≈≈≈

Michaela and Rina paced outside Eleni's room, anxiety etched on their faces. Wagner's *Tristan und Isolde* was softly playing in the background, one of Eleni's favorite operas, underscoring the melancholy mood that filled the apartment. Raindrops on the window panes provided a steady, rhythmic accompaniment to the women's soft footsteps.

The creaking sound of a door halted the pacing to and fro and the two anxious faces turned expectantly toward the ailing woman's bedroom. A man in his fifties emerged, tidying a stethoscope in a black medical bag. Before he even spoke, his somber expression announced that the news wasn't going to be good. Snapping his medical bag shut, the doctor turned to Michaela. "Her condition is more or less the same as yesterday. Stable, but I don't think she'll improve."

Michaela froze for a moment, as if she had been hoping to hear something different, then looked at Rina and tilted her head toward the bedroom. Rina swiftly returned to her post by Eleni's side, leaving Michaela and the doctor alone. "What do you mean, exactly?" Michaela asked.

"It is hard to be more specific. It's all up to her now. It would be good if you can see what her wishes are in her lucid moments. She mentioned Anita and that she wishes to see her. Is that possible?"

"I haven't told Anita about her grandmother worsening. I guess I should let her know, although it won't be easy for her to get away."

"Would you like for me to arrange a hospital stay?"

"No. She wishes to stay here until the end."

The doctor moved toward the front door. "That's fine. If you need me, at any time, be sure to call me."

Michaela accompanied the doctor to the door. Closing it behind him, she leaned against the frame trying to gather her thoughts. She thought she had prepared herself for this eventuality, but now that the end was near she felt unable to cope with the prospect of losing her mother. She wished Anita was in Berlin, someone to lean on. But Anita would not be back for another month. Should she ask her to fly back, if only for a day? She took a deep breath and entered her mother's room.

Rina sat in the armchair close to the bed, holding Eleni's feeble hand. Michaela tiptoed to the other side and gently stroked her mother's forehead. Eleni did not respond. She lay still, her eyes closed, her breathing so shallow Michaela had difficulty telling whether her chest was moving at all. She often used to get up during the night, just to check her mother was still breathing. This past week, she had moved into her mother's bedroom to be near her and give Rina some much-needed rest.

Michaela put her hand under the covers, searching for her mother's right hand. She felt something hard entwined between her mother's fingers. Pulling back the bedclothes she saw that Eleni was clasping the pocket watch that used to stand on the dressing table. Michaela gently tried to prise the watch from her mother's grasp but it was not easy. Eleni, seemingly fast asleep, tightened her grip, as if she did not want to let go.

Patiently, Michaela lifted Eleni's fingers one by one and pulled the watch free. Just as she was about to lift the watch cover, she heard Eleni's weak voice. The old woman was looking at her. "Anita...you are back. Are you back?"

Michaela moved her face closer to her mother. "No *Mamá*. It's me, Michaela. I'm here with Rina. Do you want something?"

"Where is Anita? I need to see her. Call her..." Eleni said, forming her words with great difficulty.

"She is abroad. Filming. She will be back soon. What do you want me to tell her when she calls?"

Eleni lay still for a few moments, exhausted by the effort. She closed her eyes and whispered hoarsely, "She mustn't go...they'll catch him...don't go."

She then seemed to calm down, her breathing becoming softer and slowly she drifted off once again.

Michaela stroked her mother's hair with one hand and held the watch in the other. She was trying to make sense of what Eleni had been saying. This was not the first time she was incoherent. She looked at the watch and wondered when Eleni had got hold of it. Obviously, while both women were outside with the doctor, otherwise he would have seen it when he examined her.

The watch's cover looked dented, as if it had been hit. She opened the lid and saw that the glass on the watch face was dull and cracked. She could just about make out the time, frozen still: three fifteen. As she examined the watch she noticed that a photo had been attached to the metal lid, its edges curled where the photo had come unstuck. It was the portrait of a young man, partly obscured by a dark stain. She brought the watch to the bedside lamp; it was a long-haired man laughing at something or someone in the distance, a gun slung over his shoulder.

The man was a complete stranger. Why was her mother so attached to this old watch, the photo of this man? Eleni had been a student in Italy before the outbreak of the war, had met Michaela's father at university and returned with him to Germany. Her grandfather was then sent to the front, survived the battlefield, but perished in Berlin, in the spring of 1945, in the Soviet bombing that wiped out his entire family. His young widow was pregnant with their only child at the time, a lone woman in Berlin. Michaela was born in autumn, when the war was over.

Eleni was not one to speak of the past. She had no relatives, no family pictures. It was as if her life story always began just before she got married. She never spoke of her childhood. She never spoke of Greece.

So who was the young man in the photo? Certainly not Eleni's father; the photo was too recent for that. Looking closely, she guessed it must have been taken some time in the late 1930s, early '40s.

Michaela carefully removed the photo from the watch cover. The inside of the lid was engraved: *E+M*. And in a line below, in Greek: *Forever. Together.* Michaela stared at the watch for a long moment, as if looking at it would somehow solve this mystery. She came back to the present when Rina got up to wet Eleni's lips with a moist towel.

Anita. That's what she had to focus on now, what to do about Anita. Anita had the right to know how her grandmother was doing and then she could decide whether she needed to return to Berlin or not. Not today though, Michaela decided, wishing to put off the conversation for a little bit longer. The following morning would be better, when they would have more time to talk.

She slowly walked to the dresser and replaced the watch in its case, the unknown man's photo now safely tucked under the watch cover. She patted Rina's shoulder in silent thanks and went to the kitchen.

Rummaging around the fridge, her mind was still on the photo. Those words! *Forever. Together.* It was clearly a love message. From *M* to *E*? Who was *M*? *E* had to stand for Eleni, but *M*? Maybe this was someone she'd met before her father; or after. Would her mother ever be able and willing to answer these questions? Or was this a secret that she would carry with her, another mystery from the reticent old woman's past?

≋≋≋≋≋≋≋≋≋

All was quiet on the ferry. I was alone in the seating area. The TV, now muted, replayed images of the dying woman. Except, the images were uncensored this time around. You could clearly see the faces of the executioners, filled with hatred as they hurled their stones at the unfortunate victim. Even the children's faces were distorted with malice as they struggled to pick up the heavy stones. Stone and hanging flesh became one until I couldn't stand to watch any longer.

I got up and tried to turn it off, but to no avail. I picked up a bar stool and flung it at the TV. The glass shattered but the images still played on. The volume now came on at full blast; the woman's screams as she howled in pain, the braying mob, the crack of the stones as they hit their target.

Strange music started playing in the background, a tragic soundtrack to the flickering pictures.

I tore the TV set from the wall and smashed it on the floor before the bar, leaving the entrails of naked cables hanging down from the wall. Finally, silence.

I was covered in cold sweat and could feel my drenched shirt sticking to my back. I headed to the exit and opened the door, stepped out onto the deck. I approached the railings and saw a rocky outcrop, an island close by. A house was burning on the barren hilltop, the dark smoke filling the sky.

I moved to the stern of the ship, which was tethered to the port in a dense fog that was slowly dispersing. The forlorn figures of passengers waiting at the quay started rising in the mist. They were dirty, their clothes and hands blood splattered, staring at me with naked hostility.

My heart beat faster and faster, a frenzied drumbeat of anxiety and fear. Paralyzed with terror, I wanted to run, but my feet were welded to the spot.

An old man stepped forward from the crowd. I took a closer look and started with surprise when I realized it was Thomas, slowly raising an accusing finger toward me. A woman dressed in black came to stand beside him, her white hair blowing in the wind.

I closed my eyes to shut out the scene before me.

A hand touched my shoulder and I jumped out of my skin.

"We're arriving. Wake up, my friend!"

The few seconds it took to open my eyes felt like years. Relief flooded through me at the sight of Thanasis' funny face. *Just a nightmare*, I told myself. *Just a nightmare*. The dream had been so vivid, so real, I still felt the acrid taste of fear in my mouth.

"Air-conditioning is not working. No wonder you're drenched, my friend," Thanasis said as he started clearing the tables around me.

I sat up, trying to collect myself. The warm smile of Thomas as he got up from his armchair helped push the dream further away. In my confused state, I thought about not getting off, staying on the ferry and going back. I turned to Thanasis who was stocking the fridge behind the bar and asked, as casually as I could, "How long before you return?"

"We stay on the island till Monday morning. If you feel like it, come to Lefkothea's *taverna* tonight. Best food on the island, on me. It's the *panegyri* of the Virgin Mary tomorrow, the island's biggest festival. You shouldn't miss that!" He turned away from the fridge and winked, waving two beer bottles at me to tempt me.

"Thanks, Thanasis! If I can make it, the treat will be on me," I said and picked up my rucksack, a sweat stain marking the spot I had used as a pillow.

Thomas and the few passengers who were inside had started making their way to the exit as the ferry entered the harbor. I felt the floor shake as it dropped anchor. Well, this was it. I hastily took off my wet shirt and pulled a fresh t-shirt over my head, then headed for the exit.

"It was nice meeting you, Thanasis. Maybe we'll catch up on the island."

I liked him well enough, but I didn't want to make any arrangements as a principle. I wanted to rest and find out where the spring at Mantani was, so I could carry out Uncle Nikos' final wish. I hadn't booked a place to stay. I'd been told that it would be easy to find a room when I got there, as the island was not very busy with tourists.

"Where are you staying?" Thanasis asked.

"I haven't booked anything yet. Can you recommend a place?"

He came near me and lowered his voice, as if he was about to share something confidential. "They're all more or less the same, but if you want peace and quiet go to the upper part of town and ask for Thekla's. She has the nicest rooms and makes a great breakfast. You can walk there, but it's best to rent a moped; easier to move around that way."

I hadn't driven a motorbike for a long time, but I liked his idea. It'd be convenient and a great way to tour the island.

I thanked Thanasis once more and stepped outside. For a second, the dream came back to haunt me. I half-expected to see the blood-stained mob waiting for me on the quay, burning houses in the background.

Instead, the most tranquil view was there to greet me. Three whitewashed churches perched on the hill tops, like lonely lookouts standing guard over the vast expanse of water before them. A Greek flag fluttered near one of them.

The port was a cluster of square, low houses with a couple of *taverns* on the seafront, small wooden tables on the sand and fresh octopuses drying in a row. Further up the hill stood the *hóra*— the heart of the island; a traditional amphitheater of tiny houses built almost on top of each other in a maze of winding alleys and courtyards; a searing blaze of whiteness that almost burnt your retinas in the midday sun.

I blinked and moved toward the stairs to make my way down to the port when I felt my phone vibrate, its ring tone drowned by the disembarking cars and mopeds. *Anita.* I sprinted down the few remaining steps and across the quay trying to find a quiet spot where I would be heard. All in vain. "Hi, Anita...the line is awful... I just got here, I'll call you back," was all I had time to say before the line went dead. I tried to call her back, but failed to reach her. Maybe there was no phone signal at her end.

I let out a frustrated sigh and started to walk toward the few houses. Nearby, at the center of a small square, a war memorial caught my eye. A pile of stones was randomly placed around a small marble column, which read:

IN MEMORY OF THOSE WHO GAVE UP THEIR LIVES JUSTLY OR UNJUSTLY

1940-1945

I looked around to see if there was anything else written that could shed some light on this curious inscription but found nothing. I dodged a swarm of local kids chasing a football around the square and fondly remembered my grazed knees, the battle scars of the local football matches of my childhood. *Had Uncle Nikos also played here as a child?*

I spotted the *kafeneio* nearby, a couple of tourists and a group of elderly locals sitting outside in the shade of a huge, red bougainvillea sipping Greek coffee out of tiny cups. The melody of a song drifted outside, a mournful voice singing an island tune I'd never heard before.

My beautiful island girl
Leaving these shores behind
Leaving me alone to wander
On a lonely isle...

The rest of the song was drowned out by the voice of Thomas, who stepped outside wiping his hands on an apron, a wide smile on his face. "Come on in, have a drink on us and rest. It's my *kafeneio*."

"Thank you, but I'm very tired. Let me go leave my things and I'll come back later, if you're still here. Do you know where Thekla's rooms are?"

"If I know them, he asks! I worked the stone with my own hands," he said and proudly extended his scarred and calloused palms.

I was startled by the movement. It brought back the scene from my dream, Thomas pointing an accusatory finger at me. Thankfully, Thomas did not see my start. He had turned back to toward the doorway and was calling someone.

"Sofia! My granddaughter Sofia will give you a lift on her moped. You shouldn't be walking in this heat."

"Thank you, but I'm going to rent a motorbike so I can move around freely."

"How long are you staying here?"

"I'm leaving Monday morning."

A young girl of around fifteen, tall and well- built, came out at that point. She smiled and said hello, and before I had a chance to return her greeting, Thomas spoke. "Sofia will take you to Thekla's and leave the motorbike there. You can return it on Monday. No use renting something just for a couple of days."

I was left speechless by his kind offer, spoken in a manner that clearly indicated he would not be taking no for an answer. So, I nodded my acquiescence and followed the young girl to a nearby moped.

The scene had excited the curiosity of the locals, who had fallen silent and watched us with great interest. I got on, placed my bag between us and Sofia immediately set off along a road that ran parallel to the coast line. Her hair alternately stroked and whipped my face and I turned to face the sea whizzing past us. To our right was a sharp uphill turn, and Sofia shouted out "hold on" just as she stepped on the gas to climb the steep hill. Without her warning, I would have surely flown off. I gripped her shoulders and felt her stifle a giggle.

At the top of the hill, she turned down a narrow path, drove carefully down a step, and slowed down as she made her way through the labyrinth of white-washed island houses. At every doorway she greeted someone. This was a place where everyone knew the rest of the town. She turned her head toward me to ask what I now suspected was the local ice-breaker: "First time on our island?"

"Yes, first time," I replied, distracted as I tried to balance my bag and stay on the bike.

In less than a minute she pulled up so sharply, I hit my jaw on her shoulder. She didn't seem to mind and honked to announce our arrival.

We were at the back of a large house, outside a vast wooden double door framed by island stones. That must have been Thomas' work, a fine example of island stone masonry; simple, unadorned, exquisitely showcasing the red bougainvillea that covered most of the house.

A plump woman dressed in a blue dress that matched the color of the sea, with a round, cheerful face, was making her way toward us. "Welcome, welcome to our island, come on in!"

She shook my hand, a strong manly handshake, and I was surprised at how rough her palm was. How unusual, I thought, then realized that no, of course women must be doing a lot of the rough work around here. She made to take my bag from the ground beside me, but I quickly picked it up and slung it over my shoulder. Still smiling, she turned toward Sofia. "Thank you, Sofia. You walk back down the steps. You granddad called and said you must pass by the house to pick up the sweets."

"Yes, Mrs. Thekla..." Sofia hovered awkwardly for a moment, and then, summoning all her courage, turned toward me, shyly asking, "Can I have an autograph?"

"I see Thomas hasn't wasted any time filling you in, has he?" I laughed. "Later, when I drop by the coffee shop."

Sofia hovered, still uneasy but less shy.

"And a photo of the two of us?"

Thekla spoke before I could answer. "Come now Sofia, the man is tired. Let him catch his breath. Go now, or you'll be late."

Sofia sulked but nonetheless turned and started walking down the paved steps, following the pedestrian way back to the port. She barely had time to shout out a hasty "bye" and hear my thanks before she disappeared from view.

I pointed toward the motorbike. "Won't it be in the way here?"

"Don't worry about it. If it bothers anyone, they'll move it out of the way. Come inside now and choose your room. What's your name?"

"Dimitri," I replied but I could see she was waiting for my last name. My mother's voice rang in my ears at that moment, *don't tell anyone your grandfather's name or that we come from the place. Just tell them your last name and nothing more.*

"Dimitri Voudouris"

"Voudouris. Dimitri Voudouris." She repeated my name frowning hard, as if trying to memorize it. I felt a pang of worry and looked at her quizzically. She smiled. "It's for the guest register. I don't want to ask for your passport now. You can give it to me later. I'm sorry I don't recognize you my boy, but I don't watch TV. No time."

Now I laughed. "Don't worry about it, Mrs. Thekla! I don't watch a lot of TV either, and as for being on it, that rarely happens. I wouldn't expect anyone to recognize me."

"That's strange because you look familiar and it can't be because I've seen you on TV. Have you been here before?"

Under other circumstances, I wouldn't have paid these questions any heed, but I was on my guard. I repeated the lie I'd told, Thomas that I'd been to the island once as a child but didn't remember much.

We'd arrived at one of the rooms. As Thekla opened the door, I caught sight of the uninterrupted sea view below, a painting of different shades of blue as the sea met the sky and an airy, high-ceilinged room. Plainly decorated, dominated by a large bed in the center made with white linen, the mosquito net suspended from the ceiling pulled to one side of the bed. The walls were decorated with photos depicting the usual Greek landscapes. One photo stood out, being black and white and showing the island's harbor. A lot of people had gathered on the quay, grouped together before some boats, smiling at the camera. The photo was inscribed '1938'. On the balcony, a small table and two chairs turned to face the Aegean, giving an almost aerial view of the landscape below, a feeling of being suspended in mid-air.

"I have two more free rooms you can look at, if you want. But I think this is the nicest."

The room was perfect and I wanted to call Anita and have a bath and rest. So I hastily assured her that this would be fine.

"Good. You settle in and I'll go make you something to eat, it's nearly lunchtime. You must be hungry," she said in a tone that forbade any objections.

Not that I intended to object. I'd had no breakfast, ferry food having a worse reputation than ferry coffee, and the mention of lunch made my stomach rumble.

I thanked her and flung my bag, which was starting to dig into my shoulder, on the floor.

"Come downstairs to the courtyard when you're ready," she smiled and quickly exited the room.

I stood on the balcony and tried to call Anita, but once again I could not get through, so I texted her instead. *I've arrived, it's beautiful, give me a call whenever you can.* Then I remembered my mother, who I was sure would be getting worried by now.

"Hi, *Mamá*! Yes, I just got here. Everything is fine…everyone is hospitable…very friendly….no, I'll do that tomorrow morning. I need to rest now…I'll call you again tomorrow. Bye now…bye."

She sounded calm, but I could sense her tension. I felt mildly annoyed with her and Uncle Nikos as I carefully unpacked the metal box and placed it on a small wooden table, shoving the rest of my clothes haphazardly into the closet. In the short while I'd been here everyone had been kind, friendly and seemed to genuinely like me. I could not believe that mentioning my grandfather's name would change that.

I stepped back out onto the balcony to hang my drenched t-shirt and my mood lifted as I breathed in the sea air and took in the view. Determined to enjoy my stay and relax, I moved back in and stepped into the shower, my mind once again on the food that would soon be waiting for me downstairs.

The Island, September 1938

The port was busy. Any moment now, the tug boats would be arriving to ferry all the passengers waiting on the small quay to the big steamship waiting patiently in the middle of the bay.

A sharp whistle and a thick black plume of smoke from the ship's funnel filled the air. That was the signal to hurry and the people moved en masse toward the three tugboats that were tethered to the quay and preparing to load. Goods first, passengers next. Rough sacks made of hemp, baskets, chickens, and goats, their feet bound together so they could not move, were all heaped together. Muscular workmen were picking up the goods, piling the tugboats high. Then the sailors took over, rowing the goods to the ship. Ropes would come down and heave the goods and animals on board, the sailors flinging the lighter objects expertly high up in the air where their crewmates would catch them. Once empty, the tugboats would return as many times as necessary, and then the ship would depart.

Italian soldiers were overseeing proceedings, a soldier thoroughly checking some wooden boxes, their Greek owner watching him anxiously. Basket-laden donkeys added their hoarse cries to the bleating of the goats, the human voices, the sound of carts, and the regular whistles coming from the boat making it all a scene of lively chaos.

Amidst all that noise, the sound of hammering and sawing would occasionally burst out in a flurry. Work was being carried out on some of the port buildings. The Italian occupiers had been trying to repair many of the buildings by the port, adding their own architectural touches to some of the facades, such as the Governor's headquarters and the closed market. In the midst of traditional, white-washed walls, island stone, and blue shutters, now sprang samples of contemporary Italian architecture.

Eleni and Manolis were walking side by side in front of one of those buildings, followed by Eleni's father, captain-Andreas. All three were headed toward the port, captain-Andreas leading a donkey with a large brown suitcase strapped on its side.

As soon as they reached the edge of the quay, Eleni's father unstrapped the suitcase and, with Manolis' help, placed it on the ground. At that moment a loud voice was heard, calling everyone to gather together in front of the boats to have a group photo taken.

Everyone gathered at the designated spot where the camera had been set up. Manolis took Eleni's hand and pulled her closer, putting his arm around her waist. She felt a frisson run through her and did not resist. Resting her head against his chest, she closed her eyes and breathed deeply, as if wanting the moment to permeate her, to keep its memory within her forever. That was the first time their bodies were so close. They could feel each other's breath. The heat of Manolis' body warmed her and she wondered if he felt the same. What they had never managed to do in the few moments they had found themselves alone was happening now, in the midst of a crowd. Hidden among passengers and bystanders, they felt desire grow for the first time. That stolen moment did not last for more than a few seconds.

More people had gathered and the photographer asked them to move back, so everyone could fit in the frame. They parted reluctantly but were back in each other's arms once again the moment they reached their designated place. Eleni closed her eyes once more, resting in Manolis' embrace.

The photo taken, the crowd split up and they returned to her father. Captain-Andreas hugged his daughter tightly and kissed her forehead. She held on to him and returned the kiss on his wrinkled cheek. He looked at Manolis for a moment, silent and pensive, then pulling the donkey's reins started to walk away from the port.

He'd been in this mood since the previous evening, when Manolis had come to their house and asked for Eleni's hand in marriage. Captain-Andreas had known the two were in love, but wanted his daughter to complete her studies and then marry. His was a rare point of view that went against all local customs, which dictated that girls should be married as soon as possible and have a family.

The scholarship awarded by the Italian state to Eleni was a great opportunity, and Captain Andreas had pressed his daughter to go to the University of Pisa and train as a teacher. Eleni had different plans. She intended to register at the School of Fine Arts there.

She'd learned Italian on the island; it was the language in which classes were taught. Greek was optional and only taught in the early grades.

The idea of studying in Italy was not unwelcome, although it spelled a long separation from Manolis. She kept telling herself it wasn't forever. She would graduate and then return, marry him, and then the two of them would move to Athens.

She hadn't shared these plans with her father. She was his only child and he loved her dearly, having single-handedly raised her following his wife's death in childbirth. He was Eleni's mother and father. Refusing any further help from female relations, he'd brought her up on his own ever since she was a toddler.

When Manolis had asked for his permission to marry Eleni, Captain-Andreas realized there wasn't much he could do. He could see his daughter loved the young man and was wise enough to understand that any objections he raised would only make the two lovers more determined, maybe even leading them to elope. So he turned to Manolis and said, "You have my blessing on one condition only. You will become engaged when Eleni graduates, and then we'll arrange the wedding. Until then, nothing must stand in the way of my daughter's education."

He then stood up, gave Manolis a warning look and shook the young man's hand to seal the deal. Manolis took the proffered hand and gave the old man his word of honor. He didn't have much choice in the matter anyway.

He knew his decision to marry Eleni would meet with opposition in his own home. His brother Yiannis was not supportive. A married man and the father of a young son, Yiannis kept saying it was wrong that Eleni had been taught Italian; that she was going to Italy. He was increasingly hostile to the Italians. Himself a teacher of Greek, he was aware that he would soon be out of a job, as the Italians were gradually phasing out Greek in schools. He had been forced to help Manolis out at the mill more and more as his teaching hours diminished.

Owning the only mill on the island, Manolis was a clever young man, interested in technology and good with his hands. He read everything that he could get his hands on and was often busy constructing contraptions that excited the curiosity and gossipy nature of his fellow islanders, who viewed him as something of an eccentric.

≈≈≈≈≈≈≈≈≈≈≈

Eleni and Manolis watched the older man move away, then turned and gazed at each other in silence. Both were dressed in their Sunday best, Eleni wearing a long gray dress and a red jacket, Manolis in a dark suit and a white shirt, its collar turned over the jacket lapels.

They looked at each other intently but with a slight awkwardness. Like a young couple who want nothing but to fall in each other's arms but are holding back, frozen in time. People were milling about them noisily, but there they stood, eyes locked in longing.

The spell was broken by the long whistle of the distant ship, which made them jump. Eleni bent down to lift her suitcase, but Manolis, more agile, picked it up before she could reach it. He took her hand with sudden determination and started to pull Eleni toward the tugboats which were beginning to fill with passengers.

His hand was squeezing hers so hard it almost hurt, but Eleni did not even think about letting go; did not want to let go for a single moment. It was as if this was her only way of letting him know all the feelings that were welling inside her, by holding tightly onto his hand.

A voice from the boat called everyone to hurry and they, instinctively, tightened their grasp and moved closer together. Seized by a sudden daring, by the realization that they were soon to part, they moved even closer and their lips met for the first time, there on the port, in full view of the others. The quay, the waiting boats, the remaining passengers all melted away as they tasted their first kiss.

The voice from the boat put an unwelcome end to their kiss. Reluctantly, she pulled away, placing her hand on Manolis' lips as a last farewell. Manolis somberly picked up her suitcase and handed it to the waiting sailor, then helped Eleni onto the boat. Eleni felt something cold and hard in her hand. She looked down and saw that Manolis had placed a small mirror in her palm and a photograph. She heard his voice sing softly:

> My beautiful island girl
> Leaving these shores behind
> Leaving me alone to wander
> On a lonely isle...

She smiled bravely, but her smile faded almost as soon as it appeared and her eyes welled up. She placed the mirror and the photograph in her pocket and kept her hand there, as if to still hold on to him. The sailors picked up their oars and the boat started to pull away from the shore.

"Take care of yourself, Manolis," Eleni shouted. "I love you," she mouthed silently, a message from him to her and for no one else to hear.

From that point onward, she never lost sight of him. Manolis stood still on the quay, watching the boat carry Eleni further and further away. He tried to appear calm, but a tear escaped down his cheek. Eleni was weeping openly now; Manolis could see the tears streaming down her face.

The boat soon reached the side of the great ship and hovered there while the luggage was unloaded. Then, one by one, the passengers started to climb aboard on a ladder.

Eleni stood up in the tugboat gazing at Manolis' direction, the last one to leave. Even when she was climbing the steps to the ship, she kept pausing and turning back to look at him. She disappeared from his view for a few moments and then reappeared on the deck, hoping to catch sight of him once more.

Both knew it was going to be a long separation; Eleni would not be back the following summer. But they both had faith in the love that had grown between them, the love that had been born on the evening of the *panegyri* of the Virgin Mary, a few months before.

It was one of the few festivals the Italians still allowed to take place. The moment Manolis saw Eleni dance, he was spellbound. The way she moved, the way she closed her eyes as if to shut everyone else out, mesmerized him. Enchanted, he stepped up to dance with her and she succumbed to an overwhelming, unexpected sense of belonging. They both knew then that destiny intended for them to be together.

≈≈≈≈≈≈≈≈≈≈

As the ship gave one final, sharp whistle and started to move away, Manolis caught a glimpse of Eleni's red jacket amidst the other passengers who had now gathered on the deck to take one last look at their beloved island. He kept his gaze fixed on the jacket, occasionally making out her face as the ship became smaller and smaller, until it shrunk into a faint dot on the horizon.

Manolis sprinted past Eleni's father, who gave him a stern look of disapproval at everything he had witnessed from afar. The young man paid no heed; all that mattered to him now was getting to Mantani, and seeing the boat one last time from the high vantage point of the spring.

He ran to the spot where his horse was tethered, a black mare with a white heart-shaped spot on her forehead. Karme, named at his brother's suggestion after the mythical demi-goddess of the harvest, neighed in recognition and picked up on his impatience as he untied her reins and sprang onto her back. As soon as his heels dug into her sides to spur her on, the mare dashed through the port and headed for the top of the hill.

With a tug of the reins, Manolis guided the horse and they both galloped on the plateau in a parallel line to the direction the ship had taken. Fearlessly they streamed ahead, man and horse now one, an intrepid centaur coursing through the sparse tree copses that stood on their path. Only when they reached the point where the rocks joined to make a narrow short tunnel did Manolis dismount and walk, pulling Karme behind him through the dark opening. As soon as they came out the other end, he jumped back onto Karme's back and spurred her on with even greater urgency than before.

They made it to Mantani with time to spare. This was their secret meeting place, where they would spend hours together, talking. He'd never so much as dared take her in his arms or hold her hand, even though he could sense Eleni would not resist. The memory of that first kiss at the port still made his heart beat like the ringing of church bells on Easter Sunday.

He dismounted Karme, who was shaking with exhaustion, her dark coat glistening with sweat, and he walked to the edge of the cliff, his feet getting soaked with the water from the spring as it made its way to tumble down the mountainside. With trembling hands he fumbled in his pocket, trying to get to the small mirror he had been carrying on him all day.

He stood there, in the water, and raised the mirror, angling it to catch a ray of sunlight and direct it toward the boat which had now appeared on the horizon. He gave a silent prayer that she would notice and stared at the boat hoping for a sign. He did not have to wait for long. On the side of the boat, he caught a glimmer of light, shaky at first, then steady, strong, beaming in his direction. He raised his hand, waving frantically and saw the beam from the boat shake.

Maybe she was waving back, sending her love and light in a last farewell, with the promise that they would meet again. The boat slowly drifted away and Eleni's light disappeared. Manolis stood still, the mirror turned toward the now empty spot. The light breeze cooled his face, still hot and sweaty from the ride. He did not want to turn back to an island which now felt empty and barren. As if sensing his mood, Karme approached and gave him a nudge. Taking her reins, Manolis shook the mud from his boots and guided her to the spring. Man and horse drank thirstily and rested, then started to make their way back.

≈≈≈≈≈≈≈≈≈≈≈

As soon as Anita finished shooting the scene, she grabbed her handbag and pulled out her cell phone. Still no signal. With a frustrated sigh, she put on her hat, holding the mobile tightly in her hand, and looked at the road that led to the monastery.

"I'm going to head to a higher spot, Electra. Maybe I'll get a signal there. You can pick me up on your way."

She then set off determinedly, pausing every minute or so to look at the phone. Five minutes into her journey, a small bar appeared on the screen and her heart fluttered with hope. She hastily dialed Dimitri's number and covered her left ear with her free hand to block out the noise coming from the crew, who were busily packing up their equipment and preparing to move. She longed to hear Dimitri's voice. The brief time they'd been apart had seemed like ages. She could not stop thinking about him; she fervently wished he could be there with her, right then. This was the first time they were apart since the beginning of their affair. Even when a scene did not require them to be together, he always found some excuse to be on set. And she never missed an opportunity to watch him film his scenes.

Waiting for the phone to ring, she watched the crew load their equipment onto a waiting jeep and start toward her. It was a narrow and sharp turn, and the jeep was struggling. The driver pulled open the side door and stepped outside to get a better idea of how wide the road was. He moved to the back of the jeep, motioning one of the crew members to come up and help him.

Anita gave a sharp cry of warning. The jeep started to move back downhill toward the drop at the edge of the road. The driver, alerted by her cry, barely had enough time to jump out of the moving car's way. The car kept moving toward the edge of the road, its descent luckily stopped by a great rock it promptly crashed into.

Running at full speed toward the driver and the car, Anita arrived before anyone else. The driver, visibly shaken, stood gazing at the jeep, alternately swearing and lamenting, wondering how the hand brake could have possibly slipped. The car did not seem to be greatly damaged. The equipment it had been carrying, however, was. Cameras and other machinery were now strewn all around the car. Chaos ensued as the crew arrived and tried to salvage whatever they could, arguing tensely all the while.

The driver, seeing smoke come from the jeep's engine, shouted at everyone to step away and pulled out a fire extinguisher. They all started to walk back up the hill toward the monastery. Before they reached the gate, they met a couple of monks and the old Abbot, who were making their way toward the scene of the accident.

Anita fell into step with the abbot, who was walking pensively beside her. The old man suddenly stopped, bent down, and picked something from the ground. He examined it for a moment and then handed to Anita, who had stopped mid-track and was watching the jeep.

"This must be yours, my child."

Anita absent-mindedly picked up the proffered black object and realized it was her cell phone.

"Thank you. I don't even remember dropping it."

She looked closely at the cracked, dead screen and sighed. "How unlucky," she mumbled as she placed the broken phone in her pocket.

The Abbot heard and turned toward her. "What's important, my child, is that no one was hurt. Everything else will happen in its own time."

Anita smiled politely, her attention still focused on the jeep. She declined the Abbot's offer to come wait in the shade inside the monastery and decided to wait there, in the sun, a worried frown on her face as she watched the crew approach the jeep once again and start unloading whatever equipment remained.

≈≈≈≈≈≈≈≈≈≈≈

Half an hour later, they were joined by the director and the producer. They could tell from their somber expressions that the news was not good. The producer spoke first, speaking loudly so he could be heard over the noise of the small tow-truck that was trying to pull the damaged jeep onto the road.

"We have to stop for today. Probably until Monday. We'll head back to the hotel now, and know more in a couple of hours."

Disappointed, everyone started to disperse, going to gather up their belongings. The director approached Anita and spoke softly, "Our main camera and other equipment have been damaged, and they'll have to be replaced. And we'll probably have to reshoot today's scenes as well. I hope there won't be any more delays, but in any case we won't be able to do anything before Tuesday. We'll have to start over from the scenes of you and Dimitri on the boat. If we are lucky, we might get a replacement camera on Monday, but it's unlikely."

"I'm sorry, I wish there was something I could do. These things happen, please don't be disheartened," Anita replied.

"Take this break to rest for a couple of days. Next week will be quite intense, as we'll try to make up for lost time. We'll go back to the hotel, you have the interview with the German channel in the afternoon, and then I guess you're free."

Anita gave him a small compassionate smile and started to move with everyone else toward the cars that would take them back. She did feel disappointed, but did not want to show it. As she pondered what to do with the time she suddenly had on her hands, a small knowing smile began to form on her lips. She looked at the broken phone once more, and the smile became a grin, as the idea she'd just had took hold.

≈≈≈≈≈≈≈≈≈≈≈

Everything Thekla had prepared looked delicious. It was all homemade, using local produce. An omelet, jams prepared by the hostess herself, fruit and honey and butter and warm bread... it had been a while since I'd tasted such delights.

I dug into the small dish filled with a local dessert made from rose petals that she'd just placed on the table before me. Rose petals! Who knew? I sighed, perfectly content to be enjoying this meal in the shade of a large vine, surrounded by her neatly tended geraniums. It reminded me of my mother's balcony and felt comfortingly familiar.

The longer I sat here, the more at ease I felt. Only one thing marred my good mood. It was nearing three o'clock and I still hadn't heard from Anita. I wanted to call Electra and check everything was okay, but I felt embarrassed and was trying to come up with a good excuse for calling her. At that moment, my phone rang and Electra's name and number flashed on the screen. I laughed out loud at such ludicrous serendipity and picked it up.

Electra quickly brought me up to date with everything that had happened, and reassured me countless times that Anita was fine. She then told me that I could call Anita later at the hotel where we had been staying and hung up.

I put my phone back in my pocket and tried to calm down. When Electra told me there'd been an accident, my heart missed a beat at the thought that something had happened to Anita. That's when I realized I could not bear the thought of anything happening to her. It was blindingly obvious that I was well and truly in love.

For a moment I thought about leaving the island and heading back to be with her, but then I remembered the metal box waiting on the bedside table in my room upstairs. I would be calling Anita at the hotel soon enough. Seeing my troubled expression, Thekla approached my table and asked if everything was okay. I reassured her that yes, everything was fine, just a mishap at work.

"Would you like a coffee, Dimitri?" she asked.

"No, thank you, I'm probably going to head to Thomas', go for a walk. Will you add this to my bill?" I pointed at the small pile of empty dishes.

"Oh, I didn't come for the bill. I came to tell you there is a *panegyri* tomorrow."

"I've already been invited by everyone I've met so far. I really don't think I could get out of that even if I wanted to," I joked.

She laughed, but her eyes were serious. "It's not just a religious festival for us tomorrow. It's not about the food and the dancing... it's also the day when we remember all the people we lost during the war. Many bad things happened that day on this island. Some things have been forgotten, others never will."

A chill went down my spine. Unexpectedly, I was receiving my first bit of information of what had happened then. Would I ever be able to unravel the family mystery? I was getting ready to ask what she meant, but she'd already moved on.

"Did you like the food?"

"Yes, everything was great, thank you," I replied almost apologetically. "Of course I'll come tomorrow and, at some point, I'd like to hear about the island's history. About what happened back then?"

I must have sounded more intense than I intended to, for she looked at me as if she now regretted having mentioned the war. "Come now, son, you are here on holiday. I never should have said anything that might spoil it. Go take your walk now. You can meet my mother at the *panegyri* tomorrow. She lived through it all and remembers. Anyway, she is the one who gives the blessing at the *panegyri* every year. All I know is there's no one worse than the Germans in this world."

I desperately wanted to tell her that I wanted to know right there and then, that this was a story that concerned me, my whole family. Only the promise I'd given my mother made me hold my tongue.

Someone called Thekla from inside the house. Giving me a sweet smile, she walked off.

I stood up and looked at the sea for a moment. Then I ran up to my room to pick up my camera, took one look at the moped and decided to walk to the port.

I stepped out into the alley and started to walk down the steps that led to the port to the sound of my whirling thoughts and the incessant song of the countless cicadas. My life had taken many twists and turns lately. I felt things shifting inside me and it wasn't just because of Anita. The past was being churned up and I suddenly felt a great sense of responsibility, being here on this island. I was the first member of my mother's family to return to this place after whatever mysterious events had taken place. What they were I did not know yet, but I could sense that it was something that could shake my world.

Walking to the port, my mind flitted between Anita and all the people I'd met since coming here. As if they were all part of the same story, a story which had started being written even before I was born, with a different cast of characters, but which was still being scripted up to and including this moment, dragging me into it.

I paused frequently and took as many photos as I could. Not only did I want to capture the narrow street, the bursts of color from the potted plants that contrasted so brilliantly with the island whites and blues, I also wanted to carry back to my mother as much of the island as I could. I hoped that would bring her to the present in some way and that this, in turn, would help her make peace with the past. Once I knew what had happened, I would return to the island with Anita and tell her everything.

Although I was seriously sleep deprived, the thought of staying in my room and catching up on the sleep I'd missed these last two weeks never crossed my mind. I wanted to see as much of the island as possible during my short stay. My plan was to visit the spring at Mantani the following day and go to the festival in the evening. Then, tour the island on the motorbike the day after. What I needed most at present, however, was to wind down and put my thoughts in order.

I got lost on my way down a couple of times, but enjoyed my wandering through the cobbled streets, taking in everything along the way—geraniums, red bougainvilleas, old wooden doors, and hidden courtyards shaded by climbing vines; even a group of friendly black-clad old women sitting on the steps of a small house sipping coffee out of those tiny cups and posing coquettishly for my lens with wide, toothless grins. By the time I reached the port I felt happy and relaxed.

The port was quiet. A few fishing boats dotted here and there, a couple of sailboats moored in the distance, and the 'Titanic', patiently waiting for Monday morning to depart. The booming buzz of the cicadas would occasionally get interrupted by the sound of a fishing boat making its way out to sea, an old moped or, rarely, the sound of a car.

I stood once more before the memorial with the strange inscription and added a couple of photos to my collection. At the *kafeneio* near the memorial, a group of men sat drinking and chattering quietly. Thomas was one of them, and got up the moment he saw me. "Hello! Why are you on foot? Has anything happened to the moped?"

"No, I just wanted to stretch my legs. If you need it, I can go back and fetch it."

"You'll bring it back on Monday morning, Dimitri, as we agreed. Plenty of motorbikes for us to move around. Come join us now. Have you had something to eat?" he asked, gently tugging at my arm.

"I've already eaten. Too much! Mrs. Thekla is an excellent cook, thank you."

"Oh, it's a pleasure to have you here. I wish all of you working on that film had come over. It's such a beautiful island, you should film here."

"I can see it's beautiful but it's not up to me, I'm afraid. I'll let them know though. We should all come and visit."

Sofia and two of her friends appeared at the doorway, holding pen and paper. Smiling awkwardly, I signed my name for all three of them. I wasn't actually used to it, still felt a bit embarrassed when it happened. The giggling teenagers insisted on having our photo taken.

I had asked Thomas for a coffee and raised a quizzical eyebrow as he placed a small bottle filled with clear liquid, ice, water, and tall narrow glasses on the table before me.

"*Ouzo*," he said in a tone that meant 'drink up'. "My cousin makes it. You've never tasted anything like it before. Have a drink and if you don't like it Sofia will make you a coffee. But you must have a drink, no other way to welcome a stranger to our parts."

I smiled and filled everyone's glass. No water, no ice, straight up. Then I raised my glass in salutation, clinked glasses with everyone else and took a sip. Thomas smiled.

"Are you sure you are not from around here? Never seen an Athenian know how to serve and drink ouzo the right way before," he teased but stared at me once he saw my frozen expression.

I took another sip, wondering whether that was a random remark and I was once again being paranoid. Better laugh it off, I thought. "You never know, Thomas, I just might be," I said jokingly.

Everyone joined in as if that was the funniest thing they'd ever heard.

"Don't worry, even if you aren't we'll make sure you become a local. Plenty of pretty girls on the island," someone added, sparking another round of laughter.

"I think Dimitri is already taken," winked Thomas. "Aren't you?"

"Yes—yes I am," I replied, wondering whether there was anything about my life this man had not already guessed or overheard. I was now certain that he had not missed a word of my conversations with Thanasis on the journey over.

The ouzo was starting to make my head spin and I put my glass down. I did not want to risk letting it affect me, for I was sure that in this pleasant, warm atmosphere I would let slip who I was and what I was really doing here. So I kept on raising my glass but only wetting my lips every time. The chit-chat continued as we spoke of the film and the island. Trying to sound as casual as possible, I asked, "They told me there is a spring up the mountain, I think it's called Mantani. How can I get there? I heard the view is breathtaking."

An old man in a sailor's white cap, replied, offering directions. "Mantani, yes, it's very pretty. It's a long hike on foot. You should take your bike. There are two ways to get there, the new road, which is tarred, or the old dirt road, which is prettier. If you follow the stream on foot once you get there, you'll get to Kryfó. Best beach on the island. Once you get to the beach, go into the Cave of Silence, really beautiful."

I smiled inwardly at the memories his last sentence awakened in me and thanked him. Thomas jumped in, offering to be my guide. I politely declined, saying I wanted to stop many times along the way to take photos and it was sure to be a long, tedious day for him. I offered to accompany him there on Sunday if he still fancied the outing.

"Sunday, we'll all be recovering from the festival," he laughed. "Never mind, we'll do it another time."

I felt a pang of guilt at my subterfuge, which contrasted sharply with his open, friendly disposition and was tempted to change my mind. Luckily, my phone rang at that moment. Unknown number. "Hello?" My face must have lit up at the sound of the voice at the other end because everyone looked at me, puzzled. "Anita! How are you? What happened?" I quickly got up and walked away from the table so I could speak to her without being overheard.

I was so happy to finally hear her voice. She filled me in on the news and mentioned several times that she was now free until Monday. I glanced at the Titanic and cursed the shipping schedules which held me captive here until then. I told her how wonderful and friendly the island was, and promised her we would return on holiday once filming was done. Anita was then called off to do an interview and we hung up.

I stared wistfully at the screen and looked up, realizing that I'd drifted toward the memorial while we spoke and was now sitting on the tiny marble wall that surrounded the randomly placed stones. I put my hand down to push myself up, as the wall was really very low and felt a sharp pang. A drop of blood dripped from my finger onto one of the sharp stones and I stared mesmerized as the red drop trickled down the stone, leaving a tiny mark.

I looked up at the engraved column once again. *IN MEMORY OF THOSE WHO GAVE UP THEIR LIVES JUSTLY OR UNJUSTLY.* What could it mean, 'unjustly'? Could it have anything to do with the events Thekla had alluded to?

I felt tempted to go back to the table and find out more. One look at the men sitting around the small metal table getting merrier by the minute and I changed my mind. Why spoil everyone's mood? I moved back to the table and joined them for one last drink.

Having closely observed my phone call, they were full of teasing questions about the film and acting. Did we kiss for real? How could I possibly explain that kissing Anita was not just real, that it was so much more than that?

Talk of the festival naturally led to talk of the occupation, though. I pricked up my ears and kept silent, but did not learn much more. Apparently, not much of the island had been left standing by the Nazis. The place became a ghost island for many years after the war, before locals returned and started to rebuild their lives.

It was getting hotter and hotter as the day went on, so I decided to go for a swim. I got up and paid for everyone's drink despite their protests and asked where the nearest beach was. *Galazia Petra*, they said; the blue stone, about ten minutes' walk from the port, deserted at this time of year.

I headed off in that direction, leaving the port behind. About ten minutes later I saw a small path to my left, gently sloping downwards, nearly obscured by thyme and rosemary bushes. I carefully walked down to be greeted by a small, secluded cove, empty but for a scraggly pine tree. I quickly undressed, hung my clothes on one of the lower branches, and ran into the clear, blue-green waters. I dived in and almost choked with laughter when I saw the large, gray-blue, flat stone which lay at the bottom of the sea floor.

Drying off on the beach, I snapped a photo on my mobile and sent it to Anita. Then, I lay back on the sand and stared at the vast, cloudless sky.

Cave of Silence

The Island, August 15, 1945

Eleni sat on a white sheet that had been spread over the sand. She was holding a thin square of wood on which a piece of paper had been carefully pinned. Color pencils were spread all around her. Every time she looked down to pick another pencil, she would pause and thoughtfully stare at the sea, trying to observe and capture all the shades of blue before her.

The sun was about to leave the horizon and rise up high in the sky, its rays a silver trail slithering on the surface of the water to join Eleni's feet on the shore. This was her first morning on the island after a two-year stay in Italy. It had been impossible to leave earlier and she had been forced to interrupt her studies as the gales of war swept across Europe: Poland, Norway, Denmark, Belgium, the Netherlands, and Italy were already in Hitler's hands, and Mussolini had entered the fray to satiate his ambitious hunger. Anxious about the way events were unfolding, Eleni had returned to Greece as soon as she could.

She seemed happy and relaxed now as she sat on the quiet shore, sketching the seascape and the figure of the man standing in the water, face turned toward the sun. She finished the sketch and made a quick note at the bottom of the paper: *Galazia Petra,* August 1945. She laid the piece of wood by her side, got up, and called out, "Done!"

At this, the young man turned and started swimming to the shore. Eleni lifted up her skirt and waded into the water to meet him. He rose up and walked toward her, water streaming down his bare chest. When he reached Eleni, he took her hand and the couple walked back to the shore together.

"How did I do?" Manolis asked. "Did I manage to stand still long enough?"

Eleni laughed and picked up a towel. Wrapping it around his body in a hug, she looked up at him with a bright smile. "You did well. I hope you weren't getting cold, I don't want you falling ill on my first day back."

Manolis laughed and hugged her back. Then he picked up the piece of wood and gazed at the sketch admiringly. "It's very pretty, Eleni."

"It's nothing, just a very quick sketch...I didn't want my model to freeze."

She took the towel from his hands and started drying his shoulders and back. Manolis let escape a sigh of pleasure and contentment. He'd missed her. They corresponded as often as they could, letters filled with passion and the love they felt for one another. It had given them a chance to talk, to get to know each other. Their bond had become the stronger for it, their separation and the distance between them bringing them closer together than before. Any awkwardness they felt when they first saw each other after two years apart dissipated almost immediately, and now, alone together for the first time, they felt at ease.

Her father had hoped that their love would fade once they were apart. He liked Manolis well enough but had higher hopes for his daughter. He hoped she would marry someone educated, who could take her away from the island, give her a better life. Not become the miller's wife. He had no idea that going away was what the young couple had been planning anyway. Eleni had not shared her hopes and dreams with her father, fearing that the prospect of her absence would break his heart. In any case, the world was changing and only fools made plans in such inauspicious times.

Manolis turned around and gazed into Eleni's eyes. He slowly took the towel from her hands and let it drop onto the sand. Reaching up to her face, he gently stroked her cheek and then hesitantly pulled her in for a kiss. Eleni blushed but did not resist. Their lips locked in a long tender kiss brimming with all those feelings that had flowed so frequently in their letters, but now shyness stopped them from putting into words.

Eleni pulled away from Manolis and smiled awkwardly, then bent down and opened her bag. She took out a small box, tied with a thin black ribbon. Looking down, she handed it to Manolis, who took it and peered at it questioningly.

"Open it," she said.

Manolis untied the ribbon and slowly lifted the cover. Removing the dark blue paper which protected the object in the box, he lifted out a small chain. At the end of the chain dangled a beautiful pocket watch. He put the watch in his palm and held it tightly there for a moment. "Thank you, it's beautiful. You shouldn't have spent your money on me, though."

"I bought this with my own money, Manolis, with money I earned when I worked for the painter I told you about. I'm glad you like it. Open the watch."

Manolis lifted the watch's cover and looked at the watch face.

"Not at the time," Eleni laughed, "inside the lid"

That's when Manolis noticed the inscription.

M+E

FOREVER. TOGETHER.

He stood there looking at the words for a moment, then bent down and picked up his trousers. From one of the pockets, he brought out a small, cloth purse.

"My turn now... Open it."

Eleni stared at him, not understanding at first what he meant. She had not been expecting to receive a gift of any kind. Dumbfounded, she untied the strings and brought out a silver ring. A rose had been sculpted at the top of the wide silver band. She tried to find something to say, but felt choked and the words wouldn't come out. Manolis placed a finger on her lips and took the ring in his other hand. Tenderly, he slid the silver band over her engagement finger, then lifted her face toward him. "It was my mother's."

Tears of joy were now flowing freely down Eleni's cheeks as Manolis pulled her in for another kiss. She responded, holding his face in her hands and kissing him back, passionately. Her hands gripped the back of his neck tightly as he kissed her eyes, her lips, her neck. His body was not completely dry and the salty water was now soaking Eleni's dress. Eleni pulled him down on the sheet, her heart beating faster and faster as Manolis raised the hem of her dress and gently stroked her leg. This was the first man to have kissed her, touched her, the man she still loved and she felt ready to give herself to him. It was a moment they had both thought about during their long correspondence, had alluded to in the letters that had kept their passion alive and they both felt that the moment they had been yearning for had finally arrived. His hand exploring every inch of her body, her nails digging into his bare back, she held on to Manolis as if she never wanted to let go, as if all she ever wanted was to be one with the man she loved for all eternity. He started to unbutton the front of her dress. His lips moved from her lips to her neck, to her breasts, and she let out a soft moan. Any thoughts of what tradition expected, of what was considered proper, had vanished as they gave in to their desire to be together, two bodies about to meet, passionately and with the slight awkwardness of the first time.

A distant voice calling out Manolis' name made them jump. They pulled hurriedly apart, Eleni fumbling to button up her dress with shaky fingers. Manolis stood up and scanned the beach trying to see where the voice was coming from. Up on the hill, his brother Yianni appeared. As soon as he spotted the young couple, he hurried toward them, a deep frown on his face which glistened with sweat.

"Bad news," he sputtered, trying to catch his breath. "I went to the headquarters to pick up the two bushels of corn to be milled. You remember the order, right? I walked in but no one was around. I found them all in a room, listening to the radio officer who was talking with the Italian command on Rhodes. From what I gathered, a ship had been sunk...a Greek ship, the *Elli*. At the port of Tinos. On purpose. They torpedoed it and it sunk. But that wasn't all..."

"What else did you hear?" Manolis asked and gripped Eleni's hand.

"They received an order from Rhodes for the whole army to be on standby. I stood in the corridor, and as they were leaving the room I heard the corporal say, *La guerra è in arrivo, preparatevi miei soldati.*"

Manolis still looked at him uncomprehendingly. He heard Eleni's soft voice translate the Italian words out loud, as much to let them sink in as to help Manolis understand. "War is coming, my soldiers, prepare."

All three stood there, frozen, trying to comprehend what had just happened. Only the waves carried on their soft song, crashing onto the shore, unaware and indifferent to the fact that life on the island was about to change.

≈≈≈≈≈≈≈≈≈≈≈

I returned late from my swim and sat on the balcony of my rented room to enjoy the peace and beauty of the landscape before me. It was nearly dark and I could feel my eyes getting heavier with fatigue. I was sure I would not be able to stay up for much longer.

The swim at *Galazia Petra* had relaxed me and my legs ached from all the walking. I did not want to get up, but had to because I wanted to call Anita and my phone was inside the room, charging.

Lethargically, I got up and went to get it from inside. I dialed Anita's room but there was no reply. I called reception and found out that she was still giving an interview. I left a message asking her to call me as soon as she was done.

Then, I sank back into my chair, facing the setting sun and enjoying the brilliant streaks of color running across the sky. It was a perfect harmony of sight and feeling, one of those moments when you feel at one with the world. Seagulls flew noisily over the rooftops, black shapes against the darkening sky. All that was missing to make this idyllic picture complete was Anita. No matter what you achieve or are given in life, it's worthless if you don't have someone to share it with.

In the distance, the lights of a passing cruise ship glimmered, lit up like an incongruous Christmas tree. I smiled, comparing it to the Titanic and my journey over, and started thinking about all the people I had met on my trip and on the island in just one day. Then I thought about my mother and uncle crossing those same waters on a tiny boat, a fourteen-year-old boy with a toddler in his care, and how scary it must have been. I felt a pang of compassion for poor Uncle Nikos and once again determined to carry out his last wish first thing the following morning.

I wondered whether I should visit their village, perched higher up on the hill above the town. I understood that not much had been left standing after the war. The village was now a small collection of newly-built houses and crumbling walls, the last silent remnants of the houses that used to be there and the lives that had filled them.

Perhaps my short stay would be better spent trying to find out what had happened instead. I felt at ease here, the locals seemed to like me and I could sense that, with a little bit of probing, they would be happy to open up and share their stories with me. Or so said my rational, adult self. The little boy inside me still felt that he should heed his mother's warnings.

I sighed as I realized that all those years of half-spoken words tinged with fear and the implied threat that something terrible might happen should any of us ever return still lived inside me and held me captive, unable to act as freely as I would like. With these thoughts churning through my mind and the soft breeze blowing down the mountain, I felt my eyes getting heavier and heavier and I drifted off to sleep, lulled by the distant melody of the familiar island song and a mechanical buzzing sound.

≈≈≈≈≈≈≈≈≈≈≈

Anita had just finished giving her interview and was chatting with the director in the hotel lobby, along with another ten actors who had smaller parts in the film. Most of the extras were locals, a choice made by the director who liked the thought of using them to give the film more authenticity.

Electra approached Anita as discreetly as she could, trying to keep out of the way of the photographer who was still snapping away and not to bump into any of the curious people who were milling about. She was carrying a small box, which she promptly handed to Anita. "I've replaced your old SIM card, but you'll need to charge it. Most of your contacts are saved but the photos are gone, I'm afraid," she said apologetically.

Anita felt a pang of disappointment. All her photos of Dimitri were gone. She tried not to let it show as she thanked Electra for all the trouble she had gone to, and asked her if she could go find Mihalis for her.

As Electra bounced off to fetch him, a small cheeky smile lit up her face, like a child that had just discovered a hidden stash of sweets. She quickly took leave of the others, thanked the photographer, and headed to the reception area. The receptionist handed over the message asking her to call Dimitri and impatience mingled with joy inside her. She wanted so much to finally be alone and talk to him. All day they'd barely managed to exchange more than a few words. But she needed to call her mother first and tell her she was well, worried that maybe they had been trying to reach her while her phone was not working. She was sorry that she had not been able to talk to her grandmother for days and worried that the elderly woman might have taken a turn for the worse.

As she made to go to her room, a hand gently touched her shoulder, trying to get her attention. She turned and came face to face with Mihalis' strong features, his distinctive mustache and the twinkling eyes that made him appear younger than his sixty years. Tall and lean, he seemed like a guardian angel to her at that moment.

"You were looking for me, Anita?" he asked.

"Yes. I have a favor to ask."

"Anything you want, just ask away."

"Remember when you took us across to the other island? That nice beach? The Cave of Silence?"

"Of course I do. Would you like me to take you back there?"

"Well," Anita gave a naughty little laugh, "not *exactly.*" She lowered her voice and started explaining her plan.

≈≈≈≈≈≈≈≈≈≈

Back in her room, her phone now charged, Anita switched it on. The first message to come up was the photo Dimitri had sent from *Galazia Petra*. Her heart beating faster, she dialed his number impatiently. No answer. Maybe he was out.

She lay down on her bed and exhaled deeply, the events of the day and Dimitri's absence making her feel out of sorts. Turning to her side, she noticed a small white envelope addressed to her standing on the bedside table. She opened it carefully and took out the piece of paper folded inside.

Whatever happens, always remember that the days I have spent with you have been the best days of my life. It hasn't been five minutes since you left this room and I miss you already.

She held the piece of paper and reread it as if she couldn't quite believe what it said. That was exactly how she had felt after saying goodbye to him that morning. Except Dimitri seemed to somehow have the courage, the strength to own up to those feelings, to put them into words and share them with her.

She quickly picked up the phone and dialed again—still no answer. She started to worry a little and felt frustrated that she didn't know where he was staying. Maybe Electra knew, but she felt uncomfortable asking.

She'd been puzzled by Dimitri's trip, by the urgency she could detect in his voice whenever he talked of going there and which he couldn't hide no matter how casually he tried to speak of his impending visit. Perhaps it was nothing, she told herself; some unfinished family business, paperwork, who knew? He was probably out and had forgotten to take his phone with him. She'd take a shower, call her mother, and try again later.

≈≈≈≈≈≈≈≈≈≈

Eleni was sleeping on her bed, her face the color of wax in the street light streaming through the curtains. The wind outside was making the shutters rattle. The moving branches cast eerie shadows on the walls.

Suddenly, the old woman's eyes opened wide, as if waking up from a bad dream. They darted around the room searching for something and came to rest on the framed photo of the crowded port. Her breathing was coming hard and fast, making a faint whistling sound that roused

Michaela who had been slumbering in the armchair near the bed.

"*Mamá*! Are you alright?" she asked anxiously, trying to raise the old woman's head on an extra pillow to ease her breathing. Rina, hearing movement in the room, ran inside to help her, turning on the bedside lamp. They raised the pillows behind her and Eleni seemed to breathe more easily.

"Water, please," the old woman whispered hoarsely.

Rina quickly brought the glass of water that stood on the bedside table to Eleni's lips, who managed to take a couple of sips through the straw. Exhausted by the effort, she sank back into the pillows. Summoning all her strength, she looked at Michaela and said with a newfound determination, "I need to talk to you."

Michaela glanced at Rina, who took the hint and swiftly left the bedroom. She then turned to her mother, astonished at this sudden flash of lucidity, so rare these days. She sat on the edge of the bed beside her, worried, her curiosity piqued. "Tell me *Mamá*, what is it? What's happening?

"Is Anita back? Is she okay?"

"Not yet, but she will be back in a few days. She is well, though. We'll call her in the morning and you can speak with her, she's been missing you too."

"Time is running out, you must learn the truth..."

Michaela stared at her mother unable to utter a word. She was trying to figure out whether her mother was really lucid or had now drifted off into a parallel world and was rambling.

"Tell me, *Mamá*. I'm here...I'm listening"

Eleni went quiet for a moment, as if gathering her thoughts and trying to overcome some lingering hesitation. She seemed to fight off any last doubts, regained her strength, and continued. "Upstairs, in the attic, is my trunk. Open it. Under all the papers, you'll find a wooden box. It says *Galazia Petra* on it. It's locked. Bring it to me, Michaela. Now."

Michaela wondered whether she should calm the agitated woman down and put all of this off for the following morning. What if her mother never regained this kind of lucidity, though? She looked at her watch. Midnight. She would do as her mother asked.

She called Rina back into the room to stay with Eleni and then almost ran up the stairs to the small attic.

It had been such a long time since she'd last been up here. This had been her favorite room as a little girl. She used to spend time with her mother up in the attic, listening to a wonderful story about a prince on a black, not white, horse; a horse with a white heart-shaped mark on its forehead. The prince had been forced to leave his girl behind one day and did not return for years. And she waited for him, in a castle at the top of a hill, on a warm, sunny island. Whenever she got to the end of the story, when the prince returned and married the girl he loved, tears would fill Eleni's eyes. Whenever Michaela would ask her why she cried at such a happy ending, Eleni would tell her that those were tears of joy. But Michaela knew, could tell that her mother's eyes were sad. The sadness never went away, even as the years went by and the story was passed on to Anita, who would sit on her grandmother's knees enraptured, listening to the story of the prince. Except Anita would weep with her grandmother, not quite knowing why, all the while reassuring her grandmother that her own prince would come on a black horse too and they would all be invited to the wedding.

Michaela looked around the attic, lost in the memories of her childhood. It had been a magical place, this attic with its wooden puppets hanging from the ceiling, Eleni's unfinished paintings on the walls, among them a painting of the fairy-tale prince astride his black horse at the top of a hill, looking at the sea.

She spotted the trunk sitting below the two small round windows at the far end of the room. She sat beside it, removed the old quilts and blankets that kept it almost hidden from view, and opened it. She carefully removed sheet after sheet of her mother's discarded sketches, all of the same face. She held one close to her eyes. Why did the man seem familiar? Her mind raced, trying to recall where she had seen his face before. She felt her heart stop for a second when she realized that this was the man in the pocket watch. She set the sketch aside and started to fumble beneath the remaining papers with greater urgency, her fingers looking for the wooden box. It did not take long. She pulled it out, scattering pieces of paper all around her. She'd never seen it before. At least now she could be certain her mother was lucid, the box was not the confused ramblings of a fading mind.

Michaela quickly brushed the dust off the top of the lid and could just about make out a small colored sketch: a man standing in the sea, looking at the rising sun. *Galazia Petra*, read a note in her mother's hand at the bottom of the sketch. She tried to open the box and then remembered that it was locked.

In a hurry now, not wanting to waste another second of whatever precious time was left, Michaela picked up the box and ran down the stairs. As she crossed the living room she heard Rina cry out in an alarmed voice, "Quickly, call the doctor! Call an ambulance, now!"

The doctor's recommendation was that Eleni be moved to the hospital immediately. It would be the only way to keep her alive and, hopefully, regain her consciousness at some point.

Tears streaming down her face, Michaela felt torn. She had promised her mother that she would not be hospitalized, that she would die in her own home. Now that the moment had come, she did not know if she had the strength to carry out her mother's wishes, knowing that this would precipitate her death. She also thought of Anita, how devastated she would be if her grandmother died while she was away, unable to see her one last time, to be near her at the very end. "To the hospital," she said.

She looked down at her hands and realized that she was still holding the box. As the ambulance men walked in carrying a stretcher, she placed it on the coffee table and wondered what it was that her mother had so urgently needed to tell her earlier in the evening.

≈≈≈≈≈≈≈≈≈≈

I opened my eyes as a hot ray of sun hit my face. My hands instinctively felt for Anita's body beside me on the bed and then I remembered where I was. I looked down and saw that I was still dressed. I must have walked into the room at some point during the night after falling asleep on the balcony and got into bed. I had barely had any sleep for days on end and exhaustion and sleep-deprivation had finally caught up, plunging me into a comatose slumber.

I looked at the open balcony doors and saw that my mobile was still outside on the coffee table. I got up and went to pick it up. Four missed calls, all from Anita. How could I have missed them? I cursed myself when I saw I had left it on vibrate. I looked at the time; too early to call, better text her.

The building was silent, a sure sign that everyone was still asleep at this early hour. The sound of the phone ringing startled me. Anita! I loved hearing the drowsiness in her voice as she explained that she'd just been woken up by my message. We spoke for a long time, not even thinking about going back to sleep.

She told me about a monastery she'd visited and the car accident that followed and I told her about my journey over. Without even realizing how, I told her about the real reason behind my visit. That I was here to carry out my uncle's dying wish and scatter his ashes on his favorite spot on the island.

She seemed puzzled, so I then had to explain that my mother's family came from this island but that no one had ever returned. I could guess all the unanswered questions this piece of information would raise, but she was discreet enough not to ask anything. I hoped she didn't think that I was trying to hide anything from her and felt reassured when I heard her say that she found it touching that my uncle wanted his island to be his final resting place and that I was going to carry out that wish.

I quickly changed the topic, talking about the festival and how much I missed her. She said she loved the picture I had taken at *Galazia Petra* and was going to send it to her family in Berlin.

The hours passed by quickly, seamlessly, as we talked and talked, as if we had been apart for more than a day and had to make up for lost time. By the time we hung up the sun was blazing in the clear blue sky and my stomach had started to rumble. I remembered Thekla's delicious breakfast and the smell of coffee being served in the courtyard lured me downstairs to join the other guests.

≈≈≈≈≈≈≈≈≈≈

Her face covered by an oxygen mask, Eleni lay immobile on the hospital bed, eyes closed. All that could be heard was the beeping of the heart monitors by her bedside.

Michaela, dark circles under her eyes and a worn look on her face, kept watch by her mother's bedside, holding the old woman's hand tenderly in her palm. At the sound of a beep coming from her handbag, Michaela got up, careful not to disturb the drip attached to her mother's arm. She took her phone out and stepped into the corridor. It was a message from Anita, photo attached.

She felt a pang of guilt as she recalled reassuring her daughter during the previous night's brief call that everything was okay so as not to worry her.

Anita seemed to be having a wonderful time, sounding happier than she had done in years; sounding—Michaela smiled to herself at the thought—in love. Should she interrupt whatever was happening in her daughter's life while it was still unclear how long Eleni would linger in this state? She didn't want to burden her now. On the other hand, Anita had a right to know. She had to hear what the doctors would say and then decide.

She opened the message and saw the picture of a beach, a picture which looked strangely familiar. She tried to remember where she had seen the place, bringing the phone up for a closer look. Impossible to recall, she was too tired to think clearly anyway. She quickly texted her daughter: *That's a great photo...we miss you. We are at the hospital for some checks, but all is well. We both love you, take care.*

Half a truth, the painless half. She took another look at the photo, still unable to place it. Taking a cup of coffee from Rina, she moved back into the hospital room and sat beside her mother. Her wrinkled face seemed at peace.

Michaela reflected gratefully on her mother's strength, the courage she had shown as a young widow, running her own business and raising her only child at the same time. Michaela smiled fondly as she remembered all the time she spent as a child in the antique shop that had belonged to her father's family, playing under coffee tables and pretending to help.

Even when times were hard, Eleni always remained calm, steady, a gentle woman made of steel. Whenever Anita, as a child, would knock something over in the shop, she would simply pick it up or calmly pick up the pieces and say that there are far more important things in life than lifeless objects. Thinking now of the man's picture in the pocket watch, the man whose face graced countless sketches hidden in a trunk that had housed a box now standing locked on the living-room coffee table, Michaela wondered whether there was more to those words than the fond musings of a forgiving grandmother.

The Island, November 10, 1940

It was almost dark and the bitter northerly wind shook the branches of the olive tree just outside Manolis' mill. A faint light shone through the small window, mingling with the flour dust inside the room to give the scene an ethereal, otherworldly air.

Seated on two large, round grinding stones, Manolis and Eleni were contemplating the flag stones on the floor, a heavy silence between them. He looked up first, reached across to Eleni and took her hand in his. Eleni looked up at him, her eyes moist. She was trying to be brave, to swallow her tears.

Manolis had just announced that he was leaving with a group of local boys to join the volunteer corps. They were heading to the Greek Albanian border to fight. Italy had declared war on Greece and he was eager to go; felt that it was his duty and the least he could do. An English vessel was due to pass by a nearby uninhabited islet early in the morning. It would collect the volunteers and transport them to Piraeus on the mainland.

He was sorry to leave her. He knew he might never see her again. She knew that too. That's why she did not want to let him go. Eleni was afraid, afraid of losing Manolis, afraid of staying on the island. Relations between the two populations were becoming strained; the Italians were not so friendly anymore. Her father was ill, she had no other relatives, and, with Manolis gone, she would be on her own.

She had tried to explain all this to him, but his mind was made up. He told her that everyone had reasons to stay instead of going to fight. If they all did that then the Italians would conquer the rest of Greece and things would become even worse. At some point, the Germans might come. He couldn't stay hidden out on the island, he had to do something for his country. He brought her hands up to his lips and kissed them. "I promise you, I'll be back. Everything will be different then. We'll be free, we'll get married, and we'll have a family. I just want you to wait for me. Nothing else... just wait for me to come back."

Eleni wiped her tears with the back of her hand. "I'll wait for you my whole life Manolis, so long as you come back..."

"I will come back, my love. I'll come back. I swear it."

It was the first time he'd called her *my love*. Eleni felt good hearing it from his lips and buried herself in his arms. He held her tightly, then gently pushed her back so he could see her face. Holding her gaze, he said, "Whatever the Italians say, you must deny that you know where I've gone. I don't want you to suffer if they find out why I've left. Whatever you need, you ask Yiannis, my brother. He'll look out for you. I'll come back for you, Eleni, take you to the mainland where we can live freely. That, I promise."

Eleni leaned toward Manolis and kissed him tenderly. The howling wind muffled the sound of the approaching footsteps, and they did not see the man looking in through the window. The sound of a fist on the door made them jump up with fright. Manolis quickly picked up a long piece of wood and approached the door to find out who the unexpected visitor was. Yiannis was supposed to meet him there, but much later. "Who is it?" he shouted without opening the door.

The sound of a hacking cough from behind the door was his only answer. Eleni realized it was her father and went to the door. There stood Captain- Andreas, his face indiscernible in the twilight, bent over, trying to make his coughing fit stop.

They both helped the old man inside and Manolis went to fetch some water. Taking a couple of breaths between coughs, he managed to drink some water and seemed to recover a little. He'd fallen ill during the summer and never seemed to fully recover. Winter had worsened his condition and the coughing fits were becoming more frequent and severe. Eleni was crouched by his side, gently stroking his back as the coughing became more subdued and he started to breathe normally again. He slowly raised his head and looked at Manolis. "I heard you are leaving Manolis, at dawn..."

No one other than Eleni and his brother knew about his imminent departure and the young man was stunned to hear those words. He looked questioningly at Eleni but she shook her head no, the information had not been passed on by her. Who then? Before he had a chance to ask, her father started to talk again, forming his words slowly and with great effort. "You are wondering how I know, right? If I weren't an old man and ill, don't you think I would be coming with you, my boy? What did you think? That we don't all love our country too?"

"Captain-Andreas..." Manolis stuttered, but was silenced by Andreas' raised hand.

"Go and God be with you. You'll return. And when you do, Eleni will be here waiting for you and we'll hold your wedding. I want to see my grandchildren before I die, Manolis."

The young couple looked at him, unable to utter a word. Before they could recover from their surprise, the old man got up. Straightening his jacket, he approached the window and looked out at the moon, casting its glow over the sea. "The day your mother died, Eleni, I promised myself that I would raise you and you would have a better life. I wanted you to get an education, leave this place, move to Greece and live there freely, raise your family there. When, God willing, Manolis is back, you'll pack up and leave this place. Unless this island is free by then. Only then can you stay here, if you want to. I want you to promise me that."

"I promise, father," Eleni replied, emotion choking her words. "And I also swear that you'll come with us, wherever we go, if you want to."

The hooves of a horse could now be heard pounding the ground outside, followed by Yiannis' voice. He called for his brother to let him in, as he dismounted outside. Manolis went to the door and pulled it open. Yiannis walked in, followed by his son Nikos, who stood timidly by the open doorway, casting curious glances at Eleni. She smiled at him through her tears. Yiannis hid his surprise at seeing Andreas at the mill and spoke to Manolis. "It's time to go."

Eleni bowed her head, trying to stifle a sob. Her father put on his coat, walked up to Manolis, and gripped his arm. "You take care, my boy. God be with you." He then walked out, followed by Yiannis, who gave his son a nudge to step outside too.

The ten-year-old seemed confused, trying to figure out what was going on. He looked in through the half-open doorway and saw Manolis walk up to Eleni and gently lift her chin toward him. She was looking at him intently, unable to stop crying. Wanting to feel Manolis against her one last time, she wrapped her arms around him in a tight embrace. He hugged her back and stroked her hair, which shone in the moonlight coming through the window.

They kissed passionately, as sorrow, pain, love, longing and sadness all mingled into one strong emotion that passed like a current between them. For a moment, it was as if they were breathing through one another.

The wind had turned into a gale by now and Manolis, looking into Eleni's eyes once more, removed a photo of the two of them at the port from the inside pocket of his jacket, kissed it before her and placed it back close to his heart. "I will always carry you with me, my love," he said.

Eleni started crying once more. Manolis, trying to hide his emotions, turned away abruptly, took a cloth bag hanging from a nail on the wall, and walked out to join his brother without looking back. At the door, he put his arm around his nephew who had been gaping open-mouthed at the scene and gently pulled him toward the waiting horses.

Eleni's father walked back into the mill and found her standing by the window, watching the departing riders. He went toward her and put his hand on her shoulder trying to comfort her. Eleni's gaze remained fixed on the three shadowy figures on horseback, dimly lit by the silver moonlight and knew that this could be the last time she ever saw the man she loved.

≈≈≈≈≈≈≈≈≈≈≈

After so many hours of sleep on the balcony and then my bed, and despite the early phone call with Anita, I felt truly rested. I had just finished my breakfast, made a couple of phone calls, and was getting ready to return to my room to pick up my rucksack and head for Mantani, when I saw Thekla carrying a small package wrapped in a red and white cloth.

"Home-baked bread and tomatoes," she explained. "For later, when you get hungry," she added and rushed off to serve the other guests who had arrived for that evening's festival. Most of them had traveled on private boats from the neighboring islands and would spend the night here; after a night of feasting, nobody would be fit to sail back.

Back in my room, I carefully placed the box containing my uncle's ashes into the rucksack, along with Thekla's parcel. Hoisting it over my shoulders, I slung my camera around my neck and went out to find the motorbike. I wanted to scatter the ashes first. I felt that doing so would release me from a burden I was carrying and somehow release Uncle Nikos too.

I set off toward the port, intending to pass by and say hello to Thomas before heading to Mantani. As expected, I occasionally got lost in the narrow winding streets but found myself outside the *kafeneio* quicker than I expected. Perhaps I was starting to get to know the place after all.

I pulled up and looked inside, but other than Sofia and a couple of old men, no one else seemed to be around. Noticing me, Sofia hurried outside to greet me.

"Morning! Where is your grandfather?" I asked her as she approached.

"Good morning!" she smiled back at me. "He's at our orchard; it's not far from here. He'll be back soon. Anything you want me to tell him?"

"No, Sofia, I just passed by to say hello. Maybe you could give me directions to Mantani?"

She turned to the right and pointed at a narrow alley. "If you go down this alley you'll come across a dirt track after a while. Just take it and it will lead you straight to the spring. Be careful though, it's a narrow path that passes under a big boulder at some point. Remember to duck," she laughed, "you wouldn't be the first one to come back with a headache."

I thanked Sofia and set off, passing before the monument to the war dead. As I rode past it, I once again felt a chill go down my spine. My mood had been a rollercoaster of highs and lows ever since I had set foot on this island.

I had spoken to my mother briefly that morning and she was as anxious as ever, asking me to leave the island that very afternoon. But there was no ferry crossing that day and I was thinking of leaving the day after. I'd been told by Thekla that some of her guests would be returning to the nearby island on a yacht the following day and she could arrange for me to return with them. I was desperate to return to Anita, now that she also had some time off, and spend time with her. Just that thought lifted my mood and reminded me again how much I missed her.

As promised by Sofia, I found the dirt track at the end of the uphill alley, a very narrow path fringed by rocks on one side and small steep cliffs on the other. The view from up here was impressive, and I would regularly stop to take pictures of the port and the sea views beyond it.

It did not take too long to reach the point where the dirt track became even narrower. To the left, the overhanging rocks, suspended in mid-air, left a small, low opening. I slowed down, got off the motorbike, and started to slowly walk through the opening, keeping the engine on and guiding it beside me. It was so low I wondered how people rode through on horseback in the old days. They must have dismounted and continued on foot, just as I was doing now. My heart was beating fast, but I felt calmer than I expected. The memory of Anita and our afternoon in the Cave of Silence seemed to have dulled my fear of caves and tunnels.

Beyond the tunnel, the track widened once more and moved uphill even more steeply. I got on the bike again and picked up speed, now clearly headed toward the mountain top. I welcomed the wind against my face and the heady smell of thyme it carried with it. The landscape was getting greener, a clear sign that the spring was near.

A few minutes later, I pulled to an abrupt stop. Just ahead I could spot a small copse of low trees and grass, a clear sign of water in this scraggy landscape. I killed the engine and the silence was like a slap in the face. I could only hear the sound of trickling water. The sea and the surrounding islands, which stretched out to my right, seemed to be miles away. I walked to the thicket of trees and bushes, quietly, almost reverently.

The spring was easy enough to spot, the water spouting from a fountain made of stones that had been built up against the rock from which a constant stream seemed to flow. I dropped my rucksack on one of the stones and bent down to quench my thirst. I wet my face and my hair to wash off the dust and leaned back against the rocks, catching my breath.

For a moment I imagined my uncle at this place, sitting at this same spot so many years ago, taking in the same view, singing along with the others. He always seemed happy whenever he spoke of *Mantani*, the only times I ever saw him smile. This was the spot where women would come to wash their laundry, he'd say. The men would accompany them, keep them company, sing songs, and wait until the laundry was done to carry them back to town on horseback. The strange love he had for this place puzzled me; knowing the circumstances of his departure, I was surprised that he'd wanted to return here after his death.

The time had come to carry out his wishes. I took out the box and moved it toward the mouth of the spring. I felt a strange charge pass through me, like an electric surge, as I held it in my hands. I opened it carefully and started emptying the ashes. For a moment, the water clouded as the ashes landed on its surface, but started to clear up again as the flowing current carried them in the stream.

I was sure this was what my uncle had had in mind. The beauty of the moment, as I experienced it, was his parting gift to me. I thought that this is what I would like for myself too, when the time came. I did not like the idea of being buried in the ground.

The last of the ashes in the water, I rinsed out the box and placed it by the spring, feeling like I'd just accomplished a ritual, a ceremony that had to happen this way. I looked up to the sky to let Uncle Nikos know I'd done as he'd asked, and turned to leave.

A man's voice, in the distance, sang the *Nisiotissa*, that song I had heard the previous day. I turned around, puzzled, trying to figure out where the singing was coming from. Thomas appeared from behind the low branches of a tree, astride a white horse.

I quickly shoved the box back in my rucksack and tried to act casual. He carried on singing as he approached, and only spoke to me once he'd dismounted right beside me. "Isn't it a beautiful spot, Dimitri?"

Having kept the reason for my presence on the island a secret, I felt the fear my mother had passed on wake up inside me. I suddenly realized that ever since I had arrived, Thomas kept appearing before me, as if he knew something, as if he'd been watching my every move. Had he seen me scatter the ashes? I looked furtively toward the copse of trees he'd materialized from—too far away, probably not. So I calmly replied, "Even more beautiful than I expected. I've taken many photos..."

He smiled and bent down to drink from the spring. Then, wiping his lips with the back of his hand, he looked at me sternly and said, "I know what you're doing here."

I felt the ground give way beneath my feet at that statement and the sudden appearance of three more men on horseback behind them, one of them holding a shotgun. I broke into a cold sweat, certain that they'd realized who I was, that I was just about to pay for the sins of my forefathers, whatever they may have been. I stood frozen to the spot, gaping at them.

Summoning whatever shreds of courage I had left, I turned back to Thomas keeping an eye out for the others, who had approached and were waiting to hear what we had to say. "What am I doing here?"

Thomas suddenly looked puzzled as he realized I was genuinely scared and said in a joking tone, "Stealing our water!" He laughed heartily at his joke. The three horsemen joined in, obviously used to his jests.

I felt my heart lurch back into my chest and tried to laugh along, to disguise my agitation. Before I had a chance to speak, he gave my shoulder a friendly punch and said, "Come, my lad, take a photo of us on our horses, here by the spring, with the sea behind us."

He mounted his horse and posed proudly next to his friends. Seen through the camera lens, they made quite a sight, these four proud men who looked like they'd stepped in from another era.

Although my hands were still shaky, I managed to snap away quite a few photos. "If there is a print shop on the island, I'll be able to make you some copies today," I offered.

Thomas nodded. "Great. When you are back from your outing, pass by the *kafeneio* and we'll do that. We'll move on now, maybe get lucky and catch a hare today. We'll leave you to steal more water behind our backs."

This time around, my laughter was genuine, now that I was certain he really had no idea of what I'd been doing at the spring.

Thomas tugged on the reins of his horse and spurred it on. The other three followed suit raising their hands in a gesture of farewell and set off back toward the trees they'd come from.

I watched them withdraw and vowed not to reveal to anyone who I was. The stress just was not worth it.

As soon as the men disappeared from my eyesight, I relaxed and took a few moments to enjoy the view and capture the scenery before me. Then, I started to walk downhill, following the path of the stream that trickled away from the spring.

I thought it would lead to the edge of some cliff. Instead, I spotted a small path that led to a plateau, where the water pooled to form a small lake before carrying on its winding path through the bushes, presumably all the way down to the sea.

What I saw next was one of the most memorable moments of my life. A herd of five horses was drinking at the edge of the lake, no saddles or reins on them.

I started photographing them, approaching as softly as I could. They did not seem to notice and I was able to get quite close. A branch snapped under my foot, startling the horses away from the shore. Only a tall black horse stayed where it had stood, a white heart-shaped mark on its forehead. It stood still, looking at me, as if it knew me, inviting me to approach it.

I slowly stepped toward the horse and stopped at a safe distance. That's when I noticed its front legs were in the lake, the water cloudy around its hooves with the ashes I had scattered.

I took another cautious step toward it. I was so near. The horse kept looking at me, unperturbed. Slowly, I lifted my hand and moved to pat its head. No reaction. When the tips of my fingers touched it, it turned to sniff my hand. And then suddenly, as if stung by a fly, it reared on its hind legs, neighing violently.

Startled, I took a step back and slipped on the muddy ground. I fell on my back, the horse now a dark, ominous shape against the blinding sun. Instinctively, I cradled my head in my hands and rolled to the side, eyes squeezed shut.

The thud of its front legs crashing on the ground beside my head broke like a thunderclap. Before I could even register my narrow escape, I felt the hot breath of the horse on my cheek and the nudge of its moist nostrils, like a faint, humid kiss.

I opened my eyes and stirred. It pulled back at this sign of movement and galloped off in the direction the rest of the herd had disappeared to. It only paused once more; a hundred feet away, it rose on its hind legs in a majestic farewell and disappeared behind the rocks.

I sat up trying to fully grasp what had just happened and to regain my composure. When I felt my legs could hold me, I stood up and dusted myself down. With mixed emotions, I turned back toward the spring.

Fear mingled with amazement at the horse's strange comportment. Had I really just experienced this or was it a mirage, a hallucination born out of the alluring landscape and my fragile emotional state?

As soon as I reached the spring, I sat on a stone and pulled out my phone to call Anita. I longed to hear her voice and share this strange experience.

Macedonia, April 13, 1941

Daylight had just started to break through the mist and the veil of thin rain that covered the tents set up on the muddy soil. Dim lights sparkled like stars in the fog as the village nesting on the hill slopes across the field rose from its slumber.

Manolis had heard that the village was called Vlasti. The locals had been helping out the troops as much as they could by bringing the soldiers food and clothes during their stay.

The men huddled around small campfires, trying to keep the asthmatic flames going with whatever bits of dry wood they could find to keep themselves warm and dry. Their long beards and sunken cheeks, and the uncaring way in which they carried their rifles, ignoring orders to be on guard, bore testament to their fatigue and despair.

Starved mules snorted through the mud in a desperate attempt to find some grass, sidestepping the abandoned machine guns which, bereft of any ammunition, rusted in the field.

The unnatural silence that reigned over the camp was sporadically broken by the moans of pain escaping from the tents.

Men, animals, objects... all abandoned to their fate.

His back leaning against a mossy rock, Manolis sat enveloped in the acrid smoke of the wet branches that burned before him. His eyes, empty and expressionless, stared at the meager flames. Only the imperceptible movement of his bony chest gave away that this man was still alive. His torn and muddy uniform hung loosely around his skeletal frame, cinched at the waist with an old and frayed piece of cord.

Of the three thousand islanders who had formed the volunteer corps, only a few hundred remained. The others had either lost their lives in battle or been captured by the Nazis, who were storming through the country, overrunning the Greek and allied forces.

They had fought bravely, but were no match for the German war machine. The front had collapsed, unable to hold any longer against the relentless hammering of the German artillery and the Luftwaffe. They were withdrawing, hoping to regroup and form a new defensive line. They had been instructed to camp out there and await orders for their next movements.

The war had changed Manolis. He was numb and withdrawn, hardened by the experience. As if at some point his heart had frozen over and nothing but the warm spark of Eleni's memory could thaw it.

He thought of her and put his hand in his overcoat, taking out a small, worn notebook. His diary. He turned to the page where he kept the photo of the crowd gathered at the port, the day Eleni was departing for Italy. He picked it up as gently as he could with his cold fingers, bringing it close to his eyes. He squinted and Eleni's smiling face came into focus, leaning against his chest with a smile. For a moment, his expression softened.

He was staring at the photo as if he wanted to enter the print, go into that moment, and stand beside her once again. He had not heard from her since he'd left for the front. He had written countless letters to her, but never received a reply. Neither had any of the men he was with and no one could explain why.

He did not even know whether any of his letters had reached her. He did not know if she was well and he was impatient to return to the island and see for himself. He could tell from the information and rumors circulating in the camp that the war was lost. Greece was on the verge of capitulating to Germany. It was a matter of days, hours even.

He pulled out the pocket watch she had given him and lifted the cover to read the time and see the inscription inside once more: *Forever. Together.* It had become a daily ritual, his brief snatched moments with her.

Suddenly, the sound of machine guns and loud explosions erupted. Manolis jumped up, hastily placing the photo back into the notebook and the notebook into his pocket, by his heart. He kicked the muddy soil over the fire to put it out and joined the soldiers running to the tent where the officers were gathered.

Before he could even reach it he heard they had to move, ASAP. German troops were approaching and daylight would bring the first enemy aircraft with it. *Destroy all military equipment that cannot be carried! Hurry! Hurry!*

Many had already started moving in the direction away from the sound of battle, carrying the injured on their backs or strapping them onto the exhausted mules. Men and beasts of burden had had no chance to rest after their exhausting trek through the mountains; on the road once again to avoid falling into the hands of the mighty enemy.

An hour later, Manolis was one of the few men still left at the dismantled camp. Nothing remained but trampled cloth, smoking campfires, and the heavy machinery. They doused everything in petrol and set it alight. From a safe distance, a man threw a grenade onto the flames and everything blew up in a loud flash.

Quickly they turned to follow their departing comrades—but not quickly enough. Ten German soldiers suddenly appeared before them, their guns ready to shoot, shouting a barrage of incomprehensible orders. There was nothing they could do, a small band of men with barely three rifles between them. One by one, the men raised their arms in surrender.

Manolis kept his arms firmly by his sides. He refused to budge, even when a German officer walked up toward him, barking something in a language Manolis could not understand. Another soldier walked up behind him and roughly brought the butt of his rifle down on the defiant man's head. The last image to flash before his eyes as he hit the ground losing consciousness was Eleni standing beside him, smiling, the boat waiting for them on the horizon.

≈≈≈≈≈≈≈≈≈≈

The rest of the day was relaxing and uneventful. I toured almost half the island on my motorbike. I walked miles to reach the hidden coves that could only be accessed on foot and to cool off with a swim. And I discovered the beauty of the hills; narrow dirt paths carpeted with wild flowers, occasionally dotted with the stone ruins of old buildings that sprung up among the tall grass; tiny white chapels crowned with small azure domes on deserted hillsides, casting their lonely gaze over the blue sea; tall, naked rocks, petrified giants that the hand of some ancient god had flung to earth.

The island exuded its strange allure and I slowly succumbed.

I did not meet many people during my wanderings, and I was grateful for that. People tend to destroy the nature that surrounds them, alter it with their actions and their presence; here, nature had remained largely untouched by the hand of man.

My encounter with the black horse remained with me all day. I searched in vain for a rational explanation, something that could dispel the strong feeling I had that the horse had responded to me as if I were a familiar face. Maybe I was too irrational to come up with a reasonable answer; maybe I'd spent too long in the sun without a hat.

As the day wore on, I turned full circle, coming back to the rooms from the top of the hill in the direction facing away from the port. A group of old stone houses belied the presence of a village that now lay abandoned, in ruins; a melancholy, gloomy presence. Was one of those my mother's house? As far as I knew, neither Uncle Nikos nor mother owned anything here, but the more I thought about it, the more I wished that a tiny parcel of this place could be ours. Good luck telling my mother that, of course. Maybe if I found out what had happened here, the full facts, I could figure out if it were possible to claim back what must have belonged to her family. How would that be possible without letting anyone realize who I was?

The sun was almost setting by the time I pulled up outside Thekla's rooms and all I wanted was some food. I was ravenous, the snack she'd packed long gone.

I left the motorbike at the same spot, its engine burning hot after the day's travels, and stepped into the courtyard. I immediately asked for a portion of her stuffed vegetables, the dish of the day, and ran upstairs to wash off the dust and sea salt.

I walked in and flung my rucksack on the sofa, eager to strip off my muddy clothes. As I was pulling my t-shirt over my head, my eyes fell on the framed photo on the wall. A group of people had gathered at the port. I picked it up and walked to the window for better light and a closer inspection.

A strange wave of nostalgia washed over me. I had always been intrigued by anything that allowed me a glimpse into the past and the lives of people long gone, maybe because it filled the gaping void of my past.

They were obviously preparing to depart on a long journey, on the ship that could be made out on the horizon. Where to, for how long? Their faces looked forlorn, like faces usually did in photos from that era, as if looking somber before the lens was as mandatory as the wide grins in today's photos. How had the years treated them? Was a distant relation of mine among them?

I took a closer, careful look. A woman in the arms of a man as he held her close to him stood out from the others, her blissful expression a sharp contrast to everyone's solemn looks. The man looked serious but not stern. He was enjoying the moment as much as the girl beside him. The longer I looked, the more the couple seemed to stand out, come into focus, as everything else faded into a sepia-tinted blur.

The more I looked the more the woman in the photo resembled Anita. That thought caught me by surprise and made me laugh. The tricks my mind was playing today! Love-struck, sun-struck, hunger-struck, I was starting to see her everywhere.

I sighed and placed the photo on the sofa, glass facing down to protect it, and jumped into the shower. Anita was far away, but I could do something about the heat and the hunger.

As soon as I sat down at a table in the shady courtyard, Thekla materialized with a tray filled with *gemistá*, the stuffed vegetables accompanied with a generous helping of feta cheese and her oven-baked bread.

"Would you like something to drink?" she asked.

"No, thank you, water will be fine."

"How was your day? Did you go far?"

"It was great!" I mumbled enthusiastically between bites. "I saw something unexpected up on the mountain, near Mantani."

Thekla pulled out a chair and sat down, wiping her hand on her apron.

"I saw a herd of horses, all alone and wild, but one of them let me stroke it."

"They must have escaped from someone's stable. Not many people have horses on the island. I'll keep it in mind in case I hear someone's looking for them. Near the spring at Mantani you say?"

"Yes, but then they moved away, toward the sea." I swallowed and quickly changed the topic as I saw her get up to return to the kitchen. "Your island keeps many secrets."

She looked at me, frowning. "More than you could imagine, Dimitri. I'll leave you to eat, make sure you get some rest. Festivals go on until the early hours here."

I watched her walk away and played with my bread crust. Would I get to discover some of those secrets?

Cave of Silence

The Island, August 1942

The sun had set behind the mountains, drowning the beach in a hazy golden glow. Before the Cave of Silence stood Yiannis, his wife Anna and their son, Nikos, all dressed in their Sunday best. In the sea, Eleni stood with the water reaching her knees and soaking her dress. She was holding a sheet in her arms, waiting to receive the baby that was being christened by the priest in the salty waters, his ceremonial robes wet and billowing around him. "We baptize thee, Maria...In the name of the Father, the Son, and the Holy Spirit..."

As soon as the baby was dunked in the water, three times, she burst into tears. Eleni looked fondly upon her goddaughter, happy in her new role as godmother to Manolis' niece. Manolis, who they now knew was alive in captivity. After all the silence, the news, any news, was a welcome respite.

Further news was hard to come by. She had spent so much time worrying that one day she would wake up and hear of his death. The thought was unbearable, more so at a time when her father's health was deteriorating rapidly and it looked like his end was near. Her only source of comfort had been Yiannis and his family.

Their worry over Manolis and his fate had brought them closer, they felt like family now. Any reservations Yiannis had had about his brother's proposed marriage had long been overcome, and Nikos adored his aunt-to-be.

As soon as the service was over, the three walked back to the shore. Eleni held Maria in her arms, wrapped in the small white sheet, and ceremoniously returned the baby to her mother. She took a small gold cross on a thin chain from her pocket and passed it over the baby's head. It seemed to soothe Maria.

They dressed the baby in her baptismal gown and hastily departed. They could not linger any longer; it would soon be dark and the Italian curfew was still in place. Eleni decided to stay on the beach a moment longer. The family and the priest mounted the horses that had been patiently waiting by the nearby creek and set off, leaving Karme to carry Eleni back to her house.

She sat down and pulled out a photo from her pocket. It was a portrait of Manolis, taken just after he'd joined the army. It had arrived with his first letter to her, the only letter she'd ever received. Two years had passed without a word until she heard of his capture from another soldier who'd returned to the island the previous month.

She closed her eyes and thought back to the morning at Galazia Petra, when they had been alone. Her body had not forgotten the feeling of Manolis touching her, kissing her and the same shudder now went through her. If Yiannis had not interrupted them, she would have given herself to him. Right there, on the beach.

She lived with the fervent hope that she would one day be back in his arms, fully his.

She opened her eyes and gazed at the waters lapping the shore. With all her strength she prayed to the Virgin Mary that she keep him safe, that she bring him back to her, alive. Alive. Alive. Repeating the silent prayer over and over, she got up and walked up to Karme. She'd better hurry. Her ailing father was waiting for her back home.

≈≈≈≈≈≈≈≈≈≈

It was late in the afternoon when Anita was finally able to call it a day. She hurriedly returned to her room and a few minutes later was back at reception, smiling brightly and holding a small suitcase. She placed her keys on the desk and let the young receptionist know that she would be returning late the following day. Looking through the wide glass doors, she saw Mihalis waiting for her and ran toward him.

"Ready?" he asked.

She nodded happily. "Will the weather hold?"

"Not even a breeze forecast for the next few days."

They set off for the port, Anita happily chattering beside him. No one but Mihalis knew that she was going to meet Dimitri. The production team had not been too happy when she had announced her sudden departure, but they didn't want to displease her either. They had only stipulated that she travel by a safer boat than Mihalis' speedboat, which was not fit for long crossings should the weather turn bad.

For the first time in her life, Anita felt any control of her feelings was beyond her. It was a frightening but also strangely giddy sensation. She'd decided to live this affair to the fullest whatever the outcome and was finding every passing minute away from Dimitri harder and harder to bear. She could not wait to find him, surprise him at the festival in the village square that evening. She felt he would be as happy as she was.

≈≈≈≈≈≈≈≈≈≈

They arrived at the quay and Mihalis helped her onto a small yacht that was moored next to the speedboat that had carried them to the Cave of Silence.

He switched the engine on, raised the anchor, loosened the ropes and they slowly exited the port, accompanied by some fishing boats going out to sea to cast their fishing nets.

Anita settled down on one of the couches by the prow of the boat and stared at the setting sun and the kaleidoscope of colors tinting the water around her, letting herself daydream. Before Dimitri, she'd never allowed herself to get carried away by her feelings for someone. She had always prioritized her career, her image. Somewhere deep inside her she'd yearned for the one great love, the one that would change her life forever. Now that it was happening, it felt unreal, like a fairytale. Meeting someone who completed her, who felt like a missing part of her, was a bittersweet experience; a sense of wholeness when they were together, a gaping void when apart.

Her musings were interrupted by the loud music coming from a passing fishing boat, an island song whose lyrics she could not make out. She turned and waved at the two fishermen who waved back and shouted their greetings.

"They are an exuberant lot in these parts!" commented Mihalis from his post behind the helm.

"What was that song? The tune was great, but I couldn't make out the words," Anita asked, eyes on the fishing boat that was sailing away.

"It's well known around these islands. They say a man wrote it after his lover left and never returned. He spent the rest of his days taking his fishing boat out at sea and singing his sorrow. When we return I'll find the CD for you."

Anita always loved these stories, where no one knew which part was real and which part fiction. She remembered her grandmother's tale of the prince on the black horse who had to leave his one true love. She used to feel that story so deeply, always crying in the end even though the prince returned to the castle and they all lived happily ever after. The characters loved one another so desperately in that story, faced all hardships together, and managed to reunite against all odds. That was how Anita imagined the man for her would be; and now she had found him.

"How long before we arrive, Mihalis?" she asked impatiently, gazing expectantly at the horizon.

"Soon. It won't be long," he replied sympathetically.

They'd caught up with the fishing boat, and part of the refrain drifted into the yacht.

The waves have come between us
Keeping our lips apart
I pray that you will keep
A place for me in your heart

The Island, November 1943

The port was bursting with activity. Two warships had just arrived, spewing forth German soldiers onto the pier. The speakers mounted outside the headquarters were broadcasting German military anthems, their cackling noise interrupted by the officers' voices barking orders. The swastika had replaced the Italian flag on the mast.

Mussolini's fall in the summer had changed life on the island once again. It had now passed under Nazi rule and life for the locals had become harder. They watched their new occupiers arrive with a paralyzing sense of dread. News had spread of what was happening in other parts of the country that had succumbed to the Third Reich.

Eleni and Yiannis stood on the paving stones outside a small church on the hill and watched the unfolding scene, lips pursed in a thin, grim line. Nikos, nearly a teenager now, was absentmindedly poking an anthill with a small wooden stick, casting furtive glances toward the port.

All three were lost in their thoughts. Eleni was thinking of Manolis, dressed in black head-to-toe in mourning for her father. No further news had reached her. She held onto the thought that Manolis was still being held captive, that he would somehow survive and return to her. She drew strength from that thought to fill the void that was chilling her heart and starting to etch the first worry lines on her forehead.

Whenever she would hear of someone's return to the island she would search them out and ask if their paths had somehow crossed Manolis'. She had pondered leaving the island to look for him, but she did not know where to start. She had heard that many of the captives were being sent to concentration camps in Germany and other countries, but deep in her heart, she felt that he was somewhere in Greece. Eleni felt tormented by her impotence, stuck on the island as she was.

These past few years, with her fiancé away, some of the Italian soldiers had tried to seduce her but she was quick to make it clear that she was not interested. Her forthright, brave manner, along with her education which seemed to inspire some kind of respect, discouraged her suitors.

She made a living by giving drawing lessons to the officers who had brought their families to the island. Many of the locals had been quick to point fingers, accuse her of collaborating. Unbeknownst to them, she eavesdropped on conversations and went through papers in the officers' house, gathering information that she then passed on through Yiannis to a resistance group that was forming on the island.

She now felt his hand on her shoulder, urging her to move away. "You go ahead, Yiannis, I'll come shortly," she said, eyes still on the port.

"Be careful, Eleni. The Germans are not ones to take hostages," he warned her.

"I will. Don't worry. I'll be over soon to see Maria."

Her beloved goddaughter had become like a child to her. She spent a lot of her time helping Anna look after the family, watching over the little girl. She yearned for Manolis to return, to have a large family herself.

She watched Yiannis and Nikos leave, then brought her right hand to her lips and kissed the engagement ring

Manolis had put on her finger at Galazia Petra. The day they had silently sworn to love one another forever.

She closed her eyes as if in silent prayer, but the increasing noise from the port was distracting. She knew the arrival of the Germans was bad news for everyone on the island. She was seized by cold fear and an overwhelming sense of foreboding.

≈≈≈≈≈≈≈≈≈≈≈

The house felt eerily quiet when Michaela returned from the hospital, leaving Rina behind with her mother. Eleni seemed to be doing better, so Michaela decided to leave her bedside for a while. All that time at the hospital and her constant worry over her mother's health were taking their toll. She needed a brief moment of respite to gather her strength; a warm bath, a night in her own bed, and then she would return to the bedside vigil.

She left her handbag on the living room table and went into the kitchen for a glass of water. Then she walked up to the coffee table and picked up the wooden box she'd found in the attic, the one with the drawing of the beach on the lid. She tried to lift it open but remembered it was locked.

In a sudden flash of inspiration, she grabbed her handbag and fished out her phone. Phone in one hand, box in the other, she moved to the study and placed both on the desk before her. She sat down at the desk, picked up her phone and began scrolling through the pictures on the screen. When she found what she had been looking for, she sat in stunned surprise. The photo Anita had sent and her mother's watercolor were the same. What a coincidence! She put the mobile down and started rummaging through the drawers. If her memory was not playing tricks, her mother used to keep every key to the house in one of them. She had noticed in the past that some of them did not seem to fit any of the locks in the house, but figured they must have simply been long-forgotten keys that no one had bothered to throw out.

She started testing them one by one until she found the one that fit. Barely able to contain her excitement, she turned the lock and lifted the lid. Two pieces of thick paper were inside, rolled up and tied with string. She placed them on the desk and picked up the small, red velvet box that lay beneath. Opening it, she discovered a ring decorated with a small silver rosebud.

The only other item in the box was a yellowing envelope, wedged at the bottom. She pulled it out carefully and turned it over. *ELENI DAPAKI. To be opened after my death.*

A will? Michaela was stupefied. She leaned back in the swiveling chair trying to gather her thoughts and recover from her surprise. Still confused, she untied the string around the rolled up papers hoping that they might shed some light.

The first one was another sketch of the beach, in greater detail this time. A man figured prominently in the picture, standing in the water. The colors were more vivid, livelier, and it looked even more like the photo Anita had sent. She could have sworn that the painter had sat looking out at the beach on the same spot as the photographer. The perspectives were identical. How could Anita be sending a photo that looked so much like a sketch drawn many years ago? Who was the man standing in the sea?

The second sketch showed the inside of a cave, the faint light casting strange shapes on the walls. On one of the walls of the cave *ELENI+MANOLIS FOREVER. TOGETHER.*

could be made out. The inscription at the bottom of the sketch read, *Cave of Silence.*

Michaela's head was spinning with all this new, inexplicable information. First, the pocket watch bearing the same inscription; then, the same man's face on all the sketches up in the attic; now, the beach, the cave, the ring, and the sealed letter. How could they all be connected? How could her mother have kept so many secrets?

She thought about calling Anita but then decided against it. Maybe she could find out a little bit more before sharing her discoveries with her daughter. She picked up the tablet that lay on the desk and went online. If she could at least identify the beach... She quickly entered the name of the island Anita was filming on. Predictably, the top results were about the film. Unable to resist the temptation to read about her daughter, she opened the first link and sprung up as if she'd just been stung by a bee.

She ran up to the attic and then into her mother's bedroom and returned holding one of the sketches and the watch. Back at the desk, her eyes flitted in astonishment between the image on the screen, the photo of the man in the watch, and her mother's sketch. She rubbed her eyes and looked again at all the pictures one by one, frowning hard. The resemblance was striking. The mysterious man in her mother's sketches, the man in the watch and Anita's co-star looked so alike she could have sworn they were the same man.

≈≈≈≈≈≈≈≈≈≈

Maria sat on her balcony looking out toward the dark water. It was nearly midnight, but sleep would not come. She tossed and turned while Kostas obliviously snored beside her. She gave up and stepped outside to get some air.

Seated among her beloved flowers, she held a photo of Dimitri and absentmindedly toyed with the small gold cross around her neck, a gift from her godmother when she had been christened at sea. She had few memories of life on the island. Most of her knowledge came from stories her brother had told her. All she remembered were burning houses and the two of them running away to hide.

She wished fervently for something more like a photo of her family or her godmother, all dead at the hands of the Germans according to Nikos. No matter how hard she tried to extract more information, some kind of detail from him, he would slip from that conversation like an eel, claiming that he remembered little, that it had all happened too fast. All he had confessed was that the locals had betrayed their uncle, their father's brother. And that was the main reason why they never returned to the island.

She could sense there was more. That was the reason she had chosen to say even less to Dimitri lest he start digging into the past and discover something painful or shameful. The betrayal of her uncle, an active member of the Greek Resistance, and the execution of all her family must have been only part of the story. Survival became the primary goal after the war and it had not been easy. She had had no time or energy to deal with the past.

Dimitri's father had given her that sense of security she so craved. She loved him deeply and his loss was the darkest moment of her life. Had it not been for her son, she might have collapsed. Then, Kostas had come into her life, a good man, someone to share her twilight years with. She still thought about Dimitri's father every day. She had met him in her teens, still a school girl, and he had been her only love. He and Dimitri had shared such a deep bond she could understand his rejection of Kostas. He could understand how important it was to have him in her life, her need for a companion, but deep in his heart he obviously perceived their relationship as a slight to his father's memory.

Out at sea, a sudden burst of fireworks lit up the evening sky. Maria smiled. A wedding. Her thoughts turned to Dimitri and Anita. She could tell from his few mumbled words that her son was in love and it made her happy. She had read everything in the press about Anita and felt that she already liked her. She came across as educated and down-to-earth and Maria could not wait to meet her. Dimitri had promised to introduce them once filming was over and they all returned to Athens for a few days. And she had promised herself that she would tell him then what little she knew about everything that happened toward the end of the war. She had a feeling that her brother's death, the return of his ashes to the island, spelled the final chapter to that part of her life, some kind of closure. Little did she know that the cobwebs of that time on the island were about to be lifted and reveal the atrocities they had hidden from view.

The Island, Christmas 1944

Torrential rain and a bitter northerly wind led the small fishing boats in the port in a frenetic dance and lashed the windows of the building housing the German command. A group of soldiers standing guard outside tried to shelter behind the portico's columns as best as they could, a burst of merry singing and loud voices drifting outside to join the howling wind every time the front door opened to let out a drunken guest.

Further away, in the island's only classroom that had been turned into a storeroom by the occupiers, Eleni and ten young children sang Christmas carols, their breath visible in the cold air a coal stove was struggling to warm up. She had managed to get permission to celebrate Christmas and it felt like a small blessing, adding another ray of happiness to her already grateful heart. At last, she had received news from Manolis. He was alive and would be returning to the island as soon as the weather would allow. The letter had been hand-delivered by a companion he trusted and now lay snuggled, frayed, and smudged with tears of joy, close to her heart. No one must be told of my presence, he had warned. Let people keep thinking I'm dead.

He confirmed that he had been captured by the Germans and been sent to a prisoners-of-war camp in Larissa, on the mainland. He had managed to escape after a few months and had joined the Greek Resistance, fighting against the occupiers. He was a wanted man and if he were captured he would be executed on the spot.

Eleni had kept the letter a secret even from Anna, who sat next to her holding Maria on her lap, the toddler's dark eyes and the tip of her nose peeking out from the blanket that covered her. A handful of other women were the only other audience. Most parents had kept their children at home, shunning Eleni once more for her relations with the Germans.

The truth was, of course, that she loathed the occupiers but kept her feelings to herself. She would have gained nothing by expressing her feelings to the locals and did not want to endanger the lives of those close to her. Her outward stance was not uncommon. Many islanders loathed the Germans but kept to themselves, thinking of their families, their homes. Of course, there were others who had been happy to collaborate, to actively help the Germans. Eleni felt outraged at this treason, despised those who had sided with the Nazis as soon as they had landed.

The news that had been arriving from Europe these past few months had raised the first timid flutters of hope. The war might be nearing its end. The men on the island, including Yiannis and the teenage Nikos, were in a feverish state, meeting in secret and discussing developments on the front. Reports of terrible battles and the work of the Resistance, who seemed to be striking blows at the mighty Third Reich, were reaching the island; maybe the tide was finally about to turn. So, Eleni had decided that perhaps this was a Christmas to celebrate, to give the children a taste of the normality that might be about to return.

Suddenly, the door to the classroom flung open, slamming against the wall. The children stopped singing abruptly and stared at the two German soldiers standing in the doorway.

One of the soldiers was waving a large bottle and could barely walk in a straight line. The men stumbled into the classroom shouting incoherently, shooing them out of the room. Hastily, the women started moving to the exit, shielding their frightened children. Anna and Eleni were the last to leave. Anna passed before the two men and Eleni made to follow her. She felt the strong grip of a hand on her shoulder. Anna, Maria still in her arms, hovered at the door, then stepped back in. Releasing his grip on Eleni, the soldier pushed Anna outside and slammed the door shut.

Both men turned toward Eleni. In a trembling voice, she asked them to let her go, first in Italian and then in Greek. She tried to move to the door. Both men laughed and blocked her way. She could smell the alcohol on their breath from where she stood and fully understood what their intentions were. She slowly started to back off, trying to put the school desks between her and the advancing men. The soldiers split up and circled around the desks, hunters stalking their prey. She found herself with her back pressed against the wall, trembling, trapped. One of the men violently grabbed her breast and she let out a piercing scream. She tried to run once more but they pinned her against the wall. She kept screaming, calling for help, hoping that the sound of the rain would not cover her cries and would alert someone, anyone.

The sound of the door opening and a sharp German voice made the two men spin toward the door. A German officer strode into the room and the two soldiers let go of Eleni and saluted. He walked up to them and sternly shouted something in German, pointing at the door. Eleni slumped to the floor as the two men ran out of the room, tears flowing down her face, chest heaving. Her gasping breath slowing down, she raised her head and saw the German officer leaning over her, looking at her with compassion.

He seemed to be around thirty, tall, blond, and very neat. His uniform was new and decorated with sparkling medals. He appeared embarrassed at what had just happened.

Feeling braver, Eleni stood up and smoothed down her dress, drying her tears. She had never seen him before. He must have been one of the latest arrivals.

"Thank you," she whispered, still in shock.

"Sprechen Sie Deutsch?" he asked.

She understood the question and shook her head no.

"Parla Italiano?" he persisted, trying to find some way to communicate.

Eleni looked at him puzzled and mumbled that yes, she spoke Italian. His face lit up and the words flowed. "Allow me to introduce myself and apologize for the despicable behavior of those soldiers. Captain Alexander Achermann, military filmmaker. Rest assured that they will be punished."

She was impressed by his politeness, his fluent Italian, and his strange post in the army. "I'm Eleni," she said. "Thank you for your help. If it weren't for you…"

"I'm very sorry about what just happened," he murmured. "I've only been on the island for a few days and for as long as I'm here I'll try to make sure it doesn't happen again. I'm not trying to excuse the behavior of those two, but our soldiers are exhausted from the war and can no longer control their actions. I hope, I wish, all of this ends soon," he added and went to close the door that was swinging in the wind.

Eleni was surprised by his words. She didn't think a German would say that. She watched him bend down and pick up a woolly hat that had been trampled on the floor in the hasty exit.

"I saw the women and children running in the rain and realized something was wrong, that's why I came," he said, then changed the subject. "Your Italian is very good, did you learn it here?"

"Here and I improved in Italy. I studied there for two years."

"Really? Me too, before the war. I spent five years in Rome. I started out in medicine, but quickly switched to what I had always wanted to study, history of art." He looked at her with renewed interest. "What did you study?"

"Fine Arts at the University of Pisa," Eleni replied. She felt that he was a cultured man but still felt uneasy talking with a German officer. On the other hand, had it not been for him...

"What a coincidence!" he exclaimed but was interrupted by the door swing open once more. Yiannis and Nikos rushed in, heavy sticks in their hands. Startled, the German officer pulled out his gun and aimed it at the intruders.

"Don't!" Eleni shouted in Greek and turned back to Achermann. "They are my family, they are here to help me," she quickly exclaimed and he slowly lowered his weapon.

Nikos was still staring at the German, agitated, stick raised with both hands. Eleni slowly walked up to him, took it, and threw it on the ground, saying, "I was attacked by two German soldiers and this man saved me."

Yiannis carefully examined the officer and then gave him a nod of thanks. The German put his gun back in its holster and moved toward the door, then hesitated and turned to face Eleni. "Kindly accept my regards. It was a pleasure to meet you," he said formally, clicking his heels.

"Thank you for everything you did and please make sure it doesn't happen again. Not just to me, but any other woman on the island," she replied coldly, feeling her hatred for the Germans return.

Without another word, he walked outside and made his way back in the pouring rain. Through one of the classroom windows, Eleni watched him go and realized he had not only saved her but Yiannis and Nikos as well. If the two had burst in while the two drunken men had been there, they would all be in serious trouble, probably dead.

"Are you okay? What did those pigs do to you?" Yiannis asked putting an arm around her shoulders.

"Thankfully, nothing," she replied, relieved.

"We must be very careful from now on," Yiannis said in a troubled voice. "It's being rumored that the Germans are losing, badly. They are like a wounded animal now, capable of anything. We must look out. The war will be over sooner than we think."

"How do you know all this?"

"Be patient, I'll soon tell you everything. Let's go home now. I have good news for you."

She gave him an anxious look, waiting to hear the good news. But Yiannis said no more. He covered her shoulders with his overcoat and led her outside her old classroom. Nikos followed them, pulling the door shut behind him.

≈≈≈≈≈≈≈≈≈≈

The small square by the port was a hive of activity; people were coming and going, some had already sat down at the long tables, and three musicians and a singer were running sound checks on a hastily assembled stage.

I arrived on my motorbike just as a large group of German tourists stood before the war memorial and Thomas, whose coffee shop tables had now become one with the tables laid out for the festival, was trying to find a place for them to sit.

As soon as he saw me, he waved and cheerfully called out my name. "Dimitri! Welcome! How was your day? I hope you left some water for us up in the spring!"

"Hello Thomas," I laughed. "I had a great day *and* I left some water for you!"

He took me by the shoulder and led me to one of the central tables.

"I see you have a lot of tourists today," I commented.

"Not many, just those Germans. They arrived today on a large yacht," he replied, keeping his voice low. "They were asking me what the war memorial said. I explained and then one of them told me that his grandfather had fought in Greece, on one of our islands too! I had to bite my tongue to stop myself from telling him all the crimes they committed, here and elsewhere! Ah, Dimitri, better not think about it... The younger generation had nothing to do with it. Still, it's not something that can be easily forgiven."

I listened carefully, taking note of the heavy emotion in his voice. This was not a past he had laid to rest. "I want to know what happened too, Thomas," I said, "I care."

He seemed to suddenly realize that the conversation was turning very serious and resorted to his usual sense of humor to lighten the atmosphere, presenting me to the others seated at the table. "Well, in case you haven't already met him, this is Dimitri— actor, nice guy, and can't hold his drink. Let's show him how it's done here!"

I spotted Thanasis, the ferry boat's bartender. He smiled and gestured at the empty chair beside him. He handed me a glass of wine, then raised his glass and spoke loudly, "Cheers, you big movie-star."

I felt embarrassed, but raised my glass and drank. A little stilted at first, the conversation soon flowed freely and I began to feel more at ease. They were full of questions about filming and Anita. She was on my mind all the time, and while I spoke about her I pictured her sitting beside me. I had spoken to her on the phone, told her the story of the black horse and she had been impressed and worried. She had a photo shoot scheduled for that evening, and then was going out to dinner with the crew and the producers. Someone from the German side of production was on the island and they had to take him out.

Ever more people were coming down to the square, the tables nearly full. The festivities were in full swing. I emptied my first glass faster than I normally would and Thanasis was ready with a refill. I had to pace myself; my alcohol tolerance was low. Not easy at a table where people were always quick to raise their glass for a toast and a 'bottoms up' rang out every couple of minutes. It was going to be a rough night for me.

I retrieved my cell phone and texted Anita. *This would be perfect if only you were here.* I pressed send and the reply flashed on my screen almost immediately. *Close your eyes and make a wish. It may come true, you never know.* I smiled and, in playful jest to the universe, closed my eyes and wished it.

The opening notes to the *ballos*, a local dance, rang out across the square and a high-pitched clear voice started to sing.

Suddenly, I felt two soft hands cover my eyes. I shivered at the touch. Surprised, I was unable to move for a few seconds, welded to the spot. I knew those hands so well...how could it be?

I removed her hands from my face and turned around in my chair, my face inches away from Anita's. The table had fallen silent, watching the scene.

She looked deeply into my eyes and gave me a long, lingering kiss. I was speechless with joy and surprise. I pulled her onto my lap and managed to stutter, "How? What happened?"

I handed her the glass of wine Thanasis had been quick to fill for her, and we all raised our glasses to her. Anita was now drawing the admiring glances of everyone, including those sat at neighboring tables. Soon, Mihalis came to join us, a mischievous glint in his eye.

Anita was filling me in on the details of her "great escape" and I watched her lips move. I couldn't take in a word she was saying. Her presence filled me with euphoria, dispelled all my fears and anxieties. I felt intoxicated just being near her, holding her in my arms. Happy, as if I had just discovered the meaning of life.

Still sensing everyone casting furtive glances in our direction, I suggested we go for a walk before the festival was in full swing. She jumped up from my lap, looking as eager as I was for us to spend some time alone.

I put my arms around her and we walked away from the revelers. She kept glancing around her, barely able to contain her joy.

We walked to the sea holding hands. Away from the lights in the square, the stars shone more brightly and seemed to multiply. Anita leaned her head on my shoulder and we stood gazing at the sky, listening to the soft moan of the waves against the shore. I gently pulled her around to face me and we looked into each other's eyes, silently communing the emotion that overflowed inside us. I pulled her up against me and bent down to taste her lips like a thirsty traveler coming upon a spring. I had traveled far and wide to meet her.

We abandoned ourselves to that kiss with unrestrained passion, the sounds of the square fading into silence, feeling as if we were alone in the world. Coming up for breath, our eyes met once again and we burst into laughter. It was not an unusual occurrence; I was enthralled by how easily we could share our joy, as if it were our own, secret, inside joke.

Someone must have amped up the volume of the sound system, blasting the strains of the familiar island song I had been hearing constantly ever since I'd set foot on this island.

Anita looked at me and said, "I like this song..."

I was surprised that she knew it and tried to remember if it was something we had heard together before. Laughter and whistling could be heard coming from the village square. We turned toward the noise and saw that almost everyone was on their feet, dancing, as if this song was very important; a song that meant something to everyone.

I took her hand and pulled her back toward the circle of dancers. Thomas saw us coming and let go of the hand he was holding, inviting us to join the circle. We didn't know the steps but followed their lead. They all seemed happy but also intensely focused, almost as if the song had put them in a trance. I sang along without even realizing.

My beautiful island girl
Leaving these shores behind
Leaving me alone to wander
On a lonely isle
The waves have come between us
Keeping our lips apart
I pray that you will keep
A place for me in your heart
My beautiful island girl
Leaving these shores behind
Remember I still love you
Until the end of time...

Cave of Silence

The Island, March 1945

Spring had finally arrived and the hilltops were now a sea of green, dotted with bursts of red, yellow, and pink wildflowers. The sun was just rising and drying off the morning dew on the grass as Eleni was making her way to Kryfó astride Karme. Yiannis and a few other men were waiting there. He had told her the night before that two Englishmen were arriving undercover to organize the local resistance. She was carrying food, some clothes, and blankets and kept casting furtive glances around her, trying to ensure she was not being followed.

The situation on the island was rapidly deteriorating and they all had to be very careful. The Germans had discovered a gun in the house of a local fisherman and promptly executed the man in front of his wife and children. Had it not been for Captain Achermann, she'd been told, they would have executed the entire family. Apparently, he had managed to dissuade the commanding officer from giving that order at the very last minute.

The occupiers had issued a decree that all weapons on the island be turned in. Most had obeyed, succumbing to the threat of punishment and their own fear. Only a few had refused to comply and already some of them were paying for this disobedience with their own lives.

In the months following the incident in the school classroom at Christmas, Eleni had taken on the job of restoring a number of paintings that the Germans had removed from the houses the Italians had been forced to abandon. Alexander Achermann had offered her this job, telling her that it was a way to keep her safe from further hassle. Ever since that evening, he had shown his interest at every opportunity, sometimes risking his position and even his own life, such as the time when Nikos had fallen gravely ill. He had brought the military doctor, a friend from his student days, to see the boy and give him all the medication he needed to recover.

The better acquainted she became with Alexander, the more Eleni realized he was different from everyone else. He had confessed that he did not agree with the Nazis but had been drafted into the army and forced to fight. As soon as the war ended—and the end was nearing—he would return to Berlin and take over his parents' antique shop.

She had explained that she was engaged and, even though she had no idea where her fiancé was, she would wait for him, forever. He had appreciated her dignified stance but never stopped courting her in his discreet manner, captivated by her looks and character. Using his post as a filmmaker and his current project to record life on the island, he had asked her to be his guide. One day he confided that the Ministry of Public Enlightenment and Propaganda had asked him to highlight the Greeks' barbarity, but he intended, as much as possible, to stay away from images that could imply that. He had studied ancient Greek, admired the Tragedians and Homer, and often spent time discussing the fates of those characters with her.

Eleni maintained her connection to Achermann for her own reasons. She garnered whatever information she could about the Germans' plans and movements and passed them on to Yiannis. She was careful, of course, to ensure that

Alexander remained oblivious to the way she was using him and let him hope that he may still have a chance to win her over. The truth was that she simply did not dislike him and nothing more. Her love for Manolis had not lessened in the least. She lived and breathed for the moment when they would reunite and believed that time was near. She knew he was on a neighboring island and would return at the first opportunity. She felt as if he were close to her and drew strength from that feeling. So, she kept up her double life, careful and alert at all times, knowing that the slightest misstep on her part would spell disaster for everyone involved.

Every time she set off to meet the men in the Resistance she claimed that she was off to paint various landscapes and prominently carried her art supplies. Alexander had asked to film her painting but she always politely refused, saying that it was not right to be seen together. Many people who were unaware of her activities were already gossiping, condemning her as a collaborator for the restoration work she was carrying out for Germans. She kept her head high and her mouth shut; it was impossible to know whom to trust in these turbulent times.

≈≈≈≈≈≈≈≈≈≈

When Karme set foot on the shore she suddenly stopped and neighed loudly in the direction of the cave. Eleni looked around her, puzzled. No one seemed to be on the beach, everything was quiet. The Germans would have found it difficult to set up an ambush here. It was impossible to approach the cave without being seen, whether coming down the hill or by boat.

From the rocks to her right, Nikos appeared. The young boy had had to grow up fast and was now acting as the lookout. He waved at Eleni and whistled, giving the all clear.

Yiannis was the first one to step out of the cave. He was followed by three locals and another two men Eleni had never seen before. *They must be the Englishmen*, she thought. The last man to come out wore a woolly hat and his face was covered by a bushy beard. He walked hunched, the lapels of his overcoat raised and covering the sides of his face. *A third Englishman?* Yiannis had only mentioned two.

Seeing the third man come out of the cave, Karme pricked her ears forward and sprang toward him, Eleni barely managing to stay on her back and unable to control her. She galloped through the other men, who jumped out of the way, and stopped before the bearded stranger, snorting expectantly. He removed the woolly hat and patted the horse's neck, Karme turning her head to sniff his palm.

Time stood still. Eleni looked at the man unable to believe what her eyes were telling her. She opened her mouth to speak but her words caught in her throat. Her mind was a blur. She felt dizzy and, losing her balance, she fell from the horse's back straight into his arms. Laughing and crying at the same time, she clung to him, her hands grasping his chest, his beard, his face, his hair as if she wanted to make sure that the man before her was real, made of flesh.

Manolis hugged her tightly and kissed her, filled with yearning. Five long years had passed since he'd last held her in his arms. His long hair, his beard—he looked like a different man. His eyes, however, remained unchanged, familiar. They were the same eyes Eleni saw every time she dreamed of their reunion.

The other men watched for a while the touching scene unfolding before them smiling in sympathy before moving away, one of them leading Karme by the reins. They busied themselves unpacking the sack Eleni had filled.

Not a word had passed between the two lovers in all this time, as if they had both lost their voice. They just looked at each other trying to fill the days and years that had passed in each other's absence.

As soon as they were alone, Eleni took a deep breath and said in a feverish whisper, "I missed you so much, Manolis. My God, I thought I would die if I didn't see you again. I still can't believe you are here. I did not know you were coming. I must be dreaming."

He stroked her cheek tenderly. "No, you are not dreaming, my love. I'm here. I'm never leaving you again, come what may."

"Promise?" she asked sitting on the sand and pulling him down beside her.

"I promise. Till death do us part."

Eleni snuggled in his arms and shut her eyes, enjoying the warmth of his body.

In the distance, Nikos watched them, smiling broadly. He had been so happy when his uncle had returned. The previous evening he'd stayed up listening to stories late into the night; stories of the battlefront, of Manolis' escape just before he was due to be transported to Poland, of the Resistance, and of his Odyssey to reach the island, finally arriving on the fishing boat that brought the two Englishmen along.

≈≈≈≈≈≈≈≈≈≈

Manolis and Eleni stayed on the beach for a long time, waiting for the others to leave, waiting to finally be alone, truly together. After all this time, their bodies hungered for each other and waiting for that moment felt like an eternity.

Eleni had pictured this moment countless nights in her lonely bed; Manolis sneaking into her bedroom unexpectedly in the middle of the night, coming into her bed and making her his in a burst of love and longing. Often, she would wake up feeling that it had really happened.

He, too, had been impatient for that moment to come. He remembered her passionate letters from Italy and that day they had come so close to making love on the shore at Galazia Petra. Their separation had not dampened their ardor for each other, but made the flames burn stronger, like a wild forest fire ready to consume everything in its way.

Manolis stood up, gave her his hand, and asked her to follow him. She did so without hesitation.

At the mouth of a cave, two shotguns were leaning against the rock. They crept through the narrow opening and waited for their eyes to adjust to the dark. The reflection of the water on the walls and the shapes it cast made the cave seem alive, pulsating.

They moved further into the cave and Manolis stopped, letting go of Eleni's hand to remove a large stone. The ground beneath the cave had been dug out to make a small basin, from which he removed something covered in a sheet and placed it on a dry spot on the ground before them. He kneeled down and motioned to her to come join him. He removed the sheet to reveal a machine that looked like a radio. He noticed her questioning look and immediately began explaining. "It belongs to the English, but we can keep it for a while. Find out what is going on in the world."

"The Germans have a similar one, at their headquarters," she replied. "I hear everything I can and pass it on to Yiannis..."

Manolis carefully wrapped up the radio with the sheet. "It must not stay here, the humidity will ruin it. Reception is really bad here, anyway. You will have to carry it back with you, when you return with the horse. Hide it in the mill. We'll go there tonight and turn it on. We'll come through the mountains, so we can't carry it. No one must see us. You must be careful. If the Germans catch you with a radio they'll execute you on the spot. Okay, my love?"

"I'll do anything you ask, so long as you never have to leave again."

"I won't have to leave again. The war is ending and we'll be able to live our lives, new lives. Great events are in the making. That's why we must be informed, prepared for what's coming."

Unable to resist any longer, he leaned toward her and kissed her passionately. Eyes shut, they abandoned themselves to the magic of the moment before slowly, reluctantly, rising and stepping outside.

The others were sitting on the sand eating the food Eleni had brought. The two of them approached and sat down to join them, the spring sun warming their faces, pale after the long winter.

Eleni tore a chunk of bread from one of the loaves and passed it to Manolis. He held her hand, looked at the ring which had never left her finger, stroked the carved rose bud, and smiled. Then, with a look full of meaning, he took out his pocket watch and angled the lid toward Eleni so she could read it. *Forever. Together.* She nodded. That was what they both wished, never to be parted again.

She filled him in on everything that had happened during his absence. She told him about her father's death, the christening of the young Maria on that same beach, the incident at the school and Captain Achermann's timely intervention, how much he had subsequently helped her. Manolis listened with a worried frown. He once again asked her to be very careful because German rule was sure to become harsher in the face of the impending developments. Elsewhere, they were burning down houses and executing anyone unfortunate enough to cross their path.

It was nearly noon by the time they finished talking. Eleni stood up to leave. She had been missing for quite a few hours and knew that Alexander was capable of hunting high and low for her if she did not reappear soon. Taking another path home, Yiannis and Nikos followed suit. They, too, had to return. Anna had been alone with Maria and would need help.

She gave Manolis a tight hug and they walked toward the waiting horse. They placed the radio in one of the sacks and tied it to the saddle, then stood looking at each other as if unable to believe they were there, on the beach, face to face.

He kissed her softly and helped her mount Karme, who had recognized her master and was waiting for his command to spur her on. Nikos and Yiannis approached. They would follow Eleni until a certain point, then split up so as not to raise any suspicions. Father and son had supposedly spent the morning working in their fields.

Manolis walked beside Eleni to the end of the beach, where the narrow path up the mountain began. She moved ahead followed by the others, turning back all the time to see her beloved, who did not move until he saw her disappear between the rocks and the sparse trees. Only then did he set off to rejoin his comrades, heart filled with hope that everything would be better from then on.

≈≈≈≈≈≈≈≈≈≈

Having waved goodbye to Yiannis and Nikos, Eleni moved toward the mill. It was nearly abandoned now, only used by Yiannis whenever he managed to find a little bit of corn or wheat.

She dismounted near the mill and, looking around her to make sure no one was watching, loosened the sack from the saddle and lifting it in her arms. She pushed the door open with her foot and entered the building, which was still in good condition despite the absence of human activity.

A soothing silence reigned, interrupted by the buzzing of some bees tirelessly working on the wild flowers outside and the breath of the soft breeze. She hid the radio in the narrow opening under a discarded millstone and sat down, her head spinning. She still could not believe that Manolis had returned, for good. It seemed like it was only yesterday when she was in this very room, crying her tearful farewell as he set off for the war.

Suddenly, Karme neighed and stamped her feet uneasily on the ground outside. Eleni jumped up and ran to the door. She stood on the doorstep and saw Alexander holding Karme by the reins and trying to soothe the nervous animal by patting its neck. She tried to hide her surprise with a nervous smile and stuttered out a greeting.

He was not in uniform, but wore black riding trousers tucked into tall leather boots. A leather jacket, gray shirt, and white scarf completed his outfit. A strap hung from his shoulder carrying a tripod on which his camera was mounted. He looked like an innocent traveler, an incoherent picture from an alternate time.

"I thought I'd take a long walk and film some of the landscapes, then saw your horse from afar and decided to come here. I'm sorry if I frightened you."

Eleni quickly gathered her wits about her and said calmly, "No, you did not frighten me. I was just surprised to see someone else here. I wanted to paint the mill and was just about to start..."

"But it's already late, will you have time?" he asked, looking puzzled.

"I'll make a quick sketch, then finish it at home. You've walked far today, haven't you?" she readily replied.

"Not that far. I've left my car nearby. So, this is where you mill your flour, eh?" He'd approached her as he spoke, glancing into the mill over her shoulder.

Eleni's heart was about to burst. What if he discovered the radio? No, she told herself, she had hidden it well. "We rarely mill anything these days," she said moving toward the low stone wall that circled the mill in an attempt to distract him.

Alexander took one last look inside the mill and followed her unsuspectingly. "Yes, times are hard, but not for much longer," he said, and then hesitated. "Eleni... when all this is over, would you like to come home with me?"

"I think I have already explained..." Eleni shifted uncomfortably.

"I don't mean to upset you," interrupted Alexander, "but as you haven't heard from you fiancé in such a long time...well, he is probably dead. Don't waste the best years of your life waiting for someone who may never return."

Under any other circumstances, she would have declared her undying love for Manolis vehemently, as if to ward off a bad spell. Now, knowing Manolis was alive, she spoke calmly. "I don't know if you have ever felt like this, but I wish you do someday. I wish you meet a woman and feel that you were made for each other and are unable to imagine anyone else but her by your side."

"Is this how you feel about your fiancé? Even if he is dead?"

"Even if he is dead," she said, choking the truth inside her.

She was simultaneously trying to hide both her joy and the real reason for her presence at the mill from Alexander. Who knew how he would react? She had gotten to know him better over time and he felt familiar, but it was obvious he saw her as more than someone to talk to, even though she had kept her distance, hiding behind an air of politeness and detachment.

She sat on the stone wall and pulled out her pencils and paper from the woven bag that usually carried her supplies. She attached the paper on a square piece of wood and started to sketch. Alexander came to stand behind her and watched her draw the outline of the mill. His hand stroked her hair and Eleni almost snapped the tip of her pencil digging it hard into the paper.

"You sketch beautifully," he said, breathing into her neck.

She pulled away showing her displeasure, but Alexander was not deterred. "You are beautiful, Eleni, and you know I like you. You could leave this place with me and make all your dreams come true. I don't want to press you. I just want you to know you have that option. I can make arrangements."

"I like you, Alexander, you are different from the others," she replied trying to keep her voice steady. "But my heart belongs to someone else and nothing can change that."

He backed off and turned to face the sea view. "The war is ending," he said. "Yet here you are, waiting for a ghost to return. Ghosts do not come back to life. Don't waste your life on an impossible dream. Even if we leave, others will come to take our place and they will not be any better."

She wished she could shout out the truth about Manolis; show him how wrong he was. She swallowed those words along with her outrage and firmly said, "This is my home. This is where I was born. This is where I will live. And I will wait for him to return every day for the rest of my life if I have to."

Her unshakeable faith made him admire her even more, even if it meant that it kept her from becoming his. He understood there was nothing more he could say to make her change her mind. He gazed at her silently for a while, then grabbed his camera and turned the lens toward Eleni. "Please do not refuse me this, too. Let me film you while you sketch. I will keep the film to myself, I promise. To remember the island...and you."

She was impressed by his politeness and flattered by his interest, but now that Manolis was back she didn't care about anything else. She decided not to respond and went back to sketching while he turned the camera handle recording the moment. For a while, all that could be heard was the whir of the camera and the rustle of the wind in the bushes.

Having captured as much of Eleni as he could, Alexander stopped and pulled the camera over his shoulder. He set off quickly in the direction of his car without uttering a word, then hesitated and turned around. "Soon, things will get violent, Eleni. If you change your mind…"

He turned around and walked away. Eleni watched him move swiftly down the path and wondered whether the mill was still a safe place for Manolis and the others to meet that night. It no longer felt secure or secluded. She decided to leave them a note informing them of what just happened, so they could be on their guard.

≈≈≈≈≈≈≈≈≈≈≈

At the village square, the party was at its peak. Everyone was on their feet, dancing. Anita seemed to be having a ball, this being her first *panegyri*. Not that I was holding back. I could not even remember how many glasses of wine I'd had. My head was spinning so badly I could barely follow the steps to the various folk dances. Most revelers were in the same condition as I was. They were just handling it better.

Thomas, Sofia, Thanasis, they all kept us on the dance floor. A small pause to down a glass of wine someone would hand you, *bottoms up*, and then back to swirling on the dance floor.

At some point, I realized that if I carried on like this I would soon be unable to stay upright. I left Anita on the dance floor and tried to walk back to the table in a straight line in a failed attempt to hide my drunkenness. The moment I sat down, everything started to move in slow motion before me. Any lingering anxiety about the locals had vanished. I liked them so much I no longer cared whether they found out who I was. It had been a long while since I had felt so relaxed, the alcohol washing away all my inhibitions. I'd been drunk once or twice before, but never quite like this.

I sat looking at Anita, who smiled every time she passed before me. I loved to watch her move to the music, so harmonious, so erotic. I would never tire of looking at her. She was beautiful and I was deliriously happy she had come here to be with me. I could have sat there watching her till dawn. I wanted to hold her in my arms, but did not risk getting up, worried I would stumble and make a fool of myself. For a moment I thought I was so drunk I could no longer hear the music. Then I saw everyone slowly return to their places at the tables and realized the music had actually stopped.

Anita sat in my lap again, giving me a kiss.

Thomas stumbled over, a little the worse for wear, and said, "Now we pause for the blessing and then, we keep dancing!"

Anita looked at me questioningly and then realized that I, too, had no idea what Thomas was talking about.

A hushed, expectant silence fell over the square. We both turned toward the wooden stage and saw Thekla holding a little old lady by the hand and helping her up the steps to the microphone. The woman's black dress and the loose white hair falling down her back made her look like an elf. She must have been at least ninety years old. I remembered Thekla saying something about her mother and figured that's who the old lady must be. A younger man joined the two women on the stage and spoke into the microphone.

"*Chronia Polla*, welcome everyone. I hope you are all having a good time at the festival, organized by our Cultural Association. Like every year, it's time for the blessing. Let me explain what this means, for those of you joining us for the first time tonight. Ever since the early 19th century, our ancestors have lived in this place holding onto their Greek traditions and cultures against all odds—first under the Turks, then the Italians and then, the Germans. However, what happened here just before the end of the war scarred this island, forever."

Despite the fog that was beginning to descend on my brain, I noticed that someone was translating what was being said to the German tourists. They all looked somber, listening with careful attention. Although I had been finding it hard to focus, the tension I felt made me feel more sober, alert. I pricked up my ears and listened intently too. Anita sensed my anxiety and gently stroked my back and neck.

"We do not remember so as to perpetuate hatred, but to honor those who sacrificed their lives back then...justly or unjustly," the young man continued. "Our island was deserted after the war. But life is stronger than pain, and here we all are tonight, together, with our families and you, our beloved friends and visitors who have come to join us this evening.

"Agathe is the last of those who lived through that time and returned. Few returned after everything that happened; most stayed away, were too young to remember, or have since joined our ancestors in Heaven. So, she will give the blessing and then the feasting will continue, just as life carries on no matter what."

With those words, he stepped away from the microphone and the old lady shuffled forward. There were a few, awkward claps that soon stopped when they realized the solemnity of this moment. A breeze ruffled Agathe's hair. She tucked the loose strands behind one ear and spoke in a calm, clear voice. "Good evening. *Chronia Polla.*"

She paused before continuing, as if she wanted to gather her strength for what she was about to say. For some strange reason, she turned and looked at our table, giving me the impression that she was staring at me. But I could not be sure, I was having difficulty focusing.

"Many years have passed but I remember it all as if it were yesterday. I can still see everyone gathered here, on the square, that black day..." Her voice broke, but she managed to regain her composure and continue. "Now, we shall raise our glasses and wish that no such darkness ever descends on any other place in the world. Pour the last drop of your drink on the ground, in memory of those we lost so unjustly. For, as my beloved schoolteacher Yiannis Reniotis, who died here with everyone else, used to say, you must love everyone, even those who cast their stones on you..."

Everyone had raised their glasses in silent salutation. I could not breathe, not move, not swallow at the sound of my grandfather's name. I took my glass and downed the wine in a single gulp, trying to get over my shock. Anita was looking at me worried. My insides felt alight from the drink and my thoughts were spinning out of control, a tangled web that was swaddling me in it. My mother's voice warning me not to say a word was fighting against everything that had been happening since I had set foot on this island.

In the meantime, Thekla's mother had finished giving the blessing and I had missed everything else she had said. She was now leaving the stage. Without even realizing how, I found myself gently lifting a stunned Anita from my lap and giving her my seat. I stood upright, swaying slightly, trying to ignore the spinning tables and chairs around me. With whatever clarity I had left, I spoke loudly. "Excuse me...I have something to add."

Everyone turned to look at me, smiling, and waiting to hear the rest. What I said next was difficult to utter, my lips refusing to obey me and forming an obstacle course to the letters and syllables leaving my mouth.

"Mrs. Agathe just spoke of the teacher she had at school... My mother will kill me for telling you this, but... Yiannis Reniotis was her father. My grandfather."

The last thing I remember before collapsing in Anita's arms were the frozen faces of everyone around me, just like the faces in the nightmare I'd had on the ferry. I saw some people moved toward me... I felt terrified... Then someone turned the lights off in my brain and I sank into drunken oblivion.

The Island, April 1945

A month had passed since Manolis' return. Nothing was the same anymore. The Germans had learned that some Resistance fighters were on the island. Informants were quick to notify them of anything they deemed suspicious, and raids on houses in search of weapons and men in hiding had become a daily occurrence.

Manolis and his comrades were in hiding, all the while organizing their group. On this day, they had arranged to gather at the mill for a meeting.

The radio was now working and the news coming through was positive. The German army was collapsing on all fronts and it was possibly a matter of days before the occupiers would be forced to leave the island.

Their instructions were to cause as much damage as they could, particularly to their equipment. The locals, thanks to German propaganda on the island, remained skeptical. They were not convinced that the war was nearing its end and that the time for an uprising against the occupiers had come.

Manolis' band of fighters was still small in number. With time pressing them, he had decided to call on anyone he thought could be trusted, update them on the latest developments first, and then ask them to join them. It was a great gamble. As long as the number of men involved remained low, they were safe. Now that their presence and actions would become known to many, secrecy would be compromised. But they had no choice. Weapons and men were scarce and they had to be found somehow.

Night had fallen long ago. The soft breeze rustled the leaves and spread the smell of thyme and rosemary. In the fields surrounding the trees, furtive shadows moved cautiously toward the mill, guided by the dim light that shone at one of the windows. Manolis and Yiannis were waiting inside. The two Englishmen had departed on a fishing boat for the coast of Turkey. They would make their way to one of the larger islands to help the fight there. On a rocky outcrop further up the hill, a lone guard stood as a lookout in case of trouble.

Within a half-hour, around twenty men had filled the space, all surprised to see Manolis there. They had thought he was dead, and after hugs, handshakes, and hearty slaps on the back wanted to know how he had made his way back. His decision to join the army in the first place and go to the front had impressed many of them and, in their eyes, he was a hero.

When the last man expected had joined the group, Manolis stood in the center of the room and silently gestured for them to quieten down. Eleni had trimmed his hair but he still had his beard, which made him look older than his years.

Before explaining the reason for the meeting, of which few were aware, he removed the radio from its hiding place and placed it on the mill stones. They all curiously looked on as he removed the sheet that covered it and addressed them. "Welcome, my friends. I am very glad to see you after all these years. I invited you today to inform you about the latest developments which you may not have heard yet. But the main reason I called you here today is to decide how we will fight the Germans. I have good news—the war is almost over. All the radio broadcasts confirm this. Soon we will find ourselves on our own; or with another master ruling us. But now, we must fight against the enemy, all of us. If we band together, we will achieve our goals. Otherwise, the few will be sacrificed for nothing. Then we will see what we'll do..."

A murmur broke out among the men, who were asking what exactly was expected of them. A few seemed displeased to be there.

Seeing the reaction, Manolis raised his voice. "Hear me out, and if you are with us say so. Everyone who is not is free to go back home. We have decided to fight, whether we are few or many. We'll use whatever weapons we have. We have information that the Germans might be leaving as early as the day after tomorrow. And we must catch them by surprise; inflict as much damage as we can. It must all happen very quickly, before they can react.

"I fought in the corps of soldiers who came from these islands. I left my home one evening five years ago to join the army, to stop the Italians and the Germans from taking over my homeland. To give our children a chance to finally live as free men and women. Do you know how many of our fellow men died? More than half. Some of them died in my arms. If we do not fight now, their lives will have been lost for nothing. So, before you hear the rest of what I have to say, I ask you this: How many of you are willing to fight?"

For a while, no one spoke. Then someone took a step forward, stood to attention, and declared, "I'm with you, Reniotis." More and more men came forward. Only three men stayed in their place. There were two distinct groups now in the mill. The men who had joined Manolis stood on one side and the three men who had declined on the other, the two groups staring at each other as if they had just turned into enemies.

Yiannis, who had silently been watching the scene unfold, spoke, keeping his gaze fixed on the men across the divide. "No one will force you to join us. All we ask is that you keep your mouths shut."

The oldest of the three men tried to explain, saying, "It's not that we don't want to join you, but we don't even know how to hold a gun. How are we even going to be able to fire one? Anyway, if the war is ending as you say, why provoke the Germans now and not be patient for a little longer, until they get up and go? If we fail, they will kill us all, our wives and children too. Do you forget how they shot Yiorgi in front of his house because he still had his father's old gun? That thing couldn't even fire a bullet…"

"I understand that you are scared," Manolis interrupted, "but you must know that what they'll do as they leave could be worse than what will happen if we fight back. If everyone had backed out like you, the Germans would have stayed in the countries they conquered forever. You must follow your own hearts. Just don't betray us…"

Everyone fell silent once again. Moving slowly, two of the men opened the door and left with a hasty goodnight. Only the man who had spoken stayed behind. He walked up to Manolis and hugged him. "Count me in," he said.

Yiannis then spoke again reminding everyone that time was running out. Manolis looked at the band of men around him, took a deep breath, and started explaining the plan.

≈≈≈≈≈≈≈≈≈≈

Two hours later, the men left the mill one at a time and dispersed into the darkness. Everyone looked pensive and troubled. The following day would be hard.

Yiannis loaded the weapons on Karme to carry them to a hideout close to the village. From there, he would equip the men when the time came. It was settled; they would strike the Germans at noon, to prevent whatever the enemy was planning to do before they left.

For a while, the two brothers lingered behind discussing the details. Then Yiannis led Karme by the reins into the night. Manolis hid the radio and locked up the mill before setting off for Kryfó. It was a moonless night and only the stars shone in the sky. Luckily, he knew his way around the island like the palm of his hand and could avoid the steep edges and cliffs.

The voice of the Scops Owl was the only sound in the dark wilderness. Its hooting kept him company in the dark, making him feel melancholic at the same time. He remembered the story his father had told him when he was young, of the two brothers who once loved each other. One day they had a fearsome fight. The elder boy drove his younger brother away from the home they had once shared. He got lost and never returned. When he realized what he had done he turned into a Scops Owl, forever searching for his lost sibling, calling out for him in the dark. The Scops Owl calls spring forth in the hope of finding his brother, who is wandering alone, forever lost in winter.

Spring was what Manolis waited patiently for. The spring to cast away the German winter, to avenge his sorrows and the friends he'd lost in the war. More than anything, however, he wanted the end to come so he could live with Eleni, marry her, and have lots of children who would grow up free, not live under the occupiers' boot like their parents had.

It had been a month of secret, snatched meetings and every time they felt their bodies eagerly yearn for the moment of their union. Their passion grew stronger with every passing day.

≈≈≈≈≈≈≈≈≈≈

Manolis carefully snuck onto the beach at Kryfó a couple of hours later, where he would be spending the night in the cave. He paused, all senses on the alert, when he caught a glimmer of light trembling close to the cave's mouth. No one else was supposed to be there.

He carefully crept toward the cave and stopped two feet away, listening for any sounds coming from the interior. The waves crashing on the shore drowned out every other sound.

The soft snorting of a horse made him turn around; Karme, tied to some driftwood, not far from the cave. The horse had recognized him and made no other sound. He felt relief flood through him. Yiannis. But why was he here? He was supposed to be hiding the arms somewhere near the village.

Glancing around him, he tiptoed to the cave's mouth and peeked inside. The spectacle that awaited him took his breath away. Candles filled every crack on the cave's walls and lit the cave with a soft glow, casting flickering shadows on the walls and the roof. Wildflowers were scattered here and there across the cave, as if spring had suddenly arrived in the barren cavern, their mild scent mixing with the smell of the burning candles.

In the midst of this dreamy landscape sat Eleni on a sheet spread on the soft, sandy ground. She smiled sweetly at Manolis, who could not take his eyes off her glowing face.

Without speaking she pointed to the empty spot beside her. That's when he noticed the bottle of wine and the two glasses on the sheet, two slices of bread and some cheese on a plate next to them.

"When did you do all this, Eleni? When did you find the time?" he asked her as soon as he sat down.

Ignoring the question, she poured the wine and handed him the glass, looking deeply into his eyes. "We don't have much time, but it's enough to have a drink and make a toast."

Manolis brought her hand to his lips. He gently kissed her fingertips, then raised his glass. "Forever. Together."

"Forever. Together," she echoed.

They were silent for a moment, sipping their wine. They both knew what would happen next. They had waited years for this moment, yet they now sat awkwardly next to each other.

Eleni, taking the initiative, picked up the glasses and the dish that separated them and set them aside. Kneeling down beside him she slowly, almost ritually, removed her jacket. She wore a low-cut dress, with a row of small buttons down the front. Mesmerized by the porcelain whiteness of her skin, Manolis began to kiss her neck, sending shivers down her spine. Impatiently, she unbuttoned his shirt and stroked his naked chest. His muscles quivered at her touch. He enveloped her in his arms, full of yearning, and she leaned back, pulling him down with her. She unfastened his belt while he slowly undid the buttons at the front of her dress, bending down to kiss her naked breasts.

Their momentary awkwardness had now evaporated, to be replaced by their swelling desire for each other. When the last of their clothes was discarded, they looked at each other and lost any sense of space or time. All that remained was the sensation of their bodies carrying them down the primal path of love.

A small cry of pain escaped Eleni's lips when Manolis entered her. He paused and made to pull back, but Eleni, determined to live this moment fully, held his arms and pulled him down, showing she wanted him to continue. She closed her eyes and let herself be swept away by the sensations flooding her body as her beloved started to move slowly, carefully, whispering tenderly in her ear.

Although both were inexperienced, instinct showed them the way to give one another the joy and pleasure of that first time.

A strong gale had risen outside, crashing the waves against the exterior of the cave, covering the sound of their breath coming short and fast, their moans of ecstasy as they reached a crescendo of pleasure and then subsided. Their still, entwined bodies looked like they had been born of the cave, another rocky outcrop sculpted on the land. They stayed in each other's arms trying to catch their breath and prolong the precious moment.

The chill in the air made them shiver. Manolis picked up the edges of the sheet and wrapped it around them, keeping Eleni snug against his chest. She leaned against his heart and heard it beat as loudly as hers. She glanced up at the roof of the cave and the shadows cast by the candles suddenly seemed like wandering ghosts, coming to haunt them. Frightened by that thought, she tightly gripped Manolis, who seemed unaware of her sudden distress.

They rose after a while and began to dress up. A small red bloodstain marked the white sheet. Embarrassed, Eleni bent down to pick it up, but he took it from her hands and carelessly flung it over a stone. "Come, I want to show you something," he said. He picked up one of the candles and led her further into the cave, lifting it above his head to cast its light high on the cave wall. Something had been scratched on the stone. Eleni peered more closely and read, *ELENI+MANOLIS. FOREVER. TOGETHER.*

≈≈≈≈≈≈≈≈≈≈

Opening my eyes, I felt a vice-like grip on my temples and the taste of stale alcohol in my mouth. My stomach churned like the spin cycle of a crazy washing machine. I remained still, trying to focus my blurry eyes and remember what had happened the previous night, and then glanced around the room searching for Anita.

I spotted her standing beside the balcony door, her body blocking the strong sunlight, which cast a golden halo around her and sank her figure in shadow. So her coming over had not been a dream, I thought and that joyous realization made me raise myself on my elbows and try to get up.

She heard the rustling sheets and turned around to face me. Her expression told that all was not well. "Good morning. How do you feel?" she asked, leaning down to give me a kiss.

"Still dizzy..." I looked at her, puzzled. "What's the matter, what's going on?"

"I don't know what's going on, but ever since you told the entire village who you are..."

"I did what?" I exclaimed, jumping up. "When did I say that? What did I say? I can't remember a thing. Please, tell me!"

She took me by the hand and led me to the balcony doors. "See for yourself."

I focused with difficulty on the spot she was pointing at, in the courtyard. Twenty men and women, seated at the tables. Thomas was among them, talking to some of the men I had met since coming here. A little old lady sat on a chair in the middle of the roughly formed circle. Her face rang a bell. "What are they all doing here?" I whispered, surprised.

"I think they are waiting..."

"For what?"

She paused and gave me a searching look, then sighed. "You."

I instinctively pulled away from the window, frightened. I moved back into the room and sat on the bed, desperately trying to recollect the events of the previous night. All that came were fragments, snapshots that made no sense. I looked up toward Anita. "Tell me what happened at the *panegyri*," I demanded. "When did I say who I was?"

Anita moved to the bathroom and returned with a tall glass of water in her hand. "Drink," she said, as she sat on the bed beside me. I quenched my thirst in a great gulp. "What do you remember, Dimitri?"

"I remember enough... I just don't remember telling them who I really am."

"Who you *really* are?" she snapped, worried. "Dimitri, what does all this mean?"

"I'll explain it all, Anita, just tell me what happened. I vaguely remember watching an elderly woman get on the stage. Then everything is a blur."

"Well, the elderly woman is the one sitting downstairs in the courtyard. She got up to give a blessing and spoke of the last war and everything that had happened here. I can't remember what that was exactly; I'd drunk a fair bit myself. Then she said something about her school teacher. That's when you jumped up and shouted that the teacher was your grandfather."

"And then?"

Anita raised her shoulders in a shrug. "Then you passed out and everyone was asking me if what you said was true, but I didn't know what to say."

My mind was starting to clear up, my thoughts slowly falling into place in some kind of order. I was filled with a sense of dread at the possible repercussions of my impulsiveness. But if we were in any danger, wouldn't Mihalis already be here, to whisk us away? He was a trustworthy man. Surely he wouldn't have left us alone.

I decided to come clean to Anita, who was looking at me tensely. I held her hand and took a deep breath. "I haven't told you everything about why I am here, on the island. I don't know that much myself. As you already know, I scattered my uncle's ashes at Mantani yesterday, carrying out his dying wish. He and my mother were born here, but after everything that happened during the war they left, never to return. They always discouraged me from coming here, giving a number of vague excuses. My mother made me swear to never mention my grandfather's name. He was executed in the village square, as were all her other relatives and many of the men on the island. She and her brother managed to escape at the last minute on a boat, crossing to the island where we are filming. They were discovered on the beach by a young novice, who gave them shelter at the monastery. That's how they survived."

Anita drew a sharp breath, as if suddenly recollecting something. "Dimitri, that's incredible! When I was at Aghios Mámas yesterday, I spoke to the Abbot and he told me the exact same story. He hinted that he was the young man who had rescued the children on the beach. The exact same story... how can it be?"

I stared at her blankly. Was this some kind of joke? What were the chances of such a coincidence?

"Did he tell you when that happened?" I asked.

"At the end of the war, when the Germans burned down the monastery. The two children ran off and were never seen again or something like that. Could it be they were your mother and uncle?"

"Honestly, Anita, I've been having the strangest feeling of déjà vu ever since I set foot in this place, ever since I got on the boat. So many things are happening... It *must* be my uncle and mother, what are the chances they rescued another pair of children arriving alone on a boat on the same island? I don't know what to say. I must speak to the Abbot when we go back. I wonder what my mother will say when I tell her all this..." I rubbed my eyes. "I haven't told you any of this because there is so much I still don't know. I had decided not to stir things up. But everything is now coming to light. It's making me want to find out exactly what happened. I just meant to scatter the ashes and come back to you as soon as possible. I've missed you so much these two days. I felt like you were with me all the time."

"I've missed you too. I know that perhaps I shouldn't have come, but I couldn't stand being away from you. Anyway, here we are and I think you must find your answers. I'll help you."

My mind now beginning to process all this new information, I shared my suspicions with her. "There is something very dark at the heart of all this, Anita. Something terrible must have happened here, maybe even worse than the violent death of all those people."

I stopped, remembering everyone waiting downstairs. I wondered whether I should walk downstairs and finally confront the ghosts that had been haunting my family for so many years. A small part of me shrank back from this, afraid of what the answer might be.

My thoughts were interrupted by a knock on the door. We both jumped up. Anita shouted rather too loudly, "Who is it?"

Mihalis' voice came muffled from the other side of the door. We both sighed with relief and Anita hurried to the door while I threw on some clothes. Mihalis hovered on the corridor outside. "Good morning, I saw that you were up and I knocked."

Anita did not beat about the bush. "What's happening? Why are all those people downstairs? Should we stay up here?"

"I don't think there is anything to worry about. They just want to speak to you. They tried to tell me some of it, it's all very confusing. Agathe says she will only speak to you, Dimitri. We'll leave in the afternoon when you are done. Not because there is anything to worry about, because the weather will turn bad tomorrow and it will make crossing difficult."

I looked at him suspiciously, not sure I believed what he said about the weather. I could tell something was bothering him, but what?

Anita was looking at me expectantly, letting me decide. Drawing strength from her presence beside me, I said, "We'll be downstairs in a couple of minutes, Mihalis. Thank you."

I quickly splashed some water on my face and we walked down to the courtyard, hand in hand. The chatter drifting into the house grew stronger as we approached. As soon as we stepped out into the sunshine everyone hushed. They looked at us without uttering a single word. I was no longer afraid. I wanted to know everything.

Thomas was the first one to move toward us, a restrained smile on his lips. He touched my shoulder, compassionately. "Good morning, my boy. Come sit with us."

The small circle of people shifted to let us through, and we stood before the table where Thekla and her mother were seated. Agathe had been looking at me fixedly ever since I had appeared. Everyone was waiting for her to speak. She kept examining me for a long moment and then said, "You look like him."

"Who do I look like?" I asked, guessing the answer.

"Your grandfather's brother."

I was taken aback by her reply. I had expected to hear my grandfather's name. I knew almost nothing about my great-uncle, Manolis, just that he had been executed along with everyone else. I fixed my gaze on her, stunned, neither one of us uttering a word. Her eyes were moist, but I couldn't tell whether it was emotion or old age.

The silence was broken by the running footsteps of a man who burst into the courtyard. He was the young man who had welcomed everyone to the festival. He greeted everyone and came to sit beside us. "Good morning! Antonis Kantounas, president of the Cultural Association."

"Good morning, Dimitri Voudouris," I replied, shaking his hand.

"Last night, you said Yiannis Reniotis was your grandfather," he said, suddenly serious.

"The truth is I don't really remember what I said. I had a bit too much to drink and it's all a blur." For a split second, I was tempted to say it was all a drunken outburst, nothing more. I decided not to. "Yes, I am Yiannis Reniotis' grandson, the son of Maria Reniotis. Voudouris is my father's last name."

He looked at Agathe who was watching our conversation keenly, then turned back to me and said, compassion creeping into his voice, "Let's take things one by one. If you are who you say, you are the first member of your family to visit the island after the end of the war. I have researched the history of the island and know a lot about what happened then. I've even written a book about it. Your presence here changes what we knew about your family, and maybe more. Is your mother alive?"

"Yes," I replied.

"Does she have any siblings?"

"She had a brother, Nikos," I said impatiently. I was starting to get angry; this was beginning to feel like an interrogation.

"Had? He is no longer alive?"

"No, he died earlier this year, that's why I'm on the island." I tried to keep the anger from creeping into my voice. I no longer cared what I would find out. I wanted this to be over with. "Why are you asking me all these questions? Why are we all here? I haven't done anything wrong."

He smiled at me and said reassuringly, "No, you certainly have done nothing wrong. Your family went through a lot in the war. I guess your uncle must have told you all that. What we didn't know was that your mother and her brother had survived. After everything that happened here they got lost on a boat and all trace of them disappeared. Everyone assumed they must have drowned that day."

I gave Anita a look full of meaning.

"Two children, alone at sea," he continued. "Their chances were not good. The first thing I must do is apologize. On behalf of everyone here and those who are gone, I apologize for what your family went through and what this island did to your grandfather's brother, Manolis Reniotis."

I seized upon this chance to find out what happened, untangle this web of half-spoken facts and secrets. Hide the fact that I knew nothing, in case that made them change their mind or lie to me. "I will accept your apology after I hear your version of what happened. I know enough, but not all the details. My family did not speak of it often."

"Rightly so," Agathe chimed in, interrupting us.

Antonis looked at me disbelievingly, as if he suspected that I was ignorant of what had happened, but made no comment. He turned toward Agathe and said, "The only one alive on this island who lived through what happened is you. I think it's best if you tell the story."

Agathe looked down at her hands, folded in her lap. She took a deep breath and spoke. "Your grandfather was my teacher before the war. I was already too old for school and did not know how to read and write. He took in all the children like me and taught us Greek. He was a good man. I remember your uncle, Nikos, riding past our house proudly every day. Your mother was a toddler, two, maybe three years old.

"The Germans came to our island after the Italians. Things were calm in the beginning but started to become violent as the end of the war neared. I, too, lost many people I loved then: my father, my brother, others... Manolis Reniotis had gone to the front to fight the Italians when the war broke out. We all thought he'd been killed until one day we saw him, alive." She stopped talking, tears streaming down her cheeks. Her voice broke into a heartbreaking sob as she said, "The very day we found out he was alive... that very day, we killed him."

I thought I misheard, that she meant something other than what I had just heard. Trying to understand, I asked urgently, "What do you mean, you killed him?"

She stopped crying and spoke as if in a trance. "I can see it in your eyes. Your family never told you what happened. Maybe your mother does not remember. Maybe your uncle did not see it all. There is no way you would be here if you knew the truth. I will tell you everything, my son; everything that happened to your grandfather and what we did to Manolis. Us and that cursed harlot who betrayed him."

As she heard these last words, Anita turned toward me and gave me a worried look. We were both impressed and surprised. Even if I had had no connection to the story it would have all sounded very interesting and mysterious.

I gave Anita's hand a little squeeze and turned back to Agathe, who was ready to continue her tale from the past.

The Island, April 1945

Dawn was breaking outside. The milky light crept into the small bedroom through the slats of the wooden blinds, chasing away the dark. Eleni, lying fully clothed on her bed, stared absentmindedly at the ceiling, reliving the rapture of the night with Manolis. She had never imagined that making love would satiate all her senses in this way.

The bedroom in Yiannis' house had been her home ever since her father's death. She had returned there from the cave and spent a white night lost in her thoughts. Thoughts of the evening at the cave, the pleasure, those snatched moments of bliss alternated with worry over what the coming day would bring. She hoped and prayed that everyone would be safe at the end of the day, that those she loved and her fellow countrymen would come through unscathed.

A soft, persistent tap on the blinds interrupted her thoughts. She jumped up from her bed and cautiously approached the window. "Who is it?" she whispered.

"It's me, Alexander," whispered a male voice outside. "Open the window."

She hesitated, unsure of what to do. What was he doing here, at this hour? She thought about alerting Yiannis or Nikos, but then remembered that she was alone in the house with Anna and Maria.

She decided to do as he asked and cracked the window open. Peeking outside, she saw her unexpected visitor looking ruffled and worried.

"You must come with me, right now Eleni. Hurry! There is no time to lose."

"Why should I come with you? What's happening?"

"Listen to me carefully. Any minute now they will start rounding the whole village up, at the square. We know what you are planning to do. You've been betrayed."

She stared at him feeling the panic rise, her thoughts flitting between Manolis, Yiannis, Anna, and the children...What would befall them?

"I can't come, I can't leave them."

"Anna and her children will be safe. They are looking for you and the others. Hurry up, I'm begging you!"

The sound of screeching engines broke the deathly silence. They pulled up somewhere near. Sharp orders and the thud of heavy boots, running footsteps and the crack of rifle butts on neighboring doors broke out like a sudden storm, to be followed by alarmed cries, barking dogs, and children crying.

Eleni ran to her bedroom door and peeked out. She saw three soldiers kick down the door and drag Anna outside, Maria still in her arms. She let out a small yelp, stifling the cry that was forming in her throat. Terrified, she turned to Alexander, who was beckoning her toward him. Without thinking, she grabbed her coat, shoved her feet in her shoes, and made to climb outside the window. Maria's crying and Anna's desperate screams made her freeze mid-step. Alexander grabbed her by the arm and pulled her out.

"Come, hurry before they return."

"I'm not going anywhere unless you tell me where they are taking them. I'll stay with them."

"Nothing is going to happen to them. It's you they are looking for and the others. You must believe me," he beseeched her. "Follow me now or you'll die. I'll explain everything later."

Hearing the footsteps return to the house, Eleni decided to place her fate in Alexander's hands. She followed him down the narrow alleyway behind the house and they ran to his *Kübelwagen* which he'd parked behind a neighbor's outhouse, hood raised to hide the small car's interior.

He opened the door and tried to push her into the back seat. Eleni still hesitated, something making her hold back.

"Please, get in," he said as calmly as he could. "If we don't leave now, they'll find us and kill us both. It's not just your life on the line now, it's my life too. Please understand that."

Her heart was torn. What was she about to do? Run away, leaving Anna alone with Maria? Betray Manolis' trust, everyone's trust, by running away with a German Captain to save her life?

Alexander gently pushed her into the car, onto the floor of the back seat. She obeyed unthinkingly like a sleep-walker, a puppet in someone else's hands.

"Stay still until I give you the all-clear," he warned her, covering her with a blanket and some military clothes that were scattered on the back seat. He then closed the door and hastily sat behind the wheel. His camera was lying on the passenger seat behind him.

He started the engine and drove off, trying to look as calm as he always did, but his heart was drumming out a frenzied beat. He knew that the road block was waiting at the road that led away from the village.

Thankfully, as he approached it the guards recognized him and waved him through. He heaved a big sigh of relief. The rising sun behind the mountains greeted him in all its splendor as he drove away from the village.

≈≈≈≈≈≈≈≈≈≈

A short while later, he pulled up where the road came to an abrupt stop. He stepped out of the car, carefully checking that no one was around, then walked to the back, and pulled the door open.

Eleni flung the covers away in one abrupt movement. He gave her his hand and helped her out of the car. The scene before her made her sway and she grabbed the hood of the car to stop herself from collapsing to the ground. A thick black cloud of smoke rose from the village, the houses burning. She stared at Alexander, dumbfounded. "Why? Why are they doing this? How can you think this is our fault?"

He ignored the question and determinedly said, "Eleni, I want you to listen to me very carefully and do exactly as I say. Believe me, this is not a trap. You were betrayed last night. We know about the radio. We know about the meeting and what you were planning. A few hours ago, a patrol arrested Yiannis carrying the weapons. They are keeping him at the old school. It saddens me that you are in the Resistance, but it is irrelevant now. Here is what matters—the Commander will gather everyone at the square, the entire village. Well, not everyone...you understand who will be spared. If your fiancé does not turn himself in by lunchtime, they will all be executed. They caught Yiannis' son waiting at the safe house where the guns were being taken. He was tortured but did not break. He refused to tell them where his uncle is hiding. They have now released him and asked him to take that message to his uncle."

"No," she whispered and burst into tears.

"The war is ending, Eleni, and the Nazis want to avenge their defeat. I want you to be safe from this madness. I don't know what will happen today, but I am afraid it is all out of control."

A sharp gut-wrenching spasm made Eleni double over in pain. "What will happen to Manolis if he turns himself in? I want the truth."

For a moment he did not speak, as if weighing up his answer. "If he does, I will try to persuade the Commander to punish him and maybe not—" He broke off, seeing her on the verge of collapse and reconsidered his words. "I will try for the lesser of two evils. Now I want you to go hide. Do not go anywhere near the village. Whatever happens today, I will go to the mill and wait for you there."

Eleni set off feeling the world collapse in on her. A few minutes later, she turned around and saw Alexander's car disappear down the bend. She changed direction and strode toward the path that led to Kryfó in steely determination.

≈≈≈≈≈≈≈≈≈≈

The sun was now high in the sky, its rays gently stroking the green slopes of the island. Eleni walked rapidly, constantly looking around to make sure no one was following her. She had not stopped crying ever since she saw the burning houses. Once again, her life was in ruins, from one moment to the next.

She had been so happy Manolis had returned. They had dreamt of their future, their marriage, their freedom, and just when that future seemed so real it had been snatched from their grasp. What furies were pursuing them, tormenting them at every step?

She was near Kryfó when she spied Manolis and Nikos astride Karme, riding toward her. She wiped her eyes and sprinted in their direction as fast as her feet could carry her.

With a jump, Manolis landed on the ground and they fell in each other's arms, holding onto one another in heart-breaking desperation. She tried to speak but choked, violent sobs shaking her body.

He held her tightly and stroked her hair, trying to soothe her. His face was expressionless, frozen. He had thought Eleni had been captured along with the others.

Nikos watched them, tears soaking his bruised cheeks. A trickle of blood ran down his nose. He had told his uncle everything that had happened and Manolis had made up his mind.

Eleni's sobs slowly subsided into silent tears. "Please don't go, my love," she begged him.

Manolis looked away, trying not to break down himself. He was trying to keep composed, to be strong. "At least you got away," he said. "How did you manage to escape?"

"Alexander saved me. He came to the house before the soldiers arrived and smuggled me away from the village. He told me to hide until it was over and promised to do everything he could to save your life if you turned yourself in with that radio. I don't believe him, I don't believe anyone. We've been betrayed, Manolis. The Germans know everything and they want you to surrender, otherwise they'll kill everyone... everyone!"

Manolis already knew everything except that the German officer had saved Eleni. He wondered why. From the little Eleni had told him about Alexander he had realized that the German liked her, but he hadn't expected him to go to such lengths. Was it a ploy? Did he hope that Eleni would then come find him and lead the Germans to him? In any case, he would end up in the Nazis' hands, he had no other choice. If he did not show up with the radio by noon he would be responsible for so many deaths. His torment was unspeakable. Five long years away from the woman he loved and now that they were finally together they would be parted once again. Forever. He led her to a large rock and sat her down.

"Listen to me, Eleni. I have been longing for the moment when we could finally be together more than anything I've ever longed for. My love for you has kept me alive all these years. But my life is at its end. I don't think they will let me live. And I don't think I'll be the only one to pay the price. You must swear to do as I tell you."

"I'll come with you," she interrupted. "I don't care what happens to me. I'd rather die than live without you."

Gathering all his strength, he spoke, his voice tense. "We always believed in the twists of fate. Fate reunited us after such a long time. The German officer saved you today for a reason. So you could live. That is your fate. And I need you to swear that you'll do that. You'll live the life we dreamed of. You won't waste a single day. You will marry, have children, grow old, and tell your children our story, like a fairytale. Look at all the beauty in the world around you. If you insist on coming with me, I won't go and I'll let the chips fall where they may."

This was the first time she'd heard him talk like this. She looked at him helplessly, unable to decide. Manolis left her no room for thought. "You'll hide out with Nikos for a few days. The war is ending. The Germans will leave soon. Then you'll both be free."

Eleni, in a last, desperate attempt to dissuade him fell at his feet. "But I cannot live without you!"

He bent down and lifted her in his arms. He held her like this, sobbing into his chest, and placed her on her feet when she seemed calmer. He cupped her face in his hands and gingerly placed a kiss on her lips. "You can and you will, my love. If you truly love me, you will live. It's time to go. You hide here. The Germans will not come to this place."

Eleni still resisted. She was ready to die with him if that was to be the fate of the man she loved. Realizing he was not going to back down, she played for time. "At least let me come with you until the mill," she pleaded. "Please. And when we get there, we'll see what we'll do."

Seeing the tears in her eyes, Manolis swallowed hard, trying not to cry. He acquiesced with a nod, saying "Come with me to the mill, but promise that you'll then leave and hide; that you'll try with all your might to live a beautiful life. If you promise me that, then yes, you can come."

She dried her tears and looked up at him. The mild breeze blew her hair in her eyes and Manolis brushed them away tenderly.

They started walking toward the mill. Eleni wrapped her arms around Manolis' waist and fell into step beside him, clinging to him. Her tears were the only sound that could be heard in the silent fields. She kept thinking that this was the last time she would hold him in her arms. Nikos followed behind astride Karme, stifling his sobs.

≈≈≈≈≈≈≈≈≈≈

Agathe drank a sip of water from the glass before her, prolonging our anxious wait. Anita sat forward, chin cupped in her palms, like a child listening to a fairytale. Agathe placed the glass on the table with a trembling hand and turned toward us. No one had uttered a word, all hanging from her lips. "What I am about to tell you is very painful, my child," she said. "I will not leave anything out, I remember it all.

"Your grandfather and Manolis were planning to attack the Germans that day, with a group of men from the village. They had a stash of weapons and they were planning an assault on the German headquarters and the barracks. There were fewer German soldiers on the island at that time. Many had left the previous week and the rumor was that everyone else would be leaving the following day. It didn't matter; there were still enough of them left to unleash the hounds of hell. They packed up and left the following day. But God punished them for their sins. The English sank their ship and they all drowned, may their bones rot at the bottom of the sea for all eternity!

"My father and my brother had also joined the Resistance, ready to fight. But they were betrayed before they had a chance by some of the locals... and that woman, who did not think anything of dishonoring her engagement to Manolis or causing so many deaths. And I'll tell you something else you may not know. She was your mother's godmother."

Another person in this story I had never heard of. Did my mother know any of this? I felt the burning need to ask more about her, but I did not want to interrupt Agathe, who seemed to have drifted off into another time, staring blankly at us.

"At dawn, the Germans came. They rounded us up and took us to the square, then split us up, women and children to one side, men to the other. They had already arrested your grandfather and your uncle with the weapons. Thankfully, they let the child go afterward. We never understood why.

"They knew Manolis had the radio and they threatened to kill everyone, even the women and children, if he did not surrender by noon and bring the radio with him. And that's when it all started. They caught him outside the village, at his family's mill. They set fire to the mill and burned it down. That woman I told you, she led him there and handed him over to the Germans. She betrayed everyone else. I saw her when it was all over, leaving in the arms of her German lover.

"Manolis was brought to the square, nearly unconscious. He had been badly beaten. When he came round, they made him kneel and tied him up with a rope in the center of the square. They ordered us all to group up, facing him. We knew they would execute him.

A truck drove up, the truck bed filled with stones. They made us unload them onto the square, into a pile. We obeyed, having no idea what they wanted to do with them. Their commander went up to Manolis and smacked his face with his whip, shouting something in German. The soldiers surrounded us, training their guns on us. A traitor began to translate what the commander had been saying." She paused again and turned to face the sea, tears spilling from her eyes, but her face remaining expressionless, lost in the tragic tale she was recounting.

She seemed reluctant to continue, so I touched her hand and said gently, "What happened next, Mrs. Agathe? Please tell us."

She looked at me as if waking up from a bad dream, and taking a deep breath, spoke with great difficulty. "Few know what I'm about to tell you, my child. And when you hear it, you will understand why. It is our secret. But the time has come to tell it, because guilt is a vulture that will not stop pecking away at your heart. He ordered us to do something unheard of, inhuman. He ordered that all of us, men, women, children, pick up the stones and kill Manolis."

A sob shook the old woman's shoulders and Thekla, who sat beside her, handed her a handkerchief to wipe her tears.

The images from the newscast of the previous day flashed before my eyes, the stoning of that poor woman, and I felt nauseous. Disgust flooded through me, fighting the curiosity that was driving me to find out what happened next. For a moment I thought it might be better if Anita was spared all this, but I saw that she was as gripped as I was, so I said nothing. She squeezed my hand in sympathy.

The old woman seemed to recover, and fixed her gaze on me. "When I look at you it's like I'm looking into his eyes. He gave us the same disbelieving look when he heard what the commander had said. I remember he smiled at first, as if he thought it was a prank. We didn't believe it either. But we soon realized that man was the devil himself and he was not joking.

"When that German officer, the one who later left with Manolis' fiancée, walked up to him and told him something, he pushed him away and started screaming that if we did not obey he would kill everyone. Even after that, we stood still, no one bending down to pick a stone and throw it.

"The commander ordered that they bring your grandfather forward, next to Manolis. He took out his gun and without another word, *bang!* shot him in the head. We all started screaming, but the Germans were still aiming their guns at us and we did not dare move. Manolis was cursing at the Germans; Anna, your grandmother, still holding your mother in her arms, was wailing and tearing her hair out. Still, no one bent down to pick a stone.

"The commander turned red, furious, and screamed that they would be next if we did not obey. Manolis then started shouting at us to pick up the stones and kill him, to save the lives of Anna and his niece. Still, no one moved, as if we thought that somehow the German would change his mind and spare us from this hell.

"Seeing us stand there immobile, he grabbed your mother from Anna's arms and set her down on the ground. Maria was screaming. I can still hear her cry for her mother. He shot Anna in the chest. Two people he killed, in front of us, and he never blinked once. That's what they were like. They were animals, filming everything that was happening, as if it were a movie. That officer never stopped turning the handle until..." She paused to catch her breath, and then carried on. "Manolis was begging us to kill him. When the commander aimed his gun at Maria, we realized there was nothing else we could do. He was ready to shoot the child. He would have... We picked up the stones with trembling hands, sobbing. When he saw us move, he lowered his gun and waited."

She paused once more, dissolving into tears. I felt sorry she was reliving this, tormented by the dreadful memories and as much as I yearned to know the rest, I did not ask her to continue. Her daughter hugged her and gave me a look that said, "That's enough." She lifted her up with Thomas's help and tried to lead her inside the house. But the old lady stopped, turned back toward me, and showed me her palms, sobbing. "With these hands, with these very hands... I'm so sorry, my son. Forgive us. There was nothing else we could have done."

The Island, April 1945

Time seemed to be standing still in the square, everyone frozen as if under a spell. On one side, the locals, stones in their hands; on the other, the Germans, guns raised. In the middle of the square, Manolis knelt down, bloodied and bruised, with a piece of cardboard hanging around his neck. On it, a single word had been crudely scribbled: TRAITOR. On the ground before him, Yiannis and Maria lay dead. Nearby, their daughter was crying out for her parents, unaware of the gun that the German commander was pointing at her.

The Commander nodded to Alexander, who brought his camera and set the tripod up. He started filming the scene with shaky hands.

"The Fuhrer will see what you barbarians are capable of," the Commander hollered. His voice seemed to break the spell and time sprang forward once again.

Manolis straightened his body as far as his bonds would allow and looked toward his fellow countrymen, as if he wanted to show them what to do. He saw the first hand rise and the stone fly toward him. It tore through the cardboard sign and hit him on the chest. A cry of pain escaped his lips. He looked at the crowd. Slowly, one by one, they all raised their hands, ready to cast their stones. A mortal shower rained upon him, but his screams made everyone stop. Lying on the ground covered in blood, his breath came short and raspy. Like a wounded animal, he refused to die, moaning and twisting in agony on the ground.

The Commander had not had enough. He fired a round in the air and then pointed at Manolis, showing them they were not done. As if guided by a subtle internal voice, they all decided to put an end to Manolis' torment. Frantically, men, women, and children flung as many stones as they could as fast as they could. Not to kill him, but to set him free.

He now lay still on the ground, his shredded clothes barely covering the red mass of flesh. The women lamented and cursed as the German Commander walked up to Manolis and fired a single shot into the back of his neck. He then turned to Alexander and indicated that the young officer was to keep on filming. It was not over, yet.

≈≈≈≈≈≈≈≈≈≈

At the small chapel behind the port, a pair of terrified eyes watched the unfolding scenes. Nikos, hidden behind some bushes, had seen the German kill both his parents in cold blood and his uncle die in a rain of stones flung by the very people he'd known his whole life.

He had followed Manolis and Eleni when they'd set off for the mill, but when the Germans had sprung up before them he'd run away on Karme. He'd abandoned the horse in the fields and returned on foot. He had no idea what had happened to Eleni. He tried to spot her in the crowd herded at the port, but failed.

His body trembled from the violent shock. The Germans were separating the men from the women once again and he knew what would happen next.

Suddenly, he heard the cries of his sister. A German soldier had picked her up in his arms as she'd drifted off into the narrow, winding streets of the neighborhood behind the port. Nikos carefully got up and started to walk down in the direction of the soldier. The houses were built amphitheatrically, each level separated from the one below by low, stone walls. Nikos hid behind such a wall as the German walked toward him on the street below.

Right beneath the spot where Nikos was hiding, he placed the toddler on the ground and tried to shrug his gun from his shoulder. The strap seemed to have caught on his uniform and he was struggling. He seemed annoyed, mumbling a string of oaths. Without wasting any time and afraid that the soldier would kill his sister, Nikos grabbed a large rock and flung it at the German with all his strength. It hit him on the head. Were it not for his helmet, the rock would have cracked it open.

The soldier cried out and fell, concussed. Nikos jumped over the low wall and landed behind him, landing him a furious kick in the stomach. He grabbed Maria and sprinted back toward the chapel. From there, he would make his way to the mountains.

Feeling her brother's arms around her, Maria stopped crying and smiled at him. Behind him, the soldier dizzily got to his feet and stumbled toward the port.

A little later, gunfire and screams rang out from the square. Nikos turned to look, alarmed, knowing what must be happening. He saw the soldier he had hit stumble into the square and gesture frantically. The Germans started firing at the women and children, who dispersed in despair, trying to escape. One by one the men fell dead, the Commander dispatching the injured with a shot to the head.

Another massacre was taking place before the boy's eyes and Nikos stood frozen in shock. One of the Germans spotted him and pointed in his direction. They turned their weapons on him and fired.

Bullets whistling around his head and hitting the rocks and the walls of the church, he raced up the path that led to the mountain, running as fast as he could, his sister in his arms. He could hear the voices of the soldiers giving chase, but managed to escape.

Soon, he arrived at the shore on the other side of the mountain, a small cove with a makeshift pier that served the local fishermen. A boat was tied to one of the poles. Without even thinking about it, he placed Maria inside the boat and hastily untied the ropes. Pulling on the oars as hard as he could, he pushed away from the shore. His chest was about to burst from the exertion.

Sometime later, the boat turned around the small peninsula and, heading east, disappeared from view.

An hour earlier

Manolis and Eleni arrived at the mill, where their paths would separate. Forever. Nikos, astride Karme, discretely kept some distance, waiting for Eleni to say goodbye. It was getting late and they would have to hurry if Manolis was to appear with the radio before the time expired. He did not want anyone else to die.

He paused at the door of the mill and stood before his beloved. She fell into his arms, kissing him, begging him to take her with him. He pulled back with great difficulty and pulled out the pocket watch she had given him. He placed it in her palm. Eleni stared at the watch, disoriented. He gave her the photo of them at the port. She shoved everything into her coat pocket and burst into tears. Before she could ask him again to let her follow him, three soldiers jumped out through the door. They had been lying in wait inside the mill.

They were shouting and one of them raised his gun toward Nikos, who immediately turned around and starting galloping away. He heard the gunshots but did not see Eleni push the German away to save him. Another soldier smashed the handle of his pistol against her head and she fell to the ground, unconscious. She had bought Nikos enough time to reach the trees and vanish.

Manolis kneeled over Eleni trying to revive her, but the same soldier pulled him up by the hair, placing the muzzle of his pistol against his temple. The other two went back to the mill, and doused the floor in petrol. They came back out carrying the radio, and then one of them turned, lit a match, and flung it inside. They smashed the radio and threw the pieces over the stone wall, into the ditch behind it.

Manolis could not believe he had walked into an ambush and felt like a trapped animal. His breath came hard and labored. He did not care about dying. The thought that Eleni would meet the same fate drove him crazy and he blamed himself for listening to her, for taking her with him to the mill. He should have left her at Kryfó and come here on his own. Now, it was too late.

The two Germans seemed to be arguing, then pulled Manolis and shoved him toward the path that led to the port. Not wanting to leave Eleni alone on the ground, he resisted wildly. They beat him unconscious.

The third German stayed behind with Eleni. He saw his two comrades leave, dragging Manolis behind them and when they were out of sight he took aim, ready to kill her. Something seemed to stop him. He raised his gun above his head and fired a shot into the air. He cast a furtive look around and then walked off to catch up with the others.

Eleni lay still beneath the lone olive tree in the courtyard, her breathing intermittent and shallow.

≈≈≈≈≈≈≈≈≈≈≈

Michaela had pressed the third-floor button and watched the doors of the hospital elevator close. She was holding a large bouquet of red flowers and the tablet she had brought from home. She had rushed back to the hospital as soon as Rina had called to let her know Eleni had woken up and was lucid. She couldn't wait to show her mother the photos Anita had sent from Greece.

Having failed to make any more sense of the items she had found in the box, she intended to press her mother for answers. She felt that, even at this late stage, it was important that the past become known. More than anything she wanted to see her mother's reaction to the striking resemblance between the man in the photo and Dimitri Voudouris. She suspected that her mother had had a love affair before the war, one that she could not forget but had never spoken about.

The doors of the elevator opened and she stepped out into the corridor and walked to Eleni's room. Through the glass panel on the door, she saw a doctor with her. Eleni was propped up on the bed, connected to various tubes and wires. The moment she saw Michaela, she smiled and weakly beckoned her to come in.

Michaela opened the door and placed the tablet on the table by the bed. She kissed her mother cheerfully and handed her the flowers. Eleni sniffed the roses with a happy sigh.

"How are you, mother?" Michaela asked.

"Much better now that you are here. I had asked you, though, not to bring me to hospital," she complained.

The doctor turned to Michaela and said, "Your mother is strong, a true survivor. She surprised us all today, very pleasantly."

"When will we return home, doctor?"

"We'll see about that," he replied sternly, then smiled. "As soon as you have a moment, pass by my office." He patted Eleni's hand and left the room.

Rina got up from the chair by Eleni's bed and took the flowers, then left to find a vase and leave mother and daughter alone.

Michaela warmly grasped her mother's hand and said, "You look so well, *Mamá*. I can't believe it!"

"Why can't you believe it, Michaela? I'm still a young girl!" Eleni joked.

They both laughed. It had been a while since her mother had seemed so lucid and cheerful, so like her old self. Michaela was puzzled, but happy.

"How is Anita?" Eleni asked when the giggling had stopped. "Is she well? When is she coming back?"

"She is great! She sends all her love and lots of kisses. We'll call her later so you can talk to her," Michaela replied in a vibrant tone, wanting to prolong her mother's liveliness. Eleni, however, seemed to tire and sink once again into her own world. Michaela realized that this might be her last chance to ask all the questions that were bubbling up inside her.

"Mother, I found some things in the house that make no sense. I need to ask you some questions."

Reading her daughter's mind, Eleni interrupted her. "Listen, Michaela. You are wondering about why I was so worried about Anita going to Greece, about who the man in the photo is. I heard you talk about it, but I couldn't speak. You must also be wondering about the box in the attic I asked you to bring down. Did you open it?"

Michaela was impressed her mother remembered everything. "Yes, I did. I found a key in the desk drawer. I didn't know if you'd come round and I wanted to know why you needed it."

"Did you open the letter?" Eleni asked suspiciously.

"No. No, I didn't."

"Don't. Not before I..." Eleni said, her eyes welling up. She sighed. "I know the time to say goodbye is nearing. This letter is about a part of my life. The part that is missing."

Michaela was surprised. The part that is missing? What could all this mean?

"When Anita comes back, we'll open the letter," Eleni said, "the three of us, together. Anita can read it out in her fine voice, like a fairytale. That part of my life was a fairytale with an unhappy ending. I wanted to tell it myself, but I don't think I'm strong enough."

"I am your daughter, mother. Anita is your grandchild. Whatever happened in the past, you should have told us. Why carry the burden of an unhappy secret all these years on your own? Why not share it with us, who love and understand you?"

"Come now, Michaela. Let's not talk about this any longer. All will be revealed at the right time. Be patient. Let's call Anita now, shall we? I want to hear her voice."

Michaela resisted the urge to press her mother any further. It was clear she did not want to talk about it. She pulled out her phone and dialed Anita. After a few rings, the call went to voice mail.

"She must be working, but she'll call back when she sees the missed call."

"It's Sunday. Do they work on Sundays?"

Michaela laughed. "I think they work every day."

"What was the name of that island?" Eleni fretted.

"Do you want to see a photo and see if you can guess? I have a feeling you may know." Michaela reached for the tablet and switched it on.

Eleni looked puzzled and shifted in her bed. Michaela sat down beside her and placed the screen on her lap. The first picture was the beach at Galazia Petra. Eleni pulled back with a grimace of surprise and fear. Then she picked up the tablet and brought it closer to her eyes.

"It's a beach on the island where she is. Isn't it beautiful? Does it remind you of anything?" Michaela asked.

Eleni looked at her daughter with despair. "When was this photo taken?"

"Yesterday, I think."

"Anita is there?"

"I'm not really sure if she is exactly there." Michaela picked up the tablet. "You've painted this beach, *Mamá*," she whispered, "on the box. How can that be? They are identical. Have you been to this island?"

Eleni sighed. "I was born there."

≈≈≈≈≈≈≈≈≈≈

Thomas had just finished telling the story Agathe had been unable to finish, and I felt bruised and battered at the end. Anita was equally crushed. Pain and disgust raged inside me, now that I knew what had happened to Manolis, my grandfather, my grandmother and everyone else. How could that woman have betrayed them like this? I wished she'd met a similar end.

How much did my mother know, I wondered as I tried to join pieces of the puzzle together. Nikos obviously knew everything and that is why he had never spoken about it. He had snatched his sister and run, managed to escape.

Thomas told us Agathe had managed to survive, making it to the mountains with a few of the others in the chaos that ensued. That was where she saw the woman who had betrayed them all, leaving in the arms of the German with the camera. She had flung stones at the traitor in outrage, but they were too far away. The couple disappeared from her eyesight and the Germans left the island the following day. They did not see the woman leave with them and searched all over the island to find her, to punish her. To no avail—the traitor had simply vanished.

The island was abandoned after that. No one could carry on living there, with the guilt of Manolis' murder. Because they had all been forced accomplices. They had all cast the stones that killed him. The survivors of that day and their descendants never spoke about it. It was as if everyone had taken a collective oath of secrecy, including my uncle. I was almost certain that my mother did not know about the stoning. Her brother had hidden that part of their story from her. And she had chosen not to share with me the little that she knew.

I was reeling from this encounter with the darkness that lurked in human nature, the barbarous way in which it had been unleashed. I gripped Anita's hand, glad that she was here with me, drawing strength from the fact that she was beside me, sharing these tragic revelations with me. I wondered how she felt about the crimes the Nazis had committed in this place. Did she feel some kind of collective guilt, was she uncomfortable being here? Everyone knew she was half-German.

Thomas went back inside and came out holding a large, framed photo. It was the same photo as the one that had hung in my room, a group of people gathered at the port in 1938. I remembered that I had left it lying face down on the sofa in my room.

He placed the photo before us and said, "Thekla keeps one of these in every room. It's a special photo for us and for you Dimitri. It's the only photo of Manolis Reniotis. The woman who betrayed him is there with him, in his arms. Her name was Eleni Dapaki. That's them," he pointed at the couple. "She left for Italy that day, to study. How could he know then that she would cause his death?"

I was stunned when I realized he was pointing at the same couple I had been intrigued by when I had looked at the photo in my room. I would never have imagined that the man was my relative, that the woman who snuggled happily against him would later betray him to the Germans. Even the most imaginative scriptwriter could not have dreamt all this up. Life was once again proving stranger than fiction.

I turned to Anita to share these thoughts with her and saw her staring fixedly at the photo. She had stopped breathing. Her hand had turned cold and began to shake. She turned to look at me and I saw terror in her eyes. She looked like she'd just seen a ghost.

Perplexed, I stroked her hair and asked, "Anita, what's wrong?"

She did not reply. She just kept staring at that photo. Everyone else had now noticed something was amiss and was looking at her curiously. I made another effort to snap her out of her trance. "Darling, what's the matter? Talk to me."

Finally, she reacted. She pulled her hand free and slowly placed her index finger on the glass, beneath the woman's. She tried to speak, but no words came out. Her gaze was still fixed on the photo, eyes wide open.

I reached out and gently turned her face toward me. Speaking slowly and clearly, I tried once more. "Please, tell me. What is happening?"

A tear ran down her cheek. She turned back to Thomas and asked in a trembling voice, "You said this was taken at the port, here? Are you sure that it's not someplace else?"

"Someplace else?"

"Italy?"

"No, of course not. Look, it's the same horizon in the background. And look at the shape of the harbor. It hasn't changed much since then. It was taken here, on the island. Why do you ask?"

I looked at Anita too, puzzled by her questions. What did it all mean?

"This photo cannot be accurate," she said and took another look at it, still doubting her own eyes. "The same photo hangs on the wall in my mother's house, in Germany."

"Are you sure?" I asked.

"There can be no doubt. It's the same photo."

She looked distressed. I rubbed her shoulders trying to soothe her. "Even if it's the same photo, Anita, why are you so upset? Maybe someone gave it to your mother. It's not the only copy."

Anita shook her head no and looked down at her lap, hiding her face behind her hair.

"Who brought it to your house?"

She ignored my question and looked back at Thomas. Her voice was still shaky and low. "You insist that this woman betrayed them and is morally responsible for everything that happened that day?"

"If she hadn't betrayed them, they wouldn't have been caught. The massacre would have been avoided, I am certain. I hope she burns in hell for what she did." He slammed his fist on the table, rattling the water glasses.

Anita recoiled as if she'd just been slapped, but regained her composure and asked, "Do you know the name of the German officer she ran off with?"

"No, but I can find out. His name was in some archives the Germans left behind. It's in that book Antonis wrote. Let me go get it." Thomas ran back inside the house.

I could not bear to see her like this. I hugged her and said, "My love, what does all this mean? Who brought this photo to your house? Please tell me."

She pointed at the woman and simply said, "She did."

For a moment I wondered whether she had been so swept up in the story we'd just heard that she was imagining things, thinking the faces were familiar. One look at the conviction in her eyes made me dismiss that thought. She meant every word she said.

I instantly remembered the crazy thought that had crossed my mind the first time I saw that picture—that Anita looked like the woman in the photo. At the time I'd thought that my mind was playing tricks, that I was projecting my longing for Anita everywhere. Now, I was not sure what to believe. So much information to process in such a short space of time was making it hard to think. I decided to clear things up, there and then. "Anita, that's incredible. How could this woman have brought the photo to your house? How do you know that?"

Thomas reappeared holding a book. I glimpsed the title on the cover: *Our History*. He put it down on the table and started leafing through it.

"I know, because..." Anita paused and looked at everyone around her, her gaze stopping on me. "I know, because... that woman is my grandmother."

Her words struck our hearts like a thunderbolt and we all stared at her in disbelief. A deadly silence ensued, broken by a single word.

"Alexander—" Thomas stopped short, his face darkening. Anita's chair fell to the ground in a dull thud as she jumped up and ran upstairs, crying.

The Island, April 1945

Alexander was running toward the mill, hoping to find Eleni. He had told her he would be waiting for her and prayed that she would come. He had not seen her anywhere else and feared she may have come to harm. He was shocked at what had happened in the square; at the events he had been forced to film.

He felt repulsed by his countrymen's brutality. He had been forced into this war against his will. His father, a fervent follower of Hitler, had joined the party and forced him into the Hitler youth and then the army.

He had managed to be posted on this island. A friend from medical school had been stationed here and had told him that things were calm and the locals peaceful. That was what Alexander wanted—a quiet spot to sit out the war and return to Berlin and his family's antique shop.

Just a day before it would all be over, disaster had struck. Alexander had never realized the evil that was lurking in the Commander's heart. He had been asked to film it all so they could show Hitler when they returned that the people he admired for their Ancient Greek heritage were nothing but a tribe of savages. If they truly were like their ancestors, they would have chosen to die with honor than slay one of their own.

Alexander had decided to leave the island that evening with the doctor and two more officers on a fishing boat. He did not want to leave with everyone else the following day. Had it not been for Eleni, he would have deserted days ago.

He had fallen in love at first sight with her on the night he had rescued her at the school. He had tried to spend every moment with her, fallen under her spell. He had never met someone so strong and mild at the same time.

He could tell her heart belonged to her fiancé but would not give up. After Manolis' brutal death, would she follow him? He was prepared to do all he could to persuade her.

≈≈≈≈≈≈≈≈≈≈≈

Approaching the mill, he saw a body lying in the shade of an olive tree. He could not tell if it was a man or a woman. An alarm bell went off in his head and he sprinted to the mill.

He froze when he realized it was Eleni. Her face was bloody and she looked lifeless. He turned her onto her back and felt for a pulse. Her breathing was shallow and irregular.

He raised her head and she seemed to come round. She opened her eyes and looked at him, her pupils dilated. He removed his white scarf and wiped the blood carefully, then tied it around her wound.

"How are you?" he asked anxiously. "Are you in pain?"

"Who are you?"

"I'm Alexander, dear."

"I don't know you... what am I doing here?"

"What can you remember?"

She opened her mouth to reply, then stopped. She looked at him, disorientated, and gingerly touched her head. "I can't remember anything. Why is my head bandaged?"

"There is no time to explain. Listen to me, Eleni, we must leave now, or they will kill us both. I'll explain everything later, but now you must trust me. Follow me. We have to hurry up!"

He lifted her up to her feet. She was still dizzy and could not stand up properly. He put her arm around his shoulders and held her by the waist, dragging her to the path. She let herself be led away without resisting.

They stopped at the well outside the mill, where he drew some water. Removing his scarf from around her head, he washed the wound. Cupping some water in his hands, he gave her a drink.

All the while, Eleni looked at him with a vague sense that he was a familiar face, someone who could be trusted, but she was unable to remember who he was.

Alexander took a few steps and she let out a cry of pain. She was having trouble stepping on her ankle.

"Where are we going?" Eleni asked.

"Somewhere far away."

She stopped walking, her body becoming a dead weight in his arms. "I'm not going anywhere unless you tell me who you are."

Alexander was at a loss. His life was already in danger if the Germans found out he was helping a wanted woman. Now, the locals were a threat too. The men who had betrayed Manolis had pointed their finger at Eleni, saying that she was the one who had betrayed him, using her ties to Achermann as further proof. He had no time to explain, to tell the truth. He also suspected that if she realized what had just happened, that her fiancé and her family were dead, she would choose to stay behind and die.

"I'm your husband, Eleni. We must get home, quickly." A volley of gunfire was heard from the port, dark clouds of smoke rising. Eleni was frightened and dug her nails into his shoulder. He lifted her up in both arms and started making his way down the hill, to the meeting point with the others.

Neither one noticed the young girl who was watching them from further up the hill. She had paused and was staring at them. A roar of rage echoed down the slope, followed by these words: "Traitor! Traitor! Traitor!"

A stone fell some feet behind them, then another, and another. Alexander stepped off the path and hid behind a rock. He pulled out his gun and looked up, ready to fire. No one was on the hill.

Further up, a man had pinned Agathe to the ground, hissing at her to keep quiet, not to make herself and the fortunate few who had escaped a target.

≈≈≈≈≈≈≈≈≈≈

A few hours later, Eleni, Alexander, and three other officers were sailing away, to surrender at a bigger island that was no longer under German rule.

Behind them, the island was a dark, distant spot against the pink horizon. It was getting darker, a peaceful lull descending on the calm waters.

The men were chatting at the back of the boat. Further up, Eleni stood at the prow, her head dressed in a bandage. Alexander's doctor friend had taken care of her injury when they had met. She was still at a loss, unable to remember. She believed herself to be Alexander's wife and had followed him meekly.

In her mind, the last words she had heard in Greek before leaving the island still resonated: "traitor!" She could not understand why someone had shouted that. She was convinced, though, that she was in danger.

The air was getting chilly. She put her hands in her pockets to keep warm. She felt the rustle of paper and something cold, metallic in one of them. She pulled out a photo and a pocket watch. She looked at the photo; a crowd of people at a port. In the dark, she was unable to see any of the faces clearly. She then looked at the watch, the dented cover. She pried it open and saw the photo of a man. She had no idea who he was. For the first time, she noticed the ring she was wearing, the small sculpted rose. A memory seemed to rise from the depths of her mind, but it sunk again before it had a chance to surface.

≈≈≈≈≈≈≈≈≈≈≈

She heard approaching footsteps and hurriedly shoved everything back in her pocket, instinctively feeling that she must hide them.

"Remember anything?" Alexander asked, putting his arms around her waist. She stepped away from his embrace. In the dark, her eyes sparkled. A name came to her, as if someone was whispering in her ear: 'Manolis... Manolis...'"

The moon began to rise from the waters.

≈≈≈≈≈≈≈≈≈≈≈

I dragged myself to the bedroom with great difficulty, feeling numb. Confusing thoughts swirled in my mind as I tried to understand if what was happening was real or a nightmare.

When Anita had run out of the courtyard, I felt as if my insides had turned to ice. It was a familiar feeling; that was how I'd felt when my father had died.

I walked up the stairs and hesitated before the bedroom door, fervently hoping against all reason that I would find Anita smiling inside; Anita telling me that it had all been a mistake; that she had been confused; that it was all a mix up; that her grandmother had not betrayed my great uncle; that her grandmother had not caused the massacre of innocent souls and run off with the German officer, her grandfather. If it was all true, who should I feel most sorry for? Anita or myself? We were like the two sides of the same ghoulish coin.

I slowly opened the door and saw her sobbing, face down on the bed. I approached her cautiously, unsure of how to act.

She felt my presence and turned to look at me with horror. I felt a great divide come between us. Instead of giving her a hug, like I normally would have, I sat on the couch and did not speak for a while. Taking a deep breath, I said that I was hoping it was all a big misunderstanding.

"No, Dimitri, it's not," she sniffled. "I'm convinced that woman was my grandmother. My grandfather was called Alexander. I don't even have the strength to call my mother and find out if she knows how the two met. But I will, soon."

"Before you call, we should re-examine this story. Maybe there is something we're missing. You said your grandmother is Greek..."

"All these years I've felt that she was hiding something," she interrupted me. "She didn't like talking about her past, always gave us vague answers. I could tell she was in pain. My grandfather died in Berlin, as did the rest of his family, when the Soviets bombed the city. My grandmother was the only one to survive. She inherited their shop. She is the sweetest person in the world. I can't believe what they said about her. Something else must have happened, something no one knows about."

I tried to listen to her objectively, to weigh things up: on the one side, the undisputed facts and the accusations against her grandmother; on the other, Anita's doubts and my love for her, which had transformed my life these past three months. I wanted to be impartial, unemotional, but it was impossible. "Anita, according to witnesses, that woman betrayed her fiancé and her countrymen. Because of her, my mother and her brother were orphaned and survived by pure chance. She ran away to save her own skin leaving everyone else to be slaughtered by the Nazis."

She looked at me in surprise. I did not realize how vehement my words were, how tinted with hatred, until they came out. I'd spoken as if I were certain of her grandmother's guilt.

She made no comment, just got up and started packing her bag. She went to the bathroom, splashed some water on her face and returned to pick up her luggage, then moved to the door.

I made no move to stop her, feeling that whatever had held us together had now snapped.

She paused at the door and turned toward me. "If the accusations are true, please tell your mother how deeply sorry I am for her family's suffering. I wish there was something I could do to change things. However, I will try to hear my grandmother's version of the story, as soon as she can speak to me. We still have to spend a few more days together because of work. What I want you to never forget is that from the moment I met you I felt that you were the one I had been waiting for all my life. I can't believe that I met you so suddenly only to lose you so unexpectedly."

Her phone rang on the bedside table where she'd forgotten it in her haste. She crossed the room to pick it up and sighed when she saw the name that flashed on the screen. She answered in a melancholy voice, looking at me tearfully all the while. "Hello, mother... Yes, I can. What happened?"

I saw her clench her jaws as she listened, then stifle a cry and bend over, sitting down on the floor abruptly. She spoke in German and rocked herself back and forth. I couldn't understand what was happening.

The phone lay beside her on the floor, the line dead. Once more, she burst into tears. I kneeled down beside her. "Who was it? What happened?"

"My mother... the hospital..."

"What did she say?"

"My grandmother is dead."

Berlin, earlier

Michaela was still trying to recover from her mother's revelation that she had been born on the island in the photo. For a moment she wondered whether her mother had lost her mind.

The elderly woman was looking at the tablet screen nostalgically. She touched the screen as if wanting to feel the sand between her fingers and accidentally pressed the pointer and brought up another picture. The beach was replaced by a photo of Anita and Dimitri. It was taken at their first photo shoot, when Dimitri's hair was longer.

A glimmer of recognition flashed in Eleni's eyes and a name escaped her lips: "Manolis!."

"Who is Manolis, mother?" Michaela jumped at the chance, feeling that this was her time to get some answers.

Eleni's fingers hovered over Dimitri's face on the screen. "He looks like him so much... even their eyes are the same," she murmured, lost in the depths of her mind. She suddenly noticed the woman in the picture and leaned her head back to get a better look. "Oh, it's Anita? Who is the man with her, then?"

Before answering, Michaela took out the pocket watch from her handbag and lifted the cover. "It's Dimitri Voudouris, mother, her co-star. He looks like this man, doesn't he? I guess this is Manolis."

Eleni took the watch and placed it against her heart, closing her eyes. For a moment it looked like she had fainted. Michaela touched her mother's face trying to keep her alert. She was about to call a nurse, but Eleni half-opened her eyes and seemed to be recovering.

"Mother, are you okay?"

"I'm fine, Michaela." She breathed deeply and looked at her daughter. "Sit down, next to me. There isn't much time and you must know." She looked at the photo of Dimitri and her granddaughter once more.

Michaela sat down on the armchair beside her and took her hand.

Rina entered the room with a vase filled with Michaela's roses. She took one look at the two women and placed the flowers on the bedside table, then swiftly exited without uttering a word.

As soon as the door had closed behind her, Eleni spoke. "I thought I was done with the past, but it seems like the past is not done with me. That young man looks a lot like the only man I ever loved. The resemblance, the photo... it's too much of a coincidence, it's not natural. It's as if some higher power has placed him in Anita's path to remind me of everything that happened then... But I'll leave that part for later." She paused to catch her breath, and then continued, her voice weaker. "I'll tell you my story from the start, Michaela, and then you can share it with Anita when she returns. There is no reason to hide the truth about me any longer, even if I feel ashamed."

"You'll tell her the story yourself, mother, when she returns."

Eleni paid no heed. Now that she had decided to speak, she seemed in a hurry to tell it all. "I was born on that island in 1920. I never knew my mother, she died in childbirth. I was an only child. My father raised me.

"The Italians ruled our island before the war and we lived peacefully. As soon as I finished school, the Italian state gave me a scholarship and I left for Pisa, to study.

"Manolis and I fell in love and it was destiny. He came and danced with me at a festival and we never left each other's heart, even when he joined the army and was sent to the front; even after he died.

"Just before the war broke out, I returned to the island and Manolis. That's when I gave him this watch. He returned it to me on the day we parted forever."

Eleni continued her tale, in every detail. She spoke for long, without pause, tearful with emotion, smiling whenever she spoke of their love.

"When Alexander found me, I was unconscious. When I recovered, I could not remember a thing. I did not know who I was, or what I was doing there. I still have the scar from the wound to my head.

"Everyone was after us and when he told me he was my husband, I followed him. I can't even remember how we ended up on the boat that carried us away. Random pieces of memory resurfaced, but nothing that could help me understand what had happened.

"We arrived at our destination in the morning. Alexander thought that he and the other officers would be surrendering to the Allies, but he discovered a large stash of antiquities hidden on the boat. They had been stolen by the Germans from our islands. He argued with the others when he realized that what they had planned was a smuggling operation.

"Others were waiting for us on the island and they transported us and the trunks to an airfield. I still remembered very little, mostly Manolis' name. When we got on the plane I started to remember more. By the time we landed at another airport a few hours later, I'd remembered it all. I never found out where we landed. They unloaded the trunks there.

"I knew who I was and what had happened. Not everything, though; I was unaware of the worst part. I wish I had never regained my memory and spent the rest of my life oblivious to the past.

"When Alexander realized my memory had returned, he asked me to keep quiet. He was afraid they might kill us both. He had told the others that I was a German collaborator, that I was leaving with them to escape my countrymen's reprisals. Of course, his friend, the doctor, was aware of his feelings for me.

"When we got on another plane, Alexander told me what had happened while I lay unconscious outside the mill. Inside me, I prayed that the plane would crash and I would die. I did not want to live after what I'd learned."

Eleni described what had happened at the village square, Michaela listening, stunned. "Nikos and Maria... what happened to the children?" she asked anxiously.

"Alexander did not know. I hope they lived."

Michaela was impressed by how her mother kept referring to her father as 'Alexander'. Not once did she call him 'your father', as if she was detached from the fact that she had borne him a child.

"I did not care about anything after that," Eleni said, now showing signs of strain and fatigue. It was clear she would not be able to keep talking for much longer. She hugged the watch and summoned what little strength she had left, determined to finish what she'd started. "The Germans left the island the following day. The few surviving locals also left, and the place was deserted for years. When the island became inhabited again, I thought about returning there with you. Before doing so, I paid someone to go visit and find out what had happened after we had left. He confirmed what Alexander had told me, and then I discovered the worst part: everyone thought I was a traitor; that I had betrayed the man I was engaged to and run off with my German lover. I never dared return, I was afraid for my life.

"Manolis never died for me. He lives every day, inside me. Not a day has passed that I have not thought of him. Even if I never said a word to you."

"What happened to my father?"

"We arrived in Berlin, after a long, arduous journey. We went straight to the shop. Alexander hid me there. He asked me to be patient until the end of the war, but I had already decided to end my life. I could not stand to live with all those memories. I could not stand to live without Manolis.

I thank God every day that did not come to pass, for I never would have had you. When I was getting ready to hang myself, I heard a great explosion. The Soviets had begun bombing Berlin. I ran outside the shop and there, by the entrance, I saw Alexander sprawled on the pavement, dead. He had been on his way to meet me. I felt guilty about his death. When they asked me if he was my husband, I said yes. I still don't know why. Maybe because he was the last friend I had."

"*Mamá*, I'm speechless. This is too much to take in all at once!"

"I understand, Michaela, but I can't keep any more secrets. Forgive me for keeping this from you my whole life. My end is near and I want you to know everything.

"Chaos reigned around me, but I decided to live. So, I stayed at the shop. I only came out to eat at the soup kitchens. One day, I ran into the doctor, Alexander's friend. He asked me what had happened, and I explained with the few words of German I had picked up. He arranged for me to get official papers as Alexander's wife. So the store became mine. No relation of Alexander's ever turned up. They had all perished in the war. Alexander was a good man and he loved me, I know that."

Eleni's breathing became labored, she was now gasping for air. Her body started to shake. Michaela pressed the alarm button and a doctor ran into the room, a nurse at his heels. They asked her to step outside and bent over her mother. The last thing Michaela saw before the nurse drew the curtain around the bed was the doctor trying to resuscitate Eleni.

A short while later they announced her death. As they wheeled Eleni's lifeless body on a gurney, Michaela lifted the sheet and kissed her mother's forehead. She watched them take her mother away down the corridor and into an elevator. When the doors to the elevator closed, she stepped back into the room swallowing her tears and pulled her phone out of her bag to call Anita.

≈≈≈≈≈≈≈≈≈≈

Anita walked with her head bowed, hiding her red and swollen eyes behind dark sunglasses. Mihalis walked behind her carrying her suitcase and I followed, shouldering my rucksack, lost in my thoughts.

It was late in the afternoon and we were leaving the island. As we crossed the small village square littered with the remains of the previous night's revelries, three men who were clearing up stopped what they were doing and fell silent, watching us pass. The same silence greeted us outside the nearby coffee shop, the customers standing up to look at us as solemnly, as if we were a funeral procession. The children stopped running around the war memorial and stood still, affected by the sudden silence.

We reached the edge of the port feeling their eyes on our back and headed to the boat. Only a few fishing boats were beside it. Most visitors had already left.

Mihalis helped Anita step on the boat and prepared to depart.

Following her mother's phone call, Anita was on the verge of collapse. She, too, had suffered a series of heavy blows. We had both been confronted with our families' common past, which had been stripped naked before our eyes and left us reeling. We could not believe what had happened.

Eleni Dapaki had died just as the truth about her was being revealed. Another incredible coincidence. Fate had been lenient with her, giving her more years than she had deserved. Divine justice does not always punish the wicked. I don't know how she managed to make peace with her conscience, but based on the little I knew, she hadn't seemed to suffer much, not in proportion to what she'd done. I still hated her, even now that she was dead. I hated her for what she did to my mother's family and I hated her for ruining my relationship with Anita.

Before everything came to light, I was absolutely happy. Now we were cold toward each other and, even though I knew she was not to blame, something inside me had shattered. It would be hard to regain what we'd had and there was not anything I could do about that at that moment.

I had a sense of being a character in a Greek tragedy, everything happening at the right place, at the right time. Fate had spun its wheel to build up to a resolution that restored moral order and brought catharsis.

≈≈≈≈≈≈≈≈≈≈

When I reached the boat, I turned back to face the mainland and say goodbye to the place. I saw Thomas walking toward me from the square. When he reached me, he placed his hand on my shoulder and said, "There are no words, my son, to say at a time like this. We will be waiting for you and your mother, get to know you both better— if, that is, she wants to return here after she finds out about her uncle. But tell her that there was not anything else they could have done. They thought that if they sacrificed one, the rest would live. They did not suspect... Agathe has always said that the survivors lived with this nightmare every day of their lives. They were all tormented souls. They made us swear to ask for forgiveness if anyone from Manolis' family ever returned to the island."

I did not say anything.

Nodding to the boat, he continued, "Forgiveness is a great virtue, my son. He who can give it can live a better life. Let go of your anger. We ask that you forgive what our loved ones did to Manolis; maybe Anita needs your forgiveness too. We don't hate her. How is she responsible for what her grandmother did, years ago? It means something that the woman died today. Time is a gentle god, my child. He heals the most profound wounds."

His words touched me, and I was surprised. They seemed to resonate with me and washed away some of the hatred that was burning in my heart. While he spoke, I turned to look at the war memorial. He followed my gaze. "When the islanders returned, years later, they found the stones that had killed Manolis on the square," he said. "They gathered them up and made this memorial. These stones were drenched in his blood."

Everything in the universe is linked in some way. Past and present join to push the future in a different direction. *Time present and time past. Are both perhaps present in time future.* The words of T.S. Eliot came to my mind as I bid Thomas farewell and stepped onto the boat.

As soon as I was aboard, Mihalis untied the ropes and started the engines. We slowly exited the port and I, standing at the prow, looked out at the small crowd that was watching us leave.

A woman's shout tore through the air. 'Shame on her!' Most of the others seemed to be bothered by her outburst and hushed her.

Soon we were out at sea. Anita was crying inside. She had been shaken by what the woman had shouted at her. I wanted to go near her, comfort her, but my overblown sense of pride did not let me.

Watching the coastline in the hope of spotting Kryfó, I suddenly remembered the names we had seen etched on the rock, in the Cave of Silence. *ELENI+M. Eleni and Manolis.* It must have been them. That's why they had been erased. And they had been scratched there nearly seventy years ago. Some higher force—destiny, perhaps?—had pushed me to leave our names right next to theirs.

I wanted to ask Mihalis to turn the boat around and take us there and hug her as if nothing had come between us. I wished I could. I did not feel strong enough. Nonetheless, as the soft breeze stroked my face I began to feel a sense of freedom wash over me. I had learned my family's story and it was setting me free.

Anita came outside at that moment and walked to where I was standing. She looked devastated. Her eyes were red and she slouched, as if she could no longer keep upright after the blows she'd received. Her voice was hoarse from crying and she spoke in a cold monotone devoid of any feeling. "I spoke to production. They've booked a flight to Berlin for me, tonight. They changed the schedule so I can attend the funeral. You'll shoot some of your scenes tomorrow and the day after. We'll drop you off at the island, and then I'll sail to where the airport is. My grandmother's funeral is tomorrow afternoon. I'll be back Tuesday morning. I want to speak to my mother. I haven't told her anything. I think she must know the truth. I am almost certain she knows nothing. She would have said something otherwise. I don't think the truth is exactly what they say. I know... I knew my grandmother well. She would never do something like that. All those years, she never remarried. She never seemed to have another man in her life. She always said she only fell in love once and it was forever.'

"Yes, to the German she ran off with," I said sarcastically. I regretted those words the moment they escaped my lips.

She looked like I'd slapped her. "I think it's better for both of us that I'm going away for a while. I can imagine how you feel, I understand. But put yourself in my shoes for a moment."

I opened my mouth to reply but she turned around and walked back inside. Why was I acting like this? It was as if I had two selves, one who spoke without thinking and another who thought and felt but did not speak.

Electra was waiting for us at the port. She was carrying a large suitcase and jumped on board the moment the boat was moored. She greeted me indifferently and went inside to find Anita.

I moved to the gangway, but something held me back. I turned and looked behind me. Anita was looking at me. We stared at each other for a few moments. I did not know what I felt. I tried to detect some feeling inside me but found nothing, just an ever-increasing void.

I stepped off the boat and waited. Electra walked down behind me. She mumbled something I didn't catch, and then walked off.

I picked up my rucksack and walked toward the port gates. I sat under an empty carport and looked at the boat, watching it leave the port. I watched it until it became a dot on the horizon; Anita did not appear, not once.

I took out my phone and brought up her name on the screen. My finger hovered over the dial button, but I did not call. Summoning all my courage, I dialed my mother's number.

≈≈≈≈≈≈≈≈≈≈

Maria had just hung up. The phone call with Dimitri had lasted over an hour. Kostas, listening to Maria's end, could piece together enough scraps of conversation to figure out what was being said. He held her in his arms, trying to console her. Her tears flowed freely, soaking his shirt.

She understood now why Nikos had never mentioned Manolis. She had lived all her life believing that her parents had been shot in a mass execution at the village square after an informant betrayed them and that the two of them had managed to escape. The only personal memory she had of the event was the strange blue eyes of the young novice who had found them on the beach. She always thought he may have been an angel sent to help them. She had just found out the man was real, the Abbot on the island where her son was filming. She planned to visit soon, to meet him and thank him for everything he had done for them.

Suddenly, spurred on by a new realization, she snatched the cross hanging around her neck and pulled it away, violently. The chain snapped and she flung it across the room. The only object connecting her to the past and it came from that woman! She no longer wanted to have anything from her; its touch burned her throat.

Kostas picked up the cross and placed it on the coffee table. He then took Maria out to the balcony to get some fresh air. She tearfully gazed at the sea, as if she were traveling back to the island in her mind. She felt the need to return, see the place where she'd been born, where her parents had lived and died. She realized that part of her was always missing and that, even at this late hour, she had a chance to become complete. She felt no hatred for the people there. In any case, with the exception of Agathe, they were all gone.

The premonition she'd felt when Dimitri had announced his intention to return had come true, but she could never have imagined the revelations that would follow and which she now struggled to accept. She couldn't believe that of all the women in the world Dimitri would fall in love with the granddaughter of that accursed woman. What an infernal coincidence!

She'd never interfered in his private life. She'd never proffered an opinion on the women he dated or who she thought he should date. Now she wanted to scream at him to get away from Anita as fast as he could. To give it all up and come back, if possible right there and then.

She knew her son loved her. She knew, deep down, that the young woman was not to blame for what her grandmother had done. But she couldn't stand the thought of meeting her—as her son had asked her to, when they all returned to Athens at the end of the shoot—for in her face she was certain to see the woman who had brought the reaper's scythe down on her family.

≈≈≈≈≈≈≈≈≈≈≈

Dressed in black, Michaela and Anita stood arm in arm before Eleni's open grave.

Only a few people had come to bid Eleni goodbye, for she had been a reserved woman all her life. She had kept to herself and made few friends, devoted her life to her daughter and her beloved granddaughter.

As soon as the service was over, they thanked everyone who had come to support them at this difficult time and placed a few flowers on the casket that was waiting to be covered by the heap of fresh soil at the side of the grave. Beside them, Rina sobbed loudly.

The two women turned back and started walking toward the cemetery gates. With all the funeral arrangements they had not had a chance to talk, and they both had a lot to say.

≈≈≈≈≈≈≈≈≈≈≈

The sun was setting outside but they kept the lights turned off. The strains of *Tristan und Isolde* filled the room and the two women sat on the sofa side by side, in silence.

Anita was holding the pages of Eleni's letter in her hands, the open box on her lap. On the cushions between them lay scattered Eleni's sketches and the pocket watch, which Eleni had bequeathed to Anita in her letter.

Eleni explained everything. The events that led to her leaving the island and how she had ended up in Berlin, carrying the child of the only man she had ever loved.

Anita felt drained but happy and relieved at the same time. She now knew that what she had heard on the island was untrue, that she could now return and set the record straight. Would they believe her? She did not care. She just needed one person to believe the truth—Dimitri. She wanted to run back to him and tell him the story, be with him again. Away from him, she felt incomplete; she suffered in his absence. She could not wait for filming to be over and for them to run away from everyone. To be constantly together, to touch him, to explore new worlds in each other's body, to do nothing, to be happy.

Before her trip to Greece, she could never have imagined that her life would change so radically, that she would fall in love so deeply.

Reading the letter, she recognized the striking similarities in the way she and her grandmother had experienced love. So many years divided the two affairs, yet they had so much in common. How could that be? They even shared the Cave of Silence, the place where both women had experienced the most magical moments of their life.

She had not shared what had happened on the island with her mother. Michaela had started recounting Eleni's story first, then given her the letter. Now, it was Anita's turn to describe events.

The first words to come out of Michaela's mouth when Anita stopped talking were an indictment of Dimitri's behavior: "Shame on him! How could he treat you this way?"

"Mother, he did nothing wrong," Anita said, jumping to Dimitri's defense. "He doesn't know what we know. Try to put yourself in his place. I told you, he was as nice as he could be given the circumstances."

Michaela fell silent again, trying to reorganize her thoughts in the light of this new information. Had it not been for the physical presence of the letter, she would have thought all this was a dream or the ramblings of an over-active imagination.

She got up and walked to the kitchen to get a glass of water. She wasn't thirsty, just agitated, and needed to do something. She placed the glass on the coffee table and left it there, untouched. A few minutes later, she seemed to regain her composure. She turned to Anita. "Are you sure no one knew this story beforehand? That they didn't bring you together on that island on purpose, to trigger this chain of events?"

Anita had already wondered about this in the hours that had lapsed between leaving Greece and her grandmother's funeral. No one knew she intended to surprise Dimitri on Saturday night, other than Mihalis of course, and she was ready to stake her life on the man's honesty. Besides, no one could have engineered the car accident which had led to her leaving for the island. It had happened before her very eyes. And Dimitri would never have found out about her connection to Eleni had she not spoken up about it herself, when she saw the photo of the port. No, no human could have managed to set all this up.

Michaela remained suspicious. "I want you to be careful when you return," she advised. "Don't try to convince anyone about what you know. If they don't believe you, be patient until your work is done and then leave. I keep feeling like we need to take steps to protect you from some harm." She looked at Anita's melancholic expression and realized her daughter was thinking of Dimitri. "Do you love him?" she asked, fondly stroking her daughter's hair.

"What I feel inside is just what *Yiayia* writes about in her letter, what she felt for Manolis. I miss him, terribly. I'm ashamed to say that, when *Yiayia* has just died and I should be sad about her absence…"

"Anita, don't feel bad about the way you feel. I'm sure your grandmother would be telling you the same thing, now that I've read her letter and know how passionately she loved her man. She would tell you to run to him and tell him the truth. Tell him how you feel. If he doesn't understand then you are not destined to be together. And he'd better understand or he'll have me to deal with," she joked. "I'm thinking about coming to Athens and meeting everyone."

≈≈≈≈≈≈≈≈≈≈

They sat in the dark, remembering Eleni and thinking over what the old woman had been telling them during the last months of her life. It was as if she felt the moment of revelation was coming and was trying to prepare them. All these years there was a part of her they had never known; a piece of the jigsaw puzzle that fate had suddenly decided to fling onto the table and make the picture complete.

The women fell asleep on the couch in each other's arms. Neither one of them wanted to go to their rooms and be alone that night. Anita was to take an early flight back to Greece. She was aware that what lay ahead might not be easy to deal with and sought the comfort of her mother's arms.

In Eleni's bedroom, a beam of light from the streetlamp outside her window fell on the photo that was framed on the wall, lighting up her face as she rested in her beloved's arms, eyes shut.

≈≈≈≈≈≈≈≈≈≈

Anita had returned but we weren't speaking to each other these days. We only addressed one another formally and when necessary, on matters regarding work.

When she'd arrived she had tried to speak to me about what had happened but I was still cold and furious. We had our first fight. She insisted we were wrong about her grandmother and that she could prove it. I was too upset to listen, did not give her room to explain. I'd stormed off, outraged that she was trying to excuse that woman and her actions.

The following day I apologized and tried to talk, but she was angry with me and stubbornly refused. She said there was no point to any of this.

The production had tried to shield Anita when the story began to circulate among the crew, giving everyone instructions not to comment on anything and did not allow anyone to come near her. She had asked for this herself, but I think they would have done it anyway.

Filming was purgatory for both of us, especially the scenes where we were in close proximity. Retake after retake was needed to get the scenes right, but the director never complained. Once the love scenes were over and we moved onto the part where the characters' relationship breaks down, the tension between us suited the script perfectly and the director was full of praise.

The last day of filming on the island finally arrived. I had one scene left to shoot with Anita in Athens, two months later.

Anita was flying back to Germany that evening. I badly needed to talk to her but my ego had stood in the way. I missed her but hid it well. I had let my anger at her grandmother take over all other emotions, even though reason shouted that Anita had nothing to do with this.

Finally waking up to the fact that I could lose the most beautiful thing that had ever happened to me in the storm of revelations that concerned other people, from another time, I decided to clear things up between us, even at the last moment. I wanted to find a way to erase the past. I had no memory of my grandfather or Manolis, and the initial feelings that had been stirred up when I'd learned their stories were now giving their place to what any stranger might feel when hearing a tragic tale.

Late in the afternoon, a small wrap-up party was scheduled at the hotel, a chance for everyone to say goodbye. I planned to talk to her there and then. Take her in my arms and tell her I did not care about the past, I just wanted to be with her. Would I find the courage to do it? Would I finally be able to silence the voice that still whispered that Anita was the granddaughter of the woman responsible for everything my mother and uncle had suffered?

≈≈≈≈≈≈≈≈≈≈≈

The scene had been set and they were calling my name. We were filming outside, by the sea. It was noon and the sun was burning hot. They were getting us ready at the opposite ends of the shore on purpose, to avoid the awkwardness that hovered between us.

Anita was walking toward me wearing a large hat, which she removed when she was near me. She gave me a look full of anger. Why? Could she not understand that I was the injured party here?

It didn't take long to shoot the scene. We obviously both wanted for this to be over as soon as possible. We all packed up and I quickly downed a glass of the champagne someone had popped open to celebrate our last take. Then I quickly walked back to the hotel.

I sat waiting for Anita in the lobby. She appeared a few minutes later but walked straight past me without uttering a single word and went up to her room. Feeling downcast by her behavior, I ordered a drink, although after everything that had happened during my drunken night at the festival I'd promised myself never to have more than one glass. I downed the whiskey in one shot and went to my room to change clothes.

I returned to the lobby determined to speak to her. I would not let us part like this, not without confessing what I really felt. I was fed up with the past; I wanted to live in the present.

The hotel lobby was crowded with cast members, crew, and producers. Electra was among them. As soon as she spotted me, she started to make her way through the crowd toward me. She wore a strange expression that made me feel a sense of foreboding. Something had happened and I hoped it had nothing to do with Anita.

She came up to me and said, "Mr. Voudouris, Miss Hertz asked me to give you this." She handed me a sealed envelope, my name handwritten on the back.

"Why is she not giving me this? Where is she?"

"She left with Mihalis for the airport a few minutes ago. She is catching an earlier flight."

My jaw dropped and I stared at her. She shifted uncomfortably and said, "If I may, I'd like to say how sorry I am about everything that happened. It's a shame..." She turned and quickly walked off.

I dashed out onto the street, pushing everyone out of my way. In the distance, I saw Mihalis' speedboat move away. Anita stood at the back, looking in my direction. I could not make out her face but could sense that she was staring at me.

I ran toward the sea, envelope still in my hand, and stood there watching her fade away. Once again, the void that I had been feeling inside grew and engulfed me.

Thessaloniki, two months later

I unlocked the door to the apartment and was hit by an intense musty smell that escaped from the dark interior. I fumbled for the light switch and flicked it on, but the power had been cut. Minding my step, I made my way to the balcony doors and opened the blinds.

It was nearly noon and the rays of the autumn sun sprang inside, lighting up the dusty interior. I waited for the soft sea breeze to blow away the stale air and stood at the balcony doors, watching the old port warehouses and the large cranes on the ships waiting to load their cargo.

It was my first visit to Uncle Nikos' home. Wandering from room to room I realized he had led an almost ascetic life. On a wall of his sparsely furnished living room hung an old map of the island. Beside the map stood a smaller frame—the ubiquitous photo of Eleni and Manolis at the port. I kept coming across that photo but I was surprised to see it here. How did it end up in Uncle Nikos' hands? Another mystery.

It seemed that the story had not yet reached the end.

I had tried to contact Anita many times following my return to Athens, but to no avail. Those two months were the worst time of my life. I lost all interest in anything else. I turned down all interview requests and became a recluse. Everyone wanted to know the details of what had happened as the rumors spread. Luckily, the people who had been present on the island all knew how to keep a secret.

I wondered whether Anita was also being pestered. I could sense that she was suffering too, but she kept a cold distance and refused to return my calls or reply to my emails. We only spoke through the producers on matters concerning the film. That's why I was surprised to see her name flash on the phone screen the previous week. She was cool and collected, informing me of her mother's wish to meet my mother, her first cousin. I had not been expecting that.

The evening she had left for Berlin, I read the letter she had left me. It was the letter her grandmother had written, to be opened after her death.

Eleni Dapakis' story—the "missing part" as she referred to it in the opening lines—confirmed everything we had learned on the island. The story differed as far as her relationship to Ackermann and the circumstances of her flight were concerned. Eleni had been suffering from amnesia following a blow to the head and had followed the German Captain believing that she was his wife. By the time she recovered her memory she was already far away. When she later discovered that everyone thought she was a traitor she never returned.

She went on to describe how she inherited the antique shop in Berlin and her struggles as a lone, pregnant woman in a war-torn city. I could not believe what was happening. Anita and I had met as two complete strangers. A few months later, we discover that our ancestors share a common past.

My mother refused to believe it at first. She insisted Eleni must have made it up to salvage her reputation once the truth about her past came to light. I explained that Eleni had died oblivious to what had happened on the island. That she had written the letter years before. It took a lot of talking, but in the end, I persuaded her to meet Anita and her mother when they arrived in Athens the following week. I'm still not sure she was convinced; I think she accepted seeing how much I still loved Anita.

In the meantime, Uncle Nikos' will was read. Like his apartment, it was a sparsely worded document. He left me his apartment and what little money he had went to an orphanage. The last paragraph said that the "part that's missing" can be found in his apartment. They had both chosen the exact same words to speak of that time period, the missing part of their lives.

I would have come to Thessaloniki the following day, but the notary had misplaced the keys to the apartment. I came as soon as I received the keys, went straight to the apartment, and began my search for what I felt was the last piece of the puzzle.

A small desk stood below the map of the island. I pulled up a chair and as soon as I sat down I saw the corner of a big yellow envelope sticking out of the middle drawer. I pulled it out and read: *To Dimitri Voudouris and Maria Voudouris Reniotis. The Missing Part. To be opened after my death.*

I carefully tore the envelope open and extracted a leather-bound notebook that looked like a diary. I walked out to the balcony. The sounds of the city buzzed in the distance.

I quickly flicked through the pages. Most of the book was blank. I turned back to the first page and started to read his story.

I imagine that the first one to read these words will be you, Dimitri; that's why I'll address myself to you.

If you returned to the island to carry out my last wish you will have seen for yourself the beauty of the place where your mother and I were born.

I feel at peace knowing that what is left of my body will travel from the source at Mantani through the island and out to sea. I hope you did as I asked.

I don't know what you found out about our past. When I visited I found everyone's lips were tightly sealed. The shame over everything that happened is too great.

I will write everything down and you can add it to what you may already know. What you will read here is the true story. It may resemble other versions that are being said, but this is what I lived and what I saw. Maybe you and my beloved sister can now understand why I kept to myself all these years.

I stopped reading for a moment and watched a large ship approach the port. The first new piece of information was that my Uncle had returned to the island.

I kept reading. What followed agreed with everything I had learned, and matched Eleni Dapakis' version most closely.

By the time I reached the last page, I was overcome with emotion. Now I realized how much Eleni and Manolis had loved one another; and how much my relationship to Anita resembled theirs in its intensity. I felt like Manolis in some way. He had spent all that time at the front longing for the moment he would see the woman he loved again. My battle had waged inside me, but I longed to see Anita in the same way.

The most significant revelation, however, was the confirmation that Eleni had never betrayed them. I returned to the passage that described the events of that day and reread it, wanting to make sure I had understood it all.

≈≈≈≈≈≈≈≈≈

...I did not stop running until I reached the jetty. I put my sister in a boat and rowed us away. I could hear the Germans screaming in the distance, hunting for us.

The following day, the current washed us up on a shore. A young monk found us and took us to the monastery nearby. The Germans came and torched it to the ground, but we managed to run away and hide in the mountains. We were later sent to Athens—you know the story from then onward, Dimitri.

I never managed to live with the guilt. So many women and children lost their lives because of me, because I struck that German to save Maria. As far as I know, my sister had a good life. That's why I never said anything. I didn't want Maria to feel any of the guilt that has been tormenting me since that day.

When I visited the island I did not say who I really was. I asked around but managed to learn very little. I went everywhere: Kryfó, the ruins of the mill, Galazia Petra. I only revealed my identity to one man; the man I suspected was responsible for all those deaths. He confessed his deed, begged for my forgiveness. Does it surprise you that I gave it? After all, I was as much to blame as him. Anyway, none of it matters any longer. He has now passed away and it is time to bury the past once and for all.

The day before I left, an old man told me a local story about a horse that would appear at Mantani and drink at the spring. The horse was looking for its master who'd been lost in the war, a black horse with a white mark on its forehead. Its description matched Karme, our horse. He also said that only a few had seen the horse in all these years—only those who were pure of heart. I went to Mantani three times, but did not see the horse.

The story ended there, but there was a postscript on the following page:

There is a notary's card enclosed in the envelope. Contact him, hear him out, and then do as you think.

≋≋≋≋≋≋≋≋≋≋

Just when I thought I had all the answers, more questions appeared. What could that postscript mean?

I walked back into the apartment and pulled out the card. I read the address and was surprised to note that the offices were on the island. I picked up my phone and dialed the area code.

Athens, final scene

Anita and her mother had landed in Athens the night before. When we'd spoken to set up the meeting I'd held back and said nothing about Uncle Nikos' notebook. I felt like a child that could not wait to share a happy secret. My mother and I had agreed to share its contents when we met them and suggest we all visit the island together in the coming days, to set the record straight. If they declined, I was determined to go there myself. I wanted to fill the missing part.

≈≈≈≈≈≈≈≈≈

The last scene was being filmed beneath the Acropolis and we all waited for Anita to arrive. She was running late but was on her way.

I saw her walking toward us and felt an uncontrollable urge to run up to her, take her in my arms and tell her everything, right there and then. I did not want to lose another moment. I told myself to be patient.

She stopped for a second as she walked past me and looked into my eyes. A woman around my mother's age was walking behind her. She stopped and examined me, too. I smiled awkwardly at Michaela and nodded in greeting. Michaela returned the nod. Anita walked on, expressionless. She looked pale and drawn.

She returned quickly from makeup and stood beside me. We did not exchange a single word other than the scripted dialogue. There was tension between us and she seemed out of sorts. My presence seemed to repulse her and I sensed she couldn't wait to leave.

Finally, it was all over and everyone broke into a round of applause. It was a wrap!

We just looked at each other uncomfortably; two forlorn figures surrounded by a general sense of euphoria. No one came near us. They knew what had passed between us and left us alone.

I took a step toward her. No reaction. I took another step. A spasm of disgust distorted her features, like she was just about to throw up. I was just about to speak to her when I saw her close her eyes and faint.

I managed to catch her in my arms and gently lay her on the ground. I knelt by her side trying to revive her. Her mother quickly came toward us and everyone else gathered around.

One of the bystanders, who had been watching us film, pushed his way through the throng saying he was a doctor. I moved aside and cradled her head in my lap. He quickly examined her and said she should be taken to the hospital. Her pulse was weak and erratic.

I did not let go of her until we reached the hospital in the producer's car and she was carried away on a stretcher. Her mother, visibly upset and worried, followed her into ER.

I sat in the waiting area with Electra and some of the crew who had followed us in another car. I worried that I was the cause of her malaise. She felt so stressed in my presence that she had passed out. I did not know what else to think.

The passing minutes felt like eons. I got up and walked down the corridor to where they had taken her. A nurse stepped out at that moment. "Congratulations," she said and walked off, her shoes making squeaking noises on the hospital linoleum.

I felt terrible. Even the nurse was being sarcastic, blaming me for Anita's condition.

Her mother appeared at the door with a frown on her face. She seemed pensive and said, "Go on in. She wants to see you," in a laden monotone.

I could not understand what was happening. I prayed all was well and stepped into the room.

Anita seemed to have recovered some of her color and sat up on the bed. The doctor removed his latex gloves, threw them in a bin, and came to shake my hand. "Congratulations! Mrs. Hertz is about three months pregnant. She told me you are the father. We'll run some more tests and then she is free to go. Make sure she gets plenty of rest in the coming days."

I don't remember replying or seeing him leave the room. I was dumbstruck. Anita was looking at me expectantly, waiting for my reaction.

I walked to her bedside and tenderly stroked her hair. A faint smile spread across her face.

The Island, the following summer

In the Cave of Silence, no sound penetrated the thick rock to disturb the stillness inside.

I entered the cave through the narrow opening and waited for my eyes to adjust to the darkness. Slowly, the strange shape of the rocks and the sleek surface of the small lake began to emerge.

I lay down on the ground looking up at the spot where I'd scratched our names into the rock, next to the names of Eleni and Manolis. I tried to bring them to life in my mind, drawing on everything I now knew about them. I closed my eyes and let myself drift, afloat on a sea of thoughts and memories.

There are moments in people's lives when everything seems to be going according to plan, according to their desires. Then, something happens and it all comes tumbling down. It does not have to be a significant 'something'; one small piece of information can change your course and everything you believed until that moment.

That's what had happened to me. The tragic story of my family, the incredible coincidences, and the twists of fate made me realize that, in the end, nothing is improbable. Now, deep inside me, I also knew that, whatever happened, nothing could ever diminish what I felt for Anita.

I thought about how I had actually met her because of this strange chain of events in the past. If it were up to me, of course, I would never have let any of it happen. The way in which the past had come to light, however, made me think that there was some order, some purpose to it, at least as far as I was concerned. It had brought us together. It had led us to the same emotions, the same actions, the same places after all those years. We lived the love they had wanted to live but were never allowed to. We walked in their footsteps but arrived further ahead.

Even the place where Anita had fallen pregnant was the same. Here, in the Cave of Silence, where her mother had been conceived back then. As if that event had determined what would follow in the future.

It had recently become known that in a secret, long-forgotten, Nazi warehouse, thousands of film reels shot in Greece had been discovered. Maybe the scenes of Manolis' death were hiding among them, finally part of the annals of history.

≈≈≈≈≈≈≈≈≈≈

I stood up and admired the Cave's interior, the stone figures that seemed to have been born of a talented sculptor's chisel.

I sensed Anita's presence before she even walked up to me and wrapped her arms around my waist, her hot breath brushing my neck as she kissed me. I reached back and put my arms on her hips. My fingers got tangled in the net-like fabric of her white dress.

"Careful! You'll ruin my wedding dress!" she protested with a laugh and helped me untangle them.

I turned to look at her and she started to dust my clothes down, still laughing. "Look at you! You are not fit to appear in front of all these people!"

I held her face and kissed her tenderly. "We're not even husband and wife and you are telling me off! Don't you know that I don't care what people may think? Anyway, you are the one who wanted to get married here, in the middle of nowhere."

I moved my hands further down and lifted her short dress. I pulled her toward me and pressed her against me. Desire flooded through me and I wanted to relive our first time together in the Cave of Silence, to make her mine. Anita gently pulled away.

"Dimitri, don't. You'll have to be patient until our wedding night. Isn't that what they did in the old days?"

"Not in here they didn't," I replied trying to draw her near me again.

She placed her hand on my chest and kept me away, as I looked at her like a man in the desert seeing a glass of water. That's when I noticed the ring she was wearing. It was Eleni's engagement ring to Manolis. I kissed it and pulled out the watch with Manolis' photo to show her. Michaela had given it to me as a gift, saying it was only right that I should have it.

She smoothed her wedding dress and my crumpled suit and pulled me to the mouth of the cave. Just before we walked out, I winked at her. "I suppose the babies are spending the night with their grandmothers?"

She gave me a look full of promise and put her hand on my arm. We stepped outside to meet everyone. They were all there, everyone on the island, along with those who had worked on the film and friends who had traveled from Germany and Athens. Our mothers sat under one of the large umbrellas that had been set up on the beach holding our babies. Kostas sat between them trying to keep everyone cool with a fan.

As soon as they saw us, they broke into applause, not for the first time that day. Every step that day had felt like being on stage, a round of applause for a scene well-acted.

Shortly, the ceremony at the tiny chapel on the beach would begin. After the wedding, we would christen our twins in the sea: Manolis and Eleni, named in honor of the two people who had loved one another for eternity.

We had politely declined all offers to turn their story into a film. We felt that no film could capture the reality of what had happened and wanted to keep the memory of their love rather than their suffering alive.

The film that had brought Anita and me together had hit the screens at the beginning of the year and was doing well all over Europe. Our story and all the rumors circulating had certainly helped.

Anita was being offered more parts than ever but had decided to take a break for a few years and enjoy parenthood. We'd rented a house on the outskirts of Athens by the sea, our other great common love.

The following year, we intended to build our house on the island. Uncle Nikos had bought a plot of land near Mantani in my name, as I had been informed by the notary when I called the number on that card.

≈≈≈≈≈≈≈≈≈≈

The Abbot of the monastery of Aghios Mámas, the man who had saved my mother and her brother, appeared at the doorway, flanked by two monks who would help him during the ceremony.

In the time we waited for everyone to gather around us and the ceremony to begin, I looked out to the top of the hill. I thought I saw something move there. A black horse stood at the top of the hill and, as if it could tell that I was looking at it, reared on its hind legs just like that day at Mantani. I nudged Anita and pointed to the hilltop with a nod of my head. But there was nothing there. No one else seemed to have noticed anything.

I remembered the legend the old man had told my uncle about the black horse with the heart-shaped white mark on its forehead that forever roamed the island in search of its master. From where I stood, it was impossible to tell whether the horse had a mark like Karme or the horse I had met at the spring.

I held Anita's hand tightly throughout the ceremony and we kept exchanging glances as if we could not believe it was really happening. Later on, the cries of out twins rang out on the beach as the Abbot christened them in the sea. Their godparents were Thomas, Sofia, and Thekla. Most of the guests had waded into the water to watch him perform the ceremony in his serene, unhurried manner despite the scorching sun.

Everything was now in place and nothing could ever change that.

The ceremony over and everyone back on the shore, Thomas put his fingers in his mouth and gave out a loud whistle. Music came from the footpath that went up the mountain, getting louder as the musicians approached the beach. Anita and I looked at one another, both of us instantly recognizing the tune. It was the familiar island song. One by one, the musicians who had performed on the night of the festival appeared and our guests started to join hands and fall into step in a large circle, a circle that became a giant hug enclosing us in the middle as the lyrics rang out.

My beautiful island girl
Leaving these shores behind
Leaving me alone to wander
On a lonely isle
The waves have come between us
Keeping our lips apart
I pray that you will keep
A place for me in your heart
My beautiful island girl
Leaving these shores behind
Remember I will love you
Until the end of time
And if you leave one evening
I will bear your absence
Alone with my memories
In a cave of silence

Note from the author

The story of Manolis is based on the real-life story of Dimitris Pipiliagkas and the events that took place in Vlasti, a village close to Kozani in Northern Greece, just before the end of WWII. The story was passed on to me by Dimitri Lymberopoulos, the grandson of Yiannis Pipiliagkas, (Dimitris/Manolis' brother), who appears in the book as Yianni Reniotis.

Now in his nineties, Kostas Pipiliagkas is the man depicted on the front cover. He is the son of Dimitris Pipiliagkas and does not appear in the book. He is the only member of the family to have witnessed the events described here and I was honored that he chose to share his father's tragic last moments with me.

≈≈≈≈≈≈≈≈≈≈≈

The island is a fictional place, an imaginary landscape based on the Greek islands of Andros, Leros, and Halki.

≈≈≈≈≈≈≈≈≈≈≈

I have never visited Vlasti.

K.K.

About the author

When Kostas Krommydas decided to write his first novel, he took the publishing world of his native Greece by storm. A few years later, he is an award-winning author of five bestselling novels, acclaimed actor, teacher and passionate storyteller. His novels have been among the top 10 at the prestigious Public Book Awards (Greece) and his novel "Ouranoessa" has won first place (2017). He has also received the coveted WISH writer's award in 2013. When not working on his next novel at the family beach house in Athens, you will find him acting on the acclaimed ITV series, The Durrels and on various theatre, film, and TV productions. Kostas also enjoys teaching public speaking, interacting with his numerous fans, and writing guest articles for popular Greek newspapers, magazines, and websites. If you want to find out more about Costas, visit his website, http://kostaskrommydas.gr/ or check out his books on Amazon: Author.to/KostasKrommydas

More Books

Athora

A Mystery Romance set on the Greek Islands.

A tourist is found dead in Istanbul, the victim of what appears to be a ritual killing. An elderly man is murdered in the same manner, in his house by Lake Como. The third murder is the most perplexing of all: the priest of a small, isolated Greek island lies dead in the sanctuary, his body ritualistically mutilated. Fotini Meliou is visiting her family on the island of Athora for a few days, before starting a new life in the US. She is looking forward to a brief respite and, perhaps, becoming better acquainted with the seductive Gabriel, whom she has just met. It is not the summer vacation she expects it to be. A massive weather bomb is gathering over the Aegean, threatening to unleash the most violent weather the area has ever seen. When the storm breaks out, the struggle begins. A race against the elements and a race against time: the killer is still on the island, claiming yet another victim. Locals, a boatload of newly arrived refugees, foreign residents, and stranded tourists are now trapped on an island that has lost contact with the outside world. As the storm wreaks havoc on the island, how will they manage to survive?

More Books

Dominion of the Moon

Award Winner, Public Readers' Choice Awards 2017

In the final stages of WWII, archaeologist Andreas Stais follows the signs that could lead him to unearth the face of the goddess who has been haunting his dreams for years, all the while searching for the woman who, over a brief encounter, has come to dominate his waking hours. In present day Greece, another Andreas, an Interpol officer, leaves New York and returns to his grandparents' island to bid farewell to his beloved grandmother.

Once there, he will come face to face with long-buried family secrets and the enigmatic Iro. When gods and demons pull the threads, no one can escape their fate. Pagan rituals under the glare of the full moon and vows of silence tied to a sacred ring, join men and gods in a common path.

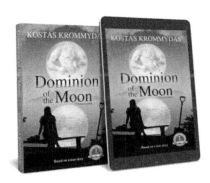

More Books

Lake of Memories

Based on a true story

In Paris, a dying woman is searching for the child that was snatched from her at birth over twenty years ago. In Athens, a brilliant dancer is swirling in ecstasy before an enraptured audience. In the first row, a young photographer is watching her for the first time, mesmerized. He knows she is stealing his heart with every swirl and turn, yet is unable to break the spell. And on the Greek island of the Apocalypse, Patmos, a man is about to receive a priceless manuscript from a mysterious benefactor. Destiny has thrown these people together, spinning their stories into a brilliant tapestry of romance, crime, and timeless love. How many memories can the past hold? Is a mother's love strong enough to find the way? Based on a true story, Krommydas' award-winning book firmly established him as one of the top Greek authors of his generation.

Very soon more novels from Kostas Krommydas will be available on Kindle. Sign up to receive our newsletter or follow Kostas on facebook, and we will let you know as soon as they are uploaded!

* * *

Want to contact Kostas? Eager for updates?

Want an e-book autograph?

Follow him on

https://www.linkedin.com/in/kostas-krommydas
https://www.instagram.com/krommydaskostas/
https://www.facebook.com/Krommydascostas/
https://twitter.com/KostasKrommydas

Amazon author page:
Author.to/KostasKrommydas

If you wish to report a typo or have reviewed this book on Amazon please email onioncostas@gmail.com with the word "review" on the subject line, to receive a free 1680x1050 desktop background.

Thank you for taking the time to read *Cave of Silence*! If you enjoyed it, please tell your friends or post a short review. Word of mouth is an author's best friend and much appreciated!

Printed in Great Britain
by Amazon

37533240R00158